Praise for the novels of

"Readers will be gratified to see the sweet ... treated with as much importance as the steamy one between Suda Kaye and Camden. This small-town contemporary is as stylish, confident, and free-spirited as its heroine."

—*Publishers Weekly* on *What the Heart Wants*

"Audrey Carlan has created a gem of a story about sisterhood, love, second chances, and the kind of wanderlust that won't be silenced, reminding us that sometimes the most important journey is the one we take home."

—*New York Times* bestselling author Lexi Ryan on *What the Heart Wants*

"A wonderful story about building a dream and loving your life, home, family, and more."

—*New York Times* bestselling author Kylie Scott on *What the Heart Wants*

"This book pulled at my heart in all the ways! An emotionally charged story of friendship, sisterhood, and love that shows us what it means to fly free."

—Elise Lee, owner of Away With Words Bookshop, on *What the Heart Wants*

"Sexy, smart, and so unique! I was completely immersed."

—Katy Evans, *New York Times* bestselling author, on the Calendar Girl series

"A fast-paced, and downright addictive read. I devoured every word of Mia's journey."

—Meghan March, *USA TODAY* bestselling author, on the Calendar Girl series

"Carlan's three brilliant and irrepressible ladies' men will have romance lovers looking forward to the next fix."

—*Publishers Weekly* on *International Guy*

"Readers will be intrigued... Recommended."

—*Library Journal* on *International Guy*

Also by Audrey Carlan

WHAT THE HEART WANTS

For a full list of books by Audrey Carlan,
please visit www.audreycarlan.com.

To Gabriela McEachern because like Evie,
you are a true light to this world.
Keep shining.

PROLOGUE

Ten years ago…

Tears track down my face as Tahsuda, my *Toko*, which is the Comanche word for "grandfather," hands me a large stack of pink envelopes tied with a ribbon. My mother's beautiful handwriting is visible on the top. He hands another stack to my eighteen-year-old sister, Suda Kaye.

"From my Catori, for her *Taabe* and *Huutsuu*," he begins, using the Comanche nicknames my mother gave us. "To have a piece of her on their birthdays. One for today, and one for each birthday and important moment in your life to come. I shall leave you to your peace but know I am here for you, forevermore." Tahsuda puts his hands together under his worn red-and-black poncho and nods his head forward. His long, silky black hair gleams a dark midnight blue in the rays of the sunlight that streak through our bedroom window. His hair is so much like my mother's I have to swallow down the sob that aches to come out in a flood of misery and grief.

Misery because I am so angry at her for all the time we could have had together. Grief because she left this world six months ago, and today, on my twentieth birthday and Suda Kaye's eighteenth, we are facing our entire lives without her.

This wasn't another one of her many adventures. We'd grown used to the routine. She'd skip around the house, packing her battered suitcase while she told us all about what she hoped to see and do on her travels. While she fluttered around the globe, we stayed behind and went to school, dropped off for an undetermined amount of time at the reservation where our grandfather lived. Months later, with a smile on her face and a song in her heart, she'd reenter our lives as though she'd never even left.

At least she'd come back.

As much as I hated our mother's wanderlust, I always knew eventually she'd find her way home. Her weary feet would be tired, and she'd come dancing into *Toko*'s home with grand tales about a world I didn't ever care to see. I didn't want to go anywhere that made me up and leave my family for months on end. Them always wondering where I was, who I was with and whether or not I was okay.

No way. That was not me. And it never would be.

I finger the ribbon on the stack of envelopes and take mine to the papasan chair in the corner of our shared room. Suda Kaye stretches out on her twin bed. We live in a two-bedroom apartment in Pueblo. Suda Kaye has just graduated high school. I attend the local community college.

The one thing Catori Ross never imagined could happen to her was illness. In all her plans to travel the globe, to experience absolutely everything she could, she didn't factor in time to get regular checkups. Since she didn't tend to get sick, Mom hadn't been to a doctor in a solid decade before she started to feel unwell. After three solid months of lethargy and depression—two things our mother never was—the first round of tests gave us the first blow.

Cancer.

Stage four.

She believed with her whole heart that she could beat it, but as *Toko* says, cancer took both his wife and his daughter. He says it was written in the stars. That was the reason he never gave Mom hell about her traveling and leaving us with him. He always said a person must do what their heart wants. Dreams are not only for the sleeping. They are meant to be chased and caught.

Our mother lived. Chased every dream with a hunger that could never be quenched. I fear my sister will do the same.

Suda Kaye sits against her headboard as I cuddle into the chair. I untie the ribbon and then set all but the top letter to the side. The first envelope has today's date on it and her nickname for me. *Taabe*, which means "sun" in Comanche.

Mom called me her sun because I am light everywhere, while she and my sister were dark. Mom was full-blooded Native American like *Toko*. Suda Kaye and I are half, and we each have different fathers. I got a lot of my coloring from my father, Adam Ross. Like Dad, my hair is golden blond and I have his ice-blue eyes. Though my high cheekbones, the shape of my eyes and my full lips are my mother's. Suda Kaye has dark, espresso-colored hair, amber eyes and will one day have a knockout figure. She already is growing into her womanly hourglass shape—full bosom, long legs and rounded hips. Me, I have the tall, lanky, athletic build. Still, there is no denying our heritage even with the play on light and dark in our coloring.

We are Catori's daughters, a vibrant mix of her and our biological fathers. Though Suda Kaye and I don't know much about her real dad. We just know what Mom told us much later in life—that she had made a mistake. She and her husband—my father, Adam—had been going through a rough time and separated for a year. In that year she'd gone on an adventure and come back pregnant with my sister. I was only two when she was born so none of that had ever mattered to me one way or the other. My father treated Suda Kaye mostly the same, which also didn't matter because he wasn't around much, either, always deployed someplace far away.

I thumb the envelope and run my fingers across her pretty handwriting.

I miss you, Mom.

Taking a full deep breath, I ease back against my chair and open the first letter.

Evie, my golden Taabe,

Never in a million years did I think I'd be in this situation. Gone from you and your sister in a way that I cannot come back from. I know you've always hated my need to wander, as it took me away from you and Suda Kaye, but you were never far from my mind or my heart. Never unloved.

I had to chase my dreams, Taabe. One day, you'll understand.

My greatest hope is that you know my love for you transcends any reality, location or final destination. It is as the sun, shining brightly each day. Never ending, always warm, forever shedding light onto you and your sister.

With me gone, without the burden of having to take care of me and Suda Kaye, I want you to think long and hard about what it is you want in life. Just you. Think big. Live out loud.

What is still out there to explore?

Where in the world do you see yourself visiting?

What new journey have you wished to undertake?

Think of all the beauty I've shared through my stories and photos over the years. Those experiences are a huge part of me. And I'm so grateful I had them. It gave me the ability to open your eyes to the fact that anything in life is possible.

My only regret was having to leave you and your sister behind. Though I hope now, you will take time out for yourself.

Evie, you are so grounded. Your feet firmly rooted to God's green earth. Pull those roots, my lovely girl. Break away from all that keeps you still and give yourself an experience unlike any other. Perhaps then you will understand my need to go, to feel the wind in my hair, the sand between my toes, the gravel under my boots. I lived every moment to the fullest and I want that for you so deeply.

Please take the inheritance I left you and use it to live.

See the world, my precious girl.

With all my love,

Mom

I grind down on my teeth and wipe my nose with the back of my hand. I fold my letter into thirds and stuff it back into the envelope. Clearing my throat, I flatten my hand along the front before lifting it to my nose and inhaling the familiar scent of citrus with a hint of patchouli.

"Smells like her." I clear my throat as a traitorous tear slides down my cheek.

Suda Kaye sniffs her letter and smiles sadly. "Mom always said if you're going to smell like anything, let it be natural. Fruit and spice."

"And everything nice!" I chuckle, then sigh as the weight of everything in my letter festers in my heart and soul, mixing with the intense sorrow I haven't shaken off in the six months since she passed.

"I miss her. Sometimes I pretend she's just gone off on another one of her adventures, you know? Then I can be pissed off and plan out all the catty things I'm going to say to her when she finally returns with a suitcase full of dirty clothes and presents to smooth over the hurt."

My sister gasps and her stunning amber eyes fill with more tears. "Evie, she didn't *want* to leave…"

I fist my hands, rekindling the anger that never seems to disappear when I think of all the years we might have had with her. "Not this time, Kaye, but what about all the other times? Years and years of time lost. And for what?" I huff and stand, pacing our small room with Mom's letters plastered to my chest like a well-loved teddy bear. "Fun. Wild experiences. Adventures! It killed her. This need to see the greener grass on the other side." Scowling, I point at myself. "Well, that won't be me. No way. No how. I've got my feet firmly planted on terra firma. I'm going to finish school, get my bachelor's in finance, then my master's, and make something of myself. And I'm going to be happy!"

How I'm going to be happy without my mother in my life, I don't know. I never knew how to fill the hole she left with each adventure she took. It just seemed that the void got bigger and bigger. But my mother…she was such a glorious woman, an incredible presence when she *was* there. She could easily fill up that gaping wound that I call my heart each and every time she came back.

Finding that the pacing isn't doing much, I toss my stack of letters onto the chair and drop onto the bed next to Kaye, face planted dramatically in the crook of my arms, my nose touching the mattress as I breathe deeply and try my best not to break down in front of my baby sister.

Slowly, she strokes my hair in long, soothing sweeps of her hand. Once I've gotten myself under control emotionally—for now, that is—I turn over.

"What did your letter say?" I ask.

Kaye licks her lips and glances away. We don't have any secrets from one another, but I can tell this is one she'd rather keep from me. Eventually she caves and hands me her letter. Pulling myself up, I sit cross-legged and read out loud.

"'Suda Kaye, my little *huutsuu*.'" I cover my mouth and close my eyes. The last word comes out as a croak. Mom's nickname for Suda Kaye meant "little bird" in Comanche. *Huutsuu* to my *Taabe*. My sister has always been the one up for a grand adventure. She could make going grocery shopping the highlight of anyone's week with her dramatic flair and interest in all things. Same goes for a laundromat, the car wash, a walk around the neighborhood. Always something to experience, to see, hear, sense. My sister soaks up life like a sponge until she's wrung out, and then starts all over again. That apple did not fall far from the tree, much to my dismay.

She smiles wide. "Always and forever, *Taabe*," she responds.

Not wanting to make Suda Kaye more emotional, I quickly read her letter. With every sentence my heart sinks. Basically, Mom has told my sister to leave home. To get in her car and travel the world, starting with the States. To leave me in order to allow me to find my own calling, without the worry of my baby sister there to hold me back. My stomach churns and acid creeps up my throat as I read the last couple sentences that tell her that if Camden, Suda Kaye's longtime boyfriend, truly loves her, he will set her free.

My hands shake as I pass it back to her, my entire body stiff as a board. I feel as though I've been staked through the heart and left for dead.

My mother wants my sister—my best friend—to leave me.

To go away for as long as it took for Mom to find herself.

"You're not going to do it, are you?" I ask, the fear clear in my tone.

She bites down on the side of her cheek and nods.

"Kaye...you can't do that. What about Camden? He won't understand. A guy like that...the life he wants to give you. No way. You just..." I let out a breath, grab my sister's hands and squeeze, trying to transfer all the worry and fear I'll experience with her leaving me behind. And yet I don't say a word. In this moment, she has to make the choice that's right for her.

I swallow down the lump of emotion swelling in my throat and whisper, "What are you going to do?"

She stares into my eyes, right through to my soul, and says the five words I never wanted to hear from her.

"I'm going to fly free."

I close my eyes, lean forward to kiss her forehead. "I love you, Suda Kaye." It's the only thing I can say. It's raw, honest and life-changing.

"You know you could come with me?" Her voice fills with hope, but the last thing she needs is me tying her down, trying to run her life for her. Mom made that very clear in her letter. Heck, she made it clear in mine.

Shaking my head, I cup her soft cheek. "You have to make your own choices."

She nods, folds up her letter, puts it back in the envelope and then ties up the stack in a bundle once more.

My sister, not one to let grass grow under her feet, pulls the big suitcase from under her bed that Mom gave her for graduation and sets it on the comforter. Methodically, without saying a word, I help my sister pack her things. The last item she puts on top of her clothes is a picture of me, Mom and her, taken last year before Mom became too sick. It had been a good day; we'd had a picnic in the park. Laughing, snacking and listening to our mother share one story after another.

I knew then that those good days would be few and far between, so I encouraged her storytelling, while Suda Kaye ate up every ounce as though it were her very favorite dish.

Holding hands, I walk my sister to her car and put her suitcase in the trunk.

"Do you know where you'll go after you see Camden?" I ask, knowing she wouldn't leave without seeing him first.

She smiles and shrugs. "We're in the middle of the country. I'm going to pick a direction and just keep driving until I get too tired. Then I'll stop and decide where I'm meant to be next."

"You call me. I'll come get you anywhere, any place. No matter w-what." My voice shakes as I pull her into my arms and inhale her fragrance—cherry-scented shampoo and lotion. I allow the scent to imprint on my memory bank for I know I'll need it in the lonely months, maybe even years, to come.

Suda Kaye walks around her car and opens the driver's side door. "Miss me," she says, and the deluge of tears falls from my eyes like a waterfall.

"Miss me more," I whisper, and hold up my hand.

She mimics the gesture, placing her palm against mine. "Always."

Then I watch for a long time as my sister's taillights eventually fade and disappear into the black night. Before long, I look up into the open sky and the wealth of sparkling stars blanketing the sky like diamonds over black velvet.

I pick a star and make the same wish I've been making since I was a child.

"One of these days, I wish someone I love would stay."

1

The present...

All I've ever wanted is a normal life. A mother who met the bus drop-off after school, helped me and my sister with our homework, made dinner and tucked us in at night. A father who was strong, committed to his family and most of all *present* for the good and bad life can bring two young, impressionable girls. Then one day, I'd marry the man of my dreams, settle down in a career of my choosing where I made enough money to contribute to the household, but also had time for my children. After my kids moved on to their own lives, I'd grow old with my love and we'd travel through our second and third acts, a retired couple desiring to see new things and spend time with their grandchildren.

A solid, beautiful life.

I think most people want what they don't have, or didn't have growing up. There was a lot of love in my family, but no consistency, no permanence. The only person I could count on for anything parental was my grandfather. My mother had a wanderer's soul and feet that could never stay in one place. I saw more of my classmates growing up throughout the years than I ever did of my own mother. Same with my father. Adam Ross was a military man with strength, grit and an unshakable sense of patriotism, but he served in other countries more than he'd ever had his boots on the ground in the States.

And then there was Suda Kaye. My whole world. My baby sister. Always by my side, her hand holding mine as we traversed the hills and valleys of an unorthodox upbringing. Except she didn't see our parents' lack of participation as something to harbor ill will and sour feelings. No, my dear Suda Kaye ate up life with every step she took. Her nature matched our mother's in the need to fly free, go where the wind took her and soak up as much as she could of what life offered.

Still, there are small moments in a person's life that ultimately define who we're meant to be. Challenges we face that take us down one path or lead us to another. Shimmers of greatness that make all the difference in deciding where we'll end up.

Choice. Life is about choices.

Which is why I'm uncertain how I made this choice. "I cannot believe you talked me into this, Kaye." I grumble through clenched teeth as I adjust the fitted hip belt with dangling cold coins around my body. It jangles and tinkles as I tie it in a knot. The bedlah I'm wearing is a stunning teal color, encrusted with gold beading all through the bra-style top. The skirt is made of a gorgeous tulle that matches the top but it flows out in swaths of fabric designed to accentuate the curves and highlight the body to its maximum.

Staring at myself in the mirror, I can see it's highlighting my half-bare body instead of hiding anything.

Suda Kaye stands next to me, sharing the mirror while putting a platinum-colored headband in her long brown locks. Her outfit is a deep crimson with silver accents. She looks like the perfect version of a belly dancer. Not that I look bad. It's just not as common to see a blond-haired, blue-eyed dancer in the traditional garments.

"You look amazing. And you've been belly dancing since you were a child. This is a corporate event. If you drop a hip roll on the wrong beat, no one is going to notice. I swear. You're really doing my dance group a solid by filling in tonight."

I roll my eyes and sigh. If my sister hadn't given me the sob story of the woman who was supposed to be in this getup tonight, I'd have never agreed. Alas, a child undergoing leukemia treatments tugged on every last one of my heartstrings. The boy's mother uses the belly dancing crew as her one small getaway from all the trauma she manages taking care of a sick child. Unfortunately, the boy took a bit of a turn for the worse and she couldn't make this evening's show, hence me agreeing to substitute.

Our mother was an amazing belly dancer and taught both of us at a very young age how to dance. One of the first presents that I can recall her giving us were the pretty little finger zills known more commonly as cymbals often used in the dance. Suda and I entertained ourselves endlessly playing with those cymbals and dancing all over the reservation where we spent most of our childhood.

"Here, let me help you." My sister places an ornate gold headband strategically in my hair on the crown of my head. It's incredibly pretty and I do feel a little like a Turkish princess in the full traditional dress.

Suda Kaye's eyes light up at the sight of us. She shimmies her hips and the coins vibrate against one another creating a lovely sound that gets my heart pumping and my excitement up. I follow her movements and together we create a beautiful harmony.

Watching us in the mirror, I can see we are two opposites attracting magically. One light, one dark.

My sister jumps up and down and pulls me into her arms for a hug. "Tonight is going to be so much fun! Just like old times."

I snuggle my girl and swing her body from left to right. "You're just saying that because your husband is in the audience. You love showing off!"

She pulls away and grins wide. "Ab-so-freakin-lutely. Any chance I get to shimmy and shake all sexified in front of Cam is a good day. He's been working godawful hours on some new project his foundation invested in," she pouts. "It's time to give my man a little relief."

I chuckle and check my lipstick in the mirror. A glossy sheen of pink suits the outfit and my naturally light brown skin tone and blond hair. My entire abdomen is exposed, which sets a few flutters of nerves skimming down my form. I rest my hands against my belly and breathe.

"Are you nervous?" Suda Kaye frowns.

I bug out my eyes. "When was the last time you saw me in something this revealing? I mean, I'm cool with showing a lot of leg, but not so used to wearing what is essentially a bikini with a sarong and shaking my booty in front of a room filled with strange men."

Suda Kaye waves her hand in the air as though it isn't even a slight bother. "Puh-leeze. You're going to have each and every one of those men salivating."

"Kaye, I'm not interested in any of those men."

She grins. "Not true. I know for a fact you're interested in *one* of them." She grins manically and my heart about drops out of my chest.

"No…"

Her face lights up as though the sun is shining straight through her. "Yes."

"You did not tell me he'd be here. Kaye, I can't do this." I gesture to my half-naked body. "Not in front of *him*."

Kaye laughs heartily, turns me around and leads me toward the other dancers. "You can, and you *will*, because some sick little boy's momma needs you to take one for the sisterhood, and I know you. My Evie would never let down the sisterhood because of a little jitter over seeing her childhood crush."

I grit my teeth and clench my hands into fists. "I hate you."

She snorts. "You love me so much you'd die for me! Now trust your baby sis. I've got you. Girl, I've *so* got you." She waggles her eyebrows and shakes her sexy hips until the coins rattle musically.

The dance troop leader comes through and hands each of us two pairs of finger cymbals. I place the loops around the appropriate fingers and press them together a few times to ensure they are in the right position.

"All right, ladies. As practiced, we flow through the tables, stopping strategically in the spots where you see a small black X taped on the ground."

I bump Kaye in the shoulder and whisper under my breath. "I wasn't here for the practice round. I don't know where to stop."

"Don't worry. Stay behind me about six to ten feet. When I stop, you stop. I'll make sure you're in the right place."

"Okay." I nod and start breathing deeply to calm my racing heart.

I can't even think about the fact that my childhood crush is somewhere in the ballroom. The man I've been avoiding for months since he reentered our lives when my sister opened her boutique, Gypsy Soul. He helped secure the connection to Camden's foundation. That one meeting changed Suda Kaye's entire life. When she met with the foundation, her first love, Camden Bryant, was in that meeting. He was then assigned to her store to assist her while he helped monitor their investment. One crazy event after another, and here we are just over half a year later and my sister is newly married to the man of her dreams and finally living in the same state as me.

I'd be lying if I didn't say I was ecstatic to have my sister back. Her presence fills a small bit of the hole inside of me but there's still a big gaping wound the size of the Grand Canyon that has never healed all these years. I've gotten used to the emptiness, the feeling of never being full. Suda Kaye's presence helps enormously. Having her in my life on a daily basis slowly started stitching up the edges of that void but not entirely. I lost hope of feeling complete a long time ago.

As the music starts, the double doors open into the huge hotel ballroom. The first set of dancers flows into the room, following one after another while leaving the appropriate amount of space between them. Closing my eyes for a moment, I allow the music to filter through my subconscious and ease away any nervousness or fear. I open my eyes and watch as my sister's arms flow out to the sides. I mimic her position and follow her in.

Every so often we spin, swaying our arms and skirts, and make exaggerated hip movements along with the music.

Suda Kaye leads me to the right side of the room where I can see her zeroing in on a table with a man with long, dirty-blond hair who only has eyes for her. I glance down at the floor to ensure I haven't hit my mark yet. I follow until she stops right in front of Camden's table. I work around a table wedged in between a group of four. She nods at me and I stop on the X.

The music changes and I watch as Suda Kaye lifts her arms and starts the routine I've had memorized since I was a child. It's one we were taught by our mother long ago. It comes to me on autopilot and I get into the music, drop my hips and use the cymbals to accentuate the beats and flow.

I'm having a blast and lose myself to the music. I do a series of hip rolls and spin around to face the other two tables. My breath is knocked right out of my chest as my gaze connects with the coal-black eyes of the only man I've ever wanted more than anything.

Milo Chavis.

Swallowing down the surprise I feel, I keep up the dance. Only this time, I feel as though I'm dancing for an audience of one.

His dark gaze leaves mine to slowly track up and down my body. It's like a featherlight caress I can almost feel from beaded sandaled feet, along my bare legs and gyrating hips, up and over my working abdominal muscles and rolling shoulders. I arch my back and thrust my chest forward as I bend back and forth.

Since I know this dance well, I can take in every inch of his masculine form. He has pitch-black hair that's parted perfectly down the center and tied tight at the nape of his neck. I know he usually fastens it with leather bands at intervals down his back. His jaw and cheekbones could have been chiseled in stone by Rodin himself they are so defined. His eyebrows are black slashes above his dark eyes and his skin tone is a toasted brown that reminds me of the desert hills on the reservation when they are shaded from the sun at dusk. He's wearing a black suit with a crisp white dress shirt underneath. At his neck is an intricate bolo tie made of black leather. Twisted rope strings hang down his massive chest; an etched medallion at his strong throat has a thumbprint-size turquoise stone in the center.

One hundred percent Native American.

One hundred percent man.

One hundred percent beautiful.

One hundred percent never meant to be mine.

Not wanting to torture myself any longer, I spin around and face the other direction, following along with the crew and glancing over at Suda Kaye. She smiles and nods her head, gesturing subtly to Milo as though she's handed me a gift.

I close my eyes and continue the dance until the music changes, sound swirling in the air around us, ramping up to the big finale right before we're supposed to take our leave.

Thank God.

I spin around and around, the finger cymbals clapping together for our dramatic ending, and stop only a few feet away from Milo's chair, as though my body gravitated toward him against my will.

His jaw is still clenched but twitches as I stare into his beautiful face. I can't help it. The man is magnificent, and I've been in love with him since I was eight years old. Not that he knows it.

Milo has never seen me in a romantic light, and I doubt he ever could. He's never so much as given me a hint that he was interested in being anything more than an acquaintance, even now that we're older and neither of us live on the reservation any longer. With the four-year age difference between us, I've always been a child to him. The awkward, skinny, gangly-limbed, little blonde girl he had to save from bullies when we were children.

Tahsuda's granddaughter. Catori's daughter. Suda Kaye's sister.

That's all I've ever been to him, and even though he's made a couple calls to my office and an official request via email to schedule an appointment for some business matter he wants to discuss, I've made sure to avoid any such meeting. I've politely requested he share the business matter he wishes to review and received another request to meet in person. With ease I professionally declined that request to meet, as I have no desire to sit face-to-face with the man. He brings up too many memories of my past, not to mention my ridiculous never-ending crush. Running into him several months ago at lunch with his *wife* ripped open that wound inside me and put out the torch I've been carrying around for him for the last twenty-two years.

I would no longer covet Milo Chavis.

He is not the man for me.

It's a newer resolution, but one I am planning to stick to until I find a nice-looking, boring, hardworking man—one who wants to be with me for me. Warts and all. Well, I don't have any warts, but I do have a lot of hang-ups, ones I've been recently discussing with a therapist.

We stare at one another for so long the music changes and I am moved into action by Suda Kaye. "Go, go, go," she urges me forward.

I hop to and dance my way back to the open doors where all the dancers are spilling through like rainbow confetti bursting through a pop gun.

Immediately my sister leads me over to a quiet corner away from the other dancers. "Okay, tell me *everything*. Was he drooling over you or what?" Her voice drips with innuendo and excitement.

I purse my lips and shake my head. "You should have told me he'd be here."

Her expression twists into one of disgust. "No way. *Nut-uh.* You'd have never come if I did."

I groan and tip my head to the ceiling. "Lord, please save me from my well-meaning sister before I run out of patience."

"He was staring at you the entire time," she gushes. "Not even so much as a glance at the other dancers. All his focus was on you."

"Because I was standing in front of him, thanks to you!" I snarl.

"Sissy, you have got to talk to him. He's made several requests to meet up with you. Just give in and listen to the man…" Her voice trails off.

"That sounds like a good, logical idea. You should listen to your younger sister, *Nizhoni,*" came a deep male voice from directly behind our huddle.

Nizhoni. Navajo for "beautiful." I close my eyes at the compliment. I don't remember when Milo had taken to calling me that, but I always thought it was sweet. Unfortunately, it also filled my head with ideas. Making me believe he could feel for me a little of what I've felt for him all these years.

Suda Kaye's eyes bulge, and a huge smile spills across her face. "Milo, so good to see you, you big hunk of hotness. We were just talking about you." She positively beams.

I glare at my sister and then plaster on a smile as I turn around and back up a few steps. As I clasp my hands in front of me, the cymbals clang stupidly.

Milo stands with his hands in his pockets, his large presence making the hallway feel smaller.

"I'm just gonna go find Cam." Suda Kaye grips my shoulders and kisses my hair before dashing off like the free bird she is.

I bite down on my bottom lip and wait for him to address me.

"You've been avoiding me." His voice is stern and straightforward.

"Well, I wouldn't exactly call it avoiding." Even though it absolutely was, I still wasn't about to admit it.

"You've ignored my calls and declined my request to meet."

"You wouldn't share what it was regarding. As I mentioned, I've been busy. You know how it is in finance. Never a dull moment." *Lie.* There are a ton of dull moments being a financial adviser. A lot of them are spent watching the market trends and following up on leads.

"Evie, why?" His voice is the low thunderous warning before a storm really hits.

I swallow and look away. "I just told you. I've been extremely busy."

He does not bite nor let me off the hook. He crosses his arms over his wide chest and the fabric of his jacket tightens around large biceps. What I wouldn't give to see them free of clothing. I used to see him running around bare-chested all the time on the reservation, but we were children. Me eight, him twelve. He hadn't really transitioned into this mammoth of a man back then. After he went through puberty, I watched with avid fascination as he grew more manly, but then he went off to college at eighteen and Mom moved us to Pueblo when I was fourteen so we could go to a public high school. I knew we were both in the same field, but nothing more.

"That is not an answer." He calls me out on my bull.

My shoulders drop as if separated from my body. "Look,

I don't answer to you, nor do I have to," is my unusual and rather uncharacteristic response. I'm almost proud of myself.

"You're attracted to me," he states flatly.

I go still. Everything around me warps and disappears as I allow the truth to seep into my conscious self.

"What?" I half gasp.

"That is why you are avoiding me. You are attracted to me."

"I am not!" I jerk back and lie through my teeth. "How dare you." More fake indignation.

His lips twitch into a half smirk. "I'm not offended. I'm rather pleased, as I have always been fond of you."

Fond of me.

I blink stupidly, trying to wrap my head around the man of my every fantasy telling me he's *fond of me*. Fond. The same way a person feels about a nice person they've just met or an acquaintance they've known for years.

I shake my head and put my hand up. "I'm outta here." I move to dash around him, but his long arm darts out and captures me at the waist, tugging me toward him and plastering me to his solid wall of a chest.

Being in his arms makes me dizzy and I place both my palms against his chest. He holds me close around the waist and back as I tip my head to look up and up. I'm tall at five foot nine, but he's at least six foot four and I'm not wearing heels.

"Let me rephrase. I'm *deeply* attracted to you, Evie Ross." His words filter straight through my brain, slither down my spine and settle hotly between my thighs.

My heart pounds and my cheeks flush. "You are?" I let the honesty fall from my lips as my body relaxes in his arms.

"Yes. Although my romantic interest in you is not why

I've cornered you. That is for another time. I have a business proposition for you to consider."

I frown and find my feet beneath me, taking on more of my own weight. "Again with the business proposition."

Him bringing up my business acumen while I stand half-naked in his arms has me stepping away from his warmth. Suddenly I'm cold, and the heat I felt before dissipates instantly.

"Of course. That's right, you want to do business with me." I huff.

He nods. "You're a shrewd businesswoman. The best financial adviser I've seen in the area, and we have common interests."

"Common interests?" I shake my head as if this is a dream and I'm about to wake up at any moment. *Please wake up.*

"Yes. Our people. Your business is far larger, and you serve the general public with their financial needs, but I carry the trust of all the tribes in the area—trust that could easily span to the surrounding states. I'd like to meet with you to discuss a merging of our businesses. Together I believe we could be even more successful, as well as help Native Americans across the country."

I close my eyes, cross my arms and rub up and down, feeling chilled to the bone. "I'm not sure I'm interested in expanding at this time." Another lie. I'd already determined that I could comfortably open another couple offices farther outside of the state, maybe even in Kansas or Utah.

"Allow me to plead my case over dinner." His dark gaze heats and he reaches across the space to finger a long blond wave of my hair.

The single touch sends a shiver down my spine. Is he using my attraction to him to get me in bed with him? Or to get me in bed with him in the business sense? My stomach plummets as I realize this is simply a ruse. He's a man that sees an opportunity to make more money and is trying to use his good looks and the longtime attraction of what used to be a young and impressionable girl to meet his current business desires.

I shake my head. "No, no thank you, Milo. I'm not interested. I've got to go. Take care of yourself, Milo."

My emotions are a whirlwind of confusion. With traitorous tears in my eyes and embarrassment in my heart, I run, literally run down the hall to the series of rooms that the dance group changed in. I don't even bother changing, just grab my bag and head for the door.

"Evie!" Suda Kaye races after me, Camden hot on her heels, but I don't stop until I'm in the safety of my Cayenne and racing home.

2

"Ms. Ross, Ms. Williamson will see you now." Shelley, the receptionist, smiles sweetly, gesturing her arm toward the door to my therapist's office.

I offer her a flat half smile, not at all in the mood to give anything more than the bare minimum. I'm still steaming from last night's epic embarrassment between Milo and me.

Since then he's left a voice mail message and texted. I was surprised at the text. Mostly because he doesn't seem the type to text when he can make a call and get straight to the heart of an issue. Though based on his two-word message of **Call me**, I'm guessing it's not his normal mode of communication.

My phone dings and I glance down at the newest text. Make that number six from Suda Kaye. She is all about the texting. Though in her defense, she tried to call me last night and again this morning. I didn't respond to either. I scan her texts and note how they get increasingly more irritated.

Why did you run out?

What happened when you talked to Milo?

You looked like you might have been crying. Call me back.
I don't care what time.

Two more came this morning.

Are you mad at me? Please don't be mad at me.

Crapola. You're mad at me. Call me back and yell at me. I
can take it.

Now this one. I huff under my breath and stand, flattening the wrinkles in my black pencil skirt.

Sissy, I'm freaking out. Call me back today or I'm going to
hunt you down.

Serves her right. She's the one that put me in the ridiculous
position to be embarrassed in the first place. She knew Milo
would be at that dinner and purposely didn't tell me. That's
right up there with being a traitor to the sisterhood, except
worse, because I'm her blood sister, not a friend or stranger
she was trying to put one over on. Suda Kaye knew exactly
what she was doing. In fact, she may have even planned it
just so I would be in the same room as Milo, dancing around
him half-naked.

I clench my teeth and smoothly walk into my therapist's
office. This is only my third visit, and after last night, I know
for a fact I need to get this off my chest.

Ms. Williamson is a petite black woman with an incredible
pair of toned legs, a bright smile and beautiful braids pulled
back into a low ponytail. She's in her late forties or early fifties, but I wouldn't dare ask one way or another.

"Hello, Evie." She holds out her hand and I shake it, giving her a genuine smile, unlike the one I gave Shelley.

"Thank you for fitting me in." I take a seat and primly cross my legs and rest the tip of my patent-leather peep-toe Louboutins where I can admire them. They cost a mint even on sale but were worth every penny. They make my legs look a mile long and give me another three to four inches on my height. When you're a woman working in a male-dominated world, you need every advantage possible. Besides, they are edgy and sexy in a classy way I adore.

"I'm glad it worked out." Ms. Williamson leans back into her chair sitting kitty-corner from the couch I'm perched on. "Now how can I help you?"

I frown, not knowing where to start.

"You obviously called this morning feeling an urgent need to discuss what's on your mind, so let's start with that."

"I had a very uncomfortable encounter last night. I couldn't sleep. Tossed and turned all night. Woke up feeling even more frustrated and out of sorts."

"And what happened in your evening that led to you feeling this way?"

For the next ten minutes I go over what happened last night, from the filling in for the original dancer to the conversation with Milo.

"You haven't mentioned a man in your life in your last two sessions," she says while scanning a yellow legal pad.

I swallow and sit up straighter. "That's because I don't have a man in my life."

"Except your sister seems to think you do and is instigating situations in which you are forced into communicating with this man."

I roll my eyes. "My sister is all of a sudden an incurable romantic. She's incapable of not pushing love, or at the very least lust, onto people, especially now that she's married to the love of her life and living the dream."

The doctor stares at me, her dark gaze unassuming yet expectant. For what, I don't know.

"It's not like she ever dreamed of love and a family before. You should have seen her. The woman has had more bed-mates than I've had years in school. Including my bachelor's and master's degrees."

"Mmm-hmm." She nods.

"So, she travels the world for a decade, leaving me behind, then reads a letter from Mom telling her to come home. She finally does, only to fall right into the arms of the man she left behind ten years ago. And get this! He was still in love with her, helped her get her boutique up and running so it's already turning a profit and then married her! He's already talking about when they can start having children. Can you believe that! My baby sister, having children. And before me." I huff and shake my head. "Insanity."

"Is it?"

I bug out my eyes. "Well, yeah. Suda Kaye is the most irresponsible person I know. Takes right after our mother. Marches to the beat of her own drum and doesn't give two figs if she's ruining your plans or leaving you behind."

"Ah, I see. So you're not mad at your sister for setting you up to be in a position to see the man you've admitted to having a crush on since you were a child, but because she left you behind when she went off on her adventures? Like your mother."

"Yes!" I point to her and it hits me what I've just said. "I mean, no. It's definitely about last night. Suda Kaye and I are trying to get past all of that. What happened before is over. We've started anew." I firm my chin and sit up straighter, uncrossing my legs and holding on to my knees.

"Have you really started over?"

"Definitely. My sister may be a menace in a lot of ways, but she's the most important person in my life. She's my best friend."

"I don't doubt that. Though it sounds as though you still have some underlying issues with the fact that she left you all those years ago."

I shrug. "I mean, it hurt, her leaving like that."

"Though she asked you to come with her, did she not?"

"Well, yes, she did, but—"

"And you chose to stay behind, go to school and, as you've put it before—" she flips through her notes "—make something of yourself. Which you have."

"Yes, I have. I'm doing exceptionally well in my career."

"And yet the fact that your sister found love after abandoning it for ten years irks you."

I open and close my mouth. "No. I want her to be happy."

"Again, that is not in question."

"As I said, she's the most important person in my world. I'd die for her. I want her to be happy and Camden makes her so happy I feel like for the first time she's actually going to stay put, put down roots here in Colorado, near me."

"And how does that make you feel?"

"Relieved."

"That's an odd choice of words. Why relieved?"

"Because I know she's safe and taken care of. Camden will ensure she's happy, protected and smiling every day. That was always my job."

"And what about you? What makes you smile?"

"Uh, um, lots of things."

Ms. Williamson waves her hand in the air. "Like what?"

I inhale full and deep and think hard. "To start, work. Work makes me happy."

"Okay, outside of work."

"My sister."

"Besides your sister." Her lips twitch with what I assume to be humor.

Sweat starts to tickle under my arms and I adjust my seat, grab at my blouse and fluff it against my chest trying to get a bit more air.

"I, um, love Camden's family. They've been great adding me into the mix, inviting me to family dinners. Those are fun."

"That's sweet of them. But what I want to know, Evie, is what do you do for *you* that makes you happy."

"I bought these shoes last week." I lift my foot. "Got a great deal on them, too."

My therapist purses her lips and then laces her fingers together and rests them on top of her legal pad.

"Evie, do you have any hobbies?"

I lick my lips and clear my throat. "There really hasn't been time for hobbies as I was setting up my career and working myself to the bone to make it successful."

"And now it is. You said so yourself. So successful that your old crush wants to go into business with you. An issue we still need to discuss."

I wave my hand. "Not necessary. I already put him off."

"Exactly. Why did you do that? If you're the successful woman you claim to be, you should want to hear more about what potential business proposition he has to offer. And yet, because it came from someone you clearly still have feelings for, you ran. Physically ran away from him *and* the opportunity. Has he tried to reach out?"

"Yes."

"And?"

"I've ignored him."

"Why?" she asks softly.

"Because I can't fathom being in the same room as him in a business capacity when all I can think about is falling into bed with him!" I blurt, desperate to get her off the subject and on to something else.

The therapist smiles wide. "Finally, we get to the truth. You ran because you felt rejected. Is it because you don't often get rejected?"

My mouth falls open as if detached from my head. "No! Oh my goodness, no."

"So, then you've been rejected by the opposite sex often?" she prods.

I shake my head. "No, because I never put myself out there."

"Ah, I see. You're angry because your expectation of Milo was too high. You wanted him to have the same feelings for you that you have for him. And when he didn't respond in the way you'd hoped, and instead discussed his business interest, you shut down any form of communication with the man."

"No. I mean, uh, hmm."

The therapist cants her head to the side and focuses on me with a warm expression covering her pretty face. "Evie, you have to let go of your expectation as it pertains to Milo. Maybe he truly is only interested in you in the business sense, even though he said he was romantically attracted to you. You'll never know one way or the other by avoiding the man and running away."

I slump back against the couch. "You want me to meet with him."

"That's up to you. Do you think you should meet with him?"

"I guess. I mean, he's the one who has been chasing me

down. I'm the one who's hiding." I tap my fingernail on my knee and think about how I'm letting this person have all the control over my thoughts and reactions. Well, not anymore. "You know what, I'll do it. I'll call him back and set up a meeting. Find out what he wants." I shrug. "If I want to prove to him that I'm the shrewd businesswoman he thinks I am, and also prove to myself that I can get past this hurdle of my childhood crush, there's only one way to do it." I nod my head as if the decision has already been signed, sealed and delivered.

"Excellent. Now let's discuss why the only things that make you happy are your job, your sister and your brother-in-law's family. What are you doing to enjoy the life you've built?"

My head feels so heavy at her question that I allow it to fall forward while I twine my fingers together in my lap.

"Honestly, I have no idea. I've spent so long preparing for the future, now that it's here, I don't know what to do with myself. It's like I don't even know who I am anymore."

"Then let's figure that out. What do you say?" she asks, chipper as a child.

"I'd like that. Lord knows I have no idea where to start."

In for four beats, out for four beats.

For a full two minutes I grip the edge of my desk and breathe, allowing all the fear and anxiety to melt away and my capable, take-charge, badass businesswoman to ease into place. Once I've let it go, I open my eyes and pick up my work phone. I dial the number I've had memorized for ages. I could have called on my mobile, but since this is a business call I'm calling from my office. Draw the lines in the sand right out of the gate.

The phone rings once, twice and then three times before a deep voice clips, "Chavis."

"Hello, Milo. It's Evie."

"Hold on." His voice sounds throaty and direct in those two simple words.

I can hear a clanking noise in the background and pop music blaring as if in the distance, getting farther and farther away the longer I wait.

"Sorry. Evie, you still there?" His words come through in a winded rush.

"Um, yes. I'm sorry, did I catch you at a bad time?" I glance at the clock. Just shy of six o'clock.

"No. At the gym. Just finished."

The gym.

Instantly a vision of Milo's six-foot-four-inch frame dressed in shorts and a pair of tennis shoes, his massive chest blanketed in sweat, flits across my mind. I fan my suddenly heated face.

"Okay, well, I just want to call and apologize for my behavior last night. It was highly unprofessional and definitely out of character."

"Apology accepted." The sound of his voice is a deep rumble that has butterflies fluttering in my stomach pleasantly.

I smile even though he can't see it. "Excellent."

"That doesn't change why you ran, *Nizhoni*. A fact we will be discussing," he states firmly.

"Milo…" I say while my heart starts to pound, the fear and anxiety flowing right back inside of me, the butterflies taking a hike instantly.

"Dinner. Tonight. No exceptions. And do not think of running."

I suck in a harsh breath and firm my resolve. He wants to talk, fine. I can take it. I can handle anything. My badass businesswoman mentally fist-bumps me. "Fine. Sure. Where?"

"You pick."

I grind my teeth. The man is infuriating. He demands dinner and then makes me pick the place?

The first place that comes to mind is Cam's brother Porter's restaurant. "Bryant Brews. My brother-in-law's family owns it. They have a great menu." Plus, if Porter is there, I'll have a friendly face and someone who can help get me out of a bind if needed.

"Fine. See you at seven," he practically purrs into the phone before hanging up.

I hear nothing but dead air as I pull the phone away from my ear and stare at the thing as though it might possibly have the answers to the weirdest conversation of my life.

Shaking my head, I place the phone back on the receiver, lean my elbows on my desk and rest my chin in my hand.

"What the heck did I just commit to? Dinner. With Milo. I'm such an idiot." I groan.

While I'm sitting there staring blankly out my window at the view from my Pueblo office, my cell phone buzzes on my desk.

It's my sister calling. For the millionth time.

"Two birds, one stone. My therapist would be thrilled." I sigh and answer the phone. "Hey, sis."

"Hey, sis? Don't 'hey, sis' me, lady! You've had me worried out of my mind and you know that worry is not a good look on me!"

The chuckle slips out of my mouth.

"Oh, sure, laugh at the poor sister who's been fretting, thinking her sister hates her for pulling a fast one. *Taabe*, I'm sorry. I'm so so so sorry."

"Are you? Really?" I know Suda Kaye too well.

"Um, should I be?" she corrects with a note of humor in her tone.

I sigh into the line and run my fingers through my long wavy hair. "What you did wasn't cool but why you did it was. Just next time you try to invade my love life, give me a heads-up? I don't like surprises, Kaye. You know that."

"I know. And for that I am sorry. I just… I don't know. I thought he'd see you all sexy and shaking your hips and his heart would explode and he'd scoop you up and make you his woman!"

"You read too many romance novels." I sigh and play with my computer mouse.

"Girl, I'm living in one! Camden is my knight in sexy slacks and cowboy boots. Of course I want that for my big sis." Her voice lowers. "Evie, I want you to be happy."

"Me, too. I'm working on that. I promise."

"Really?"

"I'm meeting Milo for dinner in less than an hour."

The line is so quiet I worry we may have been disconnected until a loud clapping sound can be heard along with a high-pitched girlie squeal. "Woo-hoo! My prayers have been answered. I'm gonna ring *Toko* and tell him to call off the elders and their prayers. This. Is. Awesome!" Her words come through the line in a rush of energy and excitement.

"Don't get too excited. We're meeting to discuss his business proposal."

"I'm sorry. What was that? You're going to discuss him giving you the business?" She chuckles wildly.

"Suda Kaye!"

Another series of raucous laughs can be heard until my sister finally gets herself together. "Man, this is great. Just great. What are you going to wear?"

I look down at my work attire. A slim pencil skirt that

hugs my curves and falls to just above the knee, the sexy peep-toe shoes and a royal-blue silk blouse. I repeat all of this to my sister.

"Boring! Stop by the shop and I'll have a dress ready."

"No! This is business, not a date. Now, stay out of it." I knew I shouldn't have told her, but in all honesty, I didn't have much by the way of excitement in my life to discuss with her.

"You ruin all my fun!" I can practically hear her pout through the phone.

"Business dinner, remember."

"Okay, well, call me the second you get into the car."

"I don't talk while driving. It's dangerous," I remind her. Ever since I had a car accident when I was a teenager, Mom hitting her head against the window and needing stitches, I don't take any risks behind the wheel.

She sighs audibly. "Then talk to me through the speakers. Just call."

"You're not going to let this go until I agree to call, are you?"

"You've known me twenty-eight years. Have I ever let something like this go?"

I close my eyes and feel the defeat eating up my defenses. "Fine. I'll call."

"Yay! Okay, don't order anything with onions or garlic."

I frown. "Why not?"

"In case he kisses you!"

I shake my head. "Do you ever listen? *Business dinner.*"

"So you've said a hundred times. Cam and I hooked back up because of our *business* relationship. It happens. Oooh, and I hope it happens to you. All that big beautiful hunk of Native American hotness. His dark to your light. Gawd! A match made in heaven. Predestined!"

I can hear her clapping through the line.

"You're insane."

"But you love me."

"Miss me," I say, forcing her to end the conversation.

"Miss me more!" she squeals in what can only be sisterly delight.

"Always. Now I gotta head out."

"Remember, no onions or garlic, and if he gives you the go sign, slip him a little tongue action!"

"Sweet mother, you cannot help yourself."

"Never! Love you. Bye!" She hangs up and I straighten my shoulders when my phone rings again. I'm just about to nail my sister thinking it's probably her with something she forgot to say when I note the caller ID says that it's Dad calling.

"Hey, you!" I answer with a smile.

"Hiya, sweetheart, how's my best girl doing?" His voice is deep and filled with warmth.

"Good, good. I'm actually on my way out to a business dinner so I only have a few minutes. I'm so glad you called. I've missed you. When are you coming home for a visit? It's been ages, Dad."

He sighs. "I know, sweetheart, but things are heating up here. You know how it is. Duty calls."

"And you always answer," I tease.

My father chuckles and it's music to my ears, so much so it lifts my spirits. "Still, Dad, you deserve some time off. You couldn't even make it for Suda Kaye's wedding." I grind down on my teeth. Not that she minded. To her it was all the same if he were there to walk her down the aisle or not. Our grandfather performed that honor.

"You're right, as usual. I'm burning the candle at both ends and I definitely need a break."

"You need to retire! You've given the military most of your life. When will it be your time to do what you want?"

Another hearty laugh comes through the line. "When will my thirty-year-old baby settle down and get married and give me some grandchildren? Maybe then I'll be more motivated to retire and move back to Colorado."

"I see what you did there, turning it around on me." I laugh. "Someday, Dad. When the right man comes calling…"

"And he will. I'm certain of it. My girl is beautiful, smart and her father's daughter."

"Absolutely!" I smile and grab my purse, setting it on my desk. "Dad, I really do have to go, though. Can we chat again soon?"

"I'd love nothing more. Be good. And get out and have some fun once in a while, will ya?"

I grin. "Sure, Dad. I promise. Love you."

"I love you, Evie. Tell your sister I love her, too, and to give her dad a call sometime."

"Will do." Though I know in my heart she'll agree and just forget.

"Bye, sweetheart."

"Bye, Dad." I toss my phone into my purse, grab my leather blazer and put it on. I glance in the big, rectangular mirror hanging along the wall in my office and assess my outfit. I think it looks hip, if not business edgy with the shoes and the blazer.

I groan and fluff my hair. "Why do I care about my looks? It's business. So, I'm going to dinner one-on-one with the only man I've ever wanted to be with. He's off-limits. Business only."

Firming my spine, I loop my purse over my shoulder and offer myself an air kiss.

"You've got this, girl." I give myself a little pep talk and head out the door.

3

Bryant Brews is hopping when I arrive at quarter to seven. When the hostess approaches, I wave her off, planning to go directly to the bar. Less date-like, more noise. Unfortunately, there's only a booth available in the bar and nothing else in the rest of the place. Sighing, I head for the single booth and pick up the drink menu. Booze will be necessary if I'm going to get through a business dinner with Milo.

While I scan the menu, I feel a familiar presence tap on my shoulder. I glance up at the smiling face of Porter Bryant, the owner and a longtime family friend.

I stand up and he pulls me into his arms for a hug.

"Hey, it's been too long." I smile, still holding his biceps and beaming into his handsome face. Porter has always been the most attractive of the Bryant brothers in my opinion but that's because he's not only good-looking but so easygoing. With dark brown hair and kind, expressive milk-chocolate-brown eyes, he could woo a woman with a simple smile but it's the comfort and confidence he exudes in his nature that gets me every time.

"How's it going, Sunshine?" He calls me the same nickname the entire Bryant clan does.

"Good. Obviously, business is booming tonight." I gesture around the room.

"Always. You meeting someone?" He runs his thumb over and around my shoulder. It's a subtle yet sensuous caress through the silk of my shirt that makes me shiver a little. He smirks at my response and cocks an arrogant brow. There's always been an edge of sexual tension simmering between me and Porter even though I've never acted on it. I've known the Bryant family for ages, and I don't want anything to risk the family connection. If we were to date and it went badly, I'd be in for a lifetime of being uncomfortable around Suda Kaye's in-laws. Still, he is a very attractive man and hard to put off after all this time.

"Actually, she's waiting for me." Milo's voice booms over the noise of the other patrons laughing and carrying on around us.

I turn my head to find Milo standing in a pair of black slacks and a pressed red dress shirt. The cuffs are rolled up his muscular forearms and his hair is down. All those glossy black strands falling over his massive chest and shoulders like a Native American god make my knees feel weak.

I open my mouth to speak when Milo gently wraps a hand around my arm and tugs me toward him. I stumble over my own feet and land flat against his chest. His arm encircles my waist and he presses his cheek to mine.

He places a kiss on my cheek and whispers in my ear. "You look amazing, *Nizhoni*."

I stand stock-still, not knowing what to do or even if I can respond. His mere presence does that to me.

"And you are?" Porter asks with a note of irritation coating his tone.

I spin around and instantly realize my mistake when Milo doesn't release his arm, his hand now resting on my abdomen and my back pressed fully against his chest. Heat warms my backside and I do everything I can not to swoon but instead remember this is supposed to be a business dinner—not a date.

"Milo Chavis, meet my friend and Camden's brother, Porter," I say, making the introduction.

"You're CJ's little brother," Milo offers, referring to Coltrane Junior, the eldest of the Bryant brothers.

Porter nods. "Yeah."

"We went to school together. I recommended Suda Kaye contact his foundation," Milo adds.

Porter snaps his fingers in recognition and points to him and smiles. "That's right. Now I remember the story. Cool, man. Good to meet you." He holds out a hand to Milo.

Instead of releasing me to shake his hand, Milo moves me bodily to his left side, curls that arm around me, keeping me close, and offers his right hand.

My friend's gaze clocks the move and he frowns. "You're dating Evie?" he asks with surprise and maybe even a hint of disappointment.

At the same time I shake my head and say, "No, we're just friends," Milo responds with, "That's the plan."

I pull away from Milo and stare up into his chiseled face and dark eyes. "What in the world?"

"I was very clear last night regarding my attraction to you."

"Are you being serious right now?" I press my hands flat against his chest.

"Yes," is his one-word stern reply.

"Yes? What the... You said you wanted to do business with me!" It takes everything I have not to stomp my foot.

"And I do."

I shake my head as if trying to clear it. "You're not making any sense. You said you were fond of me!"

"I am also that. Very fond." He grins and that expression spears through my form and makes those damn butterflies wake up and take notice in my stomach. "You're an amazing woman, Evie. I can be fond *and* attracted to you, *and* want to do business with you."

Without knowing what the heck to say I just stare into his coal-black eyes and get lost in them. I've never had the opportunity to just look into his eyes this close up. They are stunningly beautiful. Like shiny black onyx with long thick eyelashes perfectly framing them. And his high cheekbones make me want to trace them with the tips of my fingers. I can't even get into his plump pout. *Kissable* is the word I'd use but it would take my mind to a place I cannot bear to go and get rejected again.

"Uh, I'm going to go, and let you two work out your differences." Porter's suggestion surprisingly sounds a lot like dejection. "See ya, Sunshine. I'll send over that wine you liked last time."

Embarrassment burns hot at my cheeks as I glance over my shoulder at his retreating form. I can't believe I forgot Porter was even there, but that's the least of my problems. Swallowing, I lift my chin and firm my resolve and focus on the man in front of me.

"Milo, this is very awkward. We're supposed to be discussing the business proposition you have for me, not standing here in a clinch."

His beautiful lips twist up into the sexiest smirk I've ever seen. I'm a puddle of goo and have no lock on my emotions or physical desires when pressed against the man of my dreams.

"Before I let you go, you must know, I never said I didn't want to date you. Just that I wanted to discuss business first."

His words filter through my brain and the synapses start firing well enough that I'm capable of standing on my own two feet without assistance. I frown and attempt to push away. He doesn't let me go.

"I'm not done having you close, *Nizhoni*." He dips his head and presses a kiss to my temple, then runs his chin and cheek down the side of my face. The long silky strands of his hair tingle against my skin and I close my eyes, inhaling the leather-and-smoke-infused scent that has always permeated the air around him.

Before I realize what he's doing, he places a warm kiss on the side of my neck. I tremble and dig my fingers into his chest.

"Mmm, responsive. This is good," he murmurs against my skin, his breath warm and inviting.

My mind swirls with desire and I let out the breath I was holding while pushing out of his grip. "Stop. I don't even know what this is." I stagger farther away, gesturing between us before dropping into one side of the booth.

His lips twitch in what can only be amusement as he folds his large frame into the seat opposite me. A waitress rushes up and places a glass of white wine in front of me. I grab for the glass as though my life depends on it, gulping down a large amount. I swear I'm about to expire from a rapidly beating heart, an overactive libido and a whopping dose of what the heck is happening.

"I'll have the Colorado IPA. Whatever steak you offer, medium. Potato. Vegetables. Evie? You've eaten here before. What would you like?"

I physically have to watch my hand let go of the wineglass I've been clinging to like a baby to its pacifier. "Um, the same."

"That will be all until the food is ready," he states curtly, and focuses his magnetic gaze back on me.

I lick my lips and look down at my glass before clearing my throat. "You wanted to talk business?" My voice is shaky after the embrace and kisses. Sure, they were only temple and neck kisses but that was more demonstrative than I've ever seen him before. It felt so incredibly intimate coming from him.

"I've changed my mind. No business."

I frown and tip my head. "But—"

"I want you," he states directly, as he leans his elbows on the tabletop and laces his long fingers together where he rests his chin and stares me down.

Stares. Me. Down.

"I'm sorry, I don't think I heard what you said. You want what?" Two and two is definitely not adding up to four.

"You," he states flatly.

Inhaling a full breath, I let it out slowly. "Milo, I'm not sure I understand."

"Yes, you do."

I shake my head. "No, um, I don't think I do, because we've known each other for a very long time and you've never shown any interest until I made a fool of myself last night and—"

"I wasn't in the position to share my interest before. I am now."

Frowning, I reach for my glass and take a huge drink, so much so it burns the back of my throat as I swallow.

"You, me, we... I'm confused."

At this he smiles, showing no teeth, and sits back against

the booth, crossing those muscular arms over one another, an imposing king looking down at his citizens.

"Let me be clear, Evie. I want you in *every way* that matters."

I blink stupidly with my glass aloft a few inches from my face.

He smirks as he leans forward, getting closer. The table seems minuscule with his large body hovering over it. He presses his hand flat against the wooden surface.

"I want you in my life. I want you as my work partner. I want you in my home, and I want your gorgeous body in my bed. Is that clear enough for you, *Nizhoni?*"

Every sentence has me jumping out of my skin ready to catapult myself into his arms. He's saying everything I've ever dreamed of but none of it computes. I still can't comprehend how the heck we came to this scenario where he wants me as a partner in his business, in his life and in his *bed*.

"Uh, yeah. Yep, that's, yeah, that's very specific. Very clear." I stumble through my response and pound the last of the glass of wine as the server brings our plates and sets them down in front of us. "I'll take another big glass of wine. Big. Huge! Please and thank you."

Milo chuckles, unrolls his fork and knife from the napkin wrapped around it and sets the cloth to his lap. "Eat. You're going to need it. We have much to discuss."

I end up drinking my dinner. Glass after glass of wine I slosh down my gullet in order to avoid talking about anything of importance. It's as though the second he said he wanted me in his bed, my entire IQ went out the window, my brain following along, skipping, while my libido stayed and got drunk and danced the Macarena, while the rest of me shut down.

Thankfully, Milo is a true gentleman and drove me home. Though I'm not quite sure what took place after that.

Flickers of minimemories flash along the surface of my mind as I slowly wake up.

Me holding on to Milo's waist while he unlocked my door.

Him taking me into the bedroom.

Me grabbing him around the waist and pulling out his shirt, pressing my eager hands to the hot skin of his waist.

Him removing my clothes.

Me removing his shirt.

And that's when everything goes black.

I sit up in bed and press my hand to my aching forehead. "Jesus, what happened last night?" I rub at the tension pounding against my noggin.

"You drank your weight in wine, *Nizhoni*," comes the one voice in the entire world I do not want to hear.

I glance up and see Milo standing in a thin white ribbed tank top and his dress slacks. His feet are bare and crossed at the ankles. His beautiful hair is down around his shoulders blanketing the top of his upper body. He's holding a blue ceramic mug that's steaming. The scent of freshly brewed coffee fills the air.

"Milo, you're still here?" I fling the covers back and hop out of bed, finding I'm a little shaky on my bare feet.

"Well, I couldn't leave."

I frown. "Why not?"

He grins. "For one, you're wearing my shirt." I look down and my heart starts to beat so hard I cover my chest with my hand. "For two, I would never leave you unsafe in an unlocked home, nor in your condition. I wanted to be close in case you needed me in the night."

I run my hands down the length of my body and find I'm still wearing my bra and underwear but nothing else outside of his crimson-colored dress shirt…and even that's only buttoned in the center. "Did we…?" I gesture to the bed and dip my head in shame.

That has him laughing heartily, a sight I watch in equal fascination and horror. Fascination because he's absolutely magnificent when he laughs, full teeth showing, head tipped back, strong throat working, and horror because I truly cannot remember what happened after he undressed me.

"Milo, please. Did we?" I lick my lips and firm my spine, standing up straight with my shoulders pressed back, ready to be responsible for whatever my inebriated self did under the influence.

He presses off the doorjamb he was leaning against and sets his coffee on my dresser. His powerful frame moves forward and pulls me into his arms, both of them locking together around my waist. "My *adinidiin*, you amuse me."

"What's *adinidiin* mean?"

"'My light.'" He smiles softly, staring at my face as if I am the very sun giving him life.

I clench my jaw and grimace, starting to feel uncomfortable standing in my room plastered to an almost bare-chested Milo while wearing his shirt. A shirt I have no idea how I came to be wearing in the first place, and him laughing and finding me amusing while referring to me as his "light." That's it, I've woken up in another world, a parallel realm I didn't know existed.

No. "Am I awake yet? Perhaps I'm dreaming this?" I tunnel my fingers into both sides of my hair, but he just holds me tighter.

"You are not asleep, though I imagine your mind is slow from the wine."

I nod mutely.

He smiles, leans down and runs his nose along mine before kissing me at the very corner of my mouth. "Come. I have made you breakfast."

And with no further ado he grabs my hand and tugs me toward the kitchen. I follow along, attempting to keep up with his much longer strides. He brings me into my kitchen and pulls out a stool. I amble up onto it and tuck my hands under my thighs. Milo enters around the open bar and heads to the coffeepot. His large frame moves efficiently, and I watch while the muscles of his shoulders and arms contract and release as he gets me a cup from the cupboard above the machine and pours.

He's so large and his skin looks smooth. I wonder if it's soft to the touch.

"What do you take in your coffee?" he asks, breaking me out of my blatant perusal of his yummy skin.

"Creamer. Lots of it, with a side of ibuprofen," I mumble.

Shockingly he sets my ibuprofen bottle in front of me, winks and turns back to the fridge to take out the creamer. He adds a big dollop of the good stuff and sets a steaming mug in front of me.

"How did you know where to find this?" I lift the bottle and shake it, the pills inside rattling along the edges with my effort.

"Medicine cabinet in your bathroom."

"You looked inside my medicine cabinet? That's a huge no-no. You can't do that at someone's house. It's an invasion of privacy." I pick up my cup and hold it in front of my face, letting the heat of the coffee warm my palms and face.

He shrugs without a care in the world and moves to the fridge. He pulls out the eggs and sets them near the stove, which already has turkey bacon frying on low heat.

"You're making yourself rather comfortable in a woman's house you had a simple one-night stand in," I gripe.

His entire form goes still, and he stands facing the stove for a full ten seconds before he shuts off the burners, turns around and comes toward me. I set my coffee down and spin on the bar stool to face him head-on. He immediately gets the upper hand when he grabs my knees, eases them wide and steps right into my space.

Right into my space.

I gasp as he leans forward, and I lean back. He rests both of his palms on the edge of the counter behind me, caging me in.

"Listen, Evie, I'm only going to say this once. We did *not* have sex last night. We will soon, and when we do, you will be fully awake, sober and begging me to never stop. This is not a one-night anything. This is Evie and Milo."

I swallow and wait while the lump in my throat moves down far enough that I can actually speak. "And what if I don't want an Evie and Milo?"

He smiles wickedly and leans closer, his pelvis coming in direct contact with my center. I gasp and clench my thighs around his form instinctively to keep him closer.

"Your body says otherwise, *Nizhoni*." He moves his hand from the counter to the outside of my thigh. I bite down on my bottom lip and breathe as his warm palm inches up my thigh until he reaches my panty-clad booty.

In a move that defies all reason, one that must come straight out of the golden-god book he obviously owns, he curls his huge hand around my bum and squeezes while lifting up, grinding his powerful length against me until I moan and thrust my hips forward.

"Oh my." I lose my ability to speak when he places both hands on my ass and lifts me up and off the chair. I lock both of my legs to his waist and hold on for dear life.

"Milo!" I squeal.

He turns and sits in the stool with me propped up on his lap, his very sizable manhood rubbing exactly where I need him most.

"Do you want me, Evie?" he whispers, cupping my booty with one hand, my face with the other. Our mouths are only inches apart.

My entire body yearns to be taken by this man. Every pore, nerve ending and muscle throbs with the need to grab hold of what's being offered in front of me.

"Milo... I don't...this is crazy," I whisper, my mouth so close to his I can taste his breath on my tongue.

"Let's give crazy a chance." He curls his long fingers around my nape and tugs me closer. Our lips touch in the barest hint of flesh on flesh.

I close my eyes, wrap my arms around his shoulders and press my lips more firmly to his.

Gone.

Lost to his kiss.

He groans as he spears his tongue inside and I get my first real taste of Milo Chavis. My dream man. It's everything and more but I can't think straight. My entire body lights as if on fire. I let go of my inhibitions and plunge my hands into the long silky lengths of his hair and hold him to me. His lips are pillow soft and firm at the same time. He tastes of coffee and something uniquely masculine. The smoky leather scent I associate with him clings to his skin as I gasp for breath. His mouth runs down the length of my jawline and neck, then maneuvers back up for another searing kiss before he eventually pulls away.

"Gods, I knew you'd catch fire the minute I touched you." He cups my cheeks, his pitch-black gaze taking in every inch of my features. "The one woman I always wanted but couldn't have."

My stomach swirls, the acid from last night's wine mingling with the coffee of this morning as his words filter through the thick fog parading as my brain today. "I'm not sure I understand. The woman you always wanted?"

This has got to be a joke. Or maybe my mind is taking things in the wrong direction.

He pecks me on the lips. "You need food and I need to go to work. I have a meeting."

Physically, he lifts me off his lap and sets me on my feet. I grip the counter for balance.

"Milo, we just kissed," I state rather obviously.

"Yes, Evie. We will be doing a lot of that," he says while turning the stove back on. "Why don't you get dressed so I can." He smiles, glancing at the red shirt I'm wearing, then turns and pours the whisked eggs into the hot skillet.

I look down, realizing I'm still wearing his dress shirt from last night. My cheeks heat and I'm sure they match the crimson of the shirt perfectly. At least we didn't have sex. Not only would I freak out worse than I am now, I'd be so angry at myself for not remembering it.

Quickly I scamper into my room, pull off his shirt and tug on a pair of yoga pants and a tank top before dashing into the bathroom.

My lips are full, pink and swollen from his kisses. My cheeks are tinged a rosy color I haven't seen in ages. My eye makeup is a bit smudged but for the most part it stayed put. Now the hair is another thing entirely. It's a wild lion's mane of wavy long hair, natural volume for days and worse after Milo had his hands in it. I take a brush to it and put the lengths up in a messy bun on top of my head and brush my teeth.

By the time I make it back to the kitchen with Milo's wrinkled shirt, he's already eating. Sitting in front of my empty chair is a steaming plate of eggs, turkey bacon and toast.

I settle on the seat next to him and hang his shirt on the back of his chair. I want to know how I got the damn thing on in the first place, but am too afraid and embarrassed to ask.

"Thank you for breakfast." I put the first bite of eggs into my mouth and find I'm famished.

Before long we both obliterate the food and I grab the plates and bring them to the sink. "I'll clean up."

"I have to get home, shower and head to work. We still have much to discuss, Evie."

I nod, not wanting to commit to anything. I'm not even sure which way is up or down right now.

"I'll call you later."

"Yep. Okay," I agree, thinking there is no way I'm going to answer that call. I need time to figure out what's going on and how I want to handle it. But right now, I need him to go.

"Walk me to the door," he requests.

"Uh, okay." I set down the dishes and dry my hands, then follow him to the door.

He unlocks it and stands just inside. "Now kiss me."

Those three little words have my heart racing a mile a minute.

"I don't think that's such a good idea. You know, this all happened kinda fast and I for one think we need to take a step back and evaluate the situation."

Before I can react or respond further with myriad reasons why kissing again is a bad thing, he's got his arm around my form, my body once again smack-dab against his chest, and his face peers down at mine. "No steps back, only steps forward. You'll learn. I'll teach you," he says before his lips crash down on mine.

His tongue tantalizes the seam of my lips and I can't help

but open for him. He invades my mouth and kisses me deep. I forget all my concerns, wrap my arms around him, stand on my tiptoes and indulge.

Whoo boy, do I indulge. Gripping his hair at the roots and taking his mouth, nibbling on the bottom lip and sucking on his tongue. Delicious.

Eventually he pulls away and grins. "Now that's how you kiss your man, *Nizhoni*."

My man?

"Uh..."

He cups my face, slides his thumb along my cheekbone and lets me go. "I'll call. You'll answer."

"Mmm-hmm." I stand numb as he smiles and walks away. I shut the door and rest my back against it.

I'm the weakest woman alive. What did I just commit to?

4

Once I get showered and dressed, I head to work. Fortunately, I don't have any meetings today as it's after eleven when I finally make an appearance in my Colorado Springs office.

My assistant, Regina Procopio, is a petite Italian woman in her early sixties, a mother of four daughters that drive her absolutely bonkers but worship the ground she walks on. She treats me like her fifth daughter, is always in my business, griping about my lack of a love life and worrying about my workaholic ways.

"You're free of meetings today but you still have Mr. Chavis to call back. He's persistent, that fella, I'll give him that." She sifts through the stack of messages as she gives me her morning update.

"I've already spoken to him. Well, that's not exactly true. I had dinner with him last night and we, uh, well, just toss that one." I gesture to the note she has in her hand.

I move around to my desk and fall into my leather chair, blowing a breath of air over my face to shift the long side bang that fell into my eyes.

Regina stands mutely at my desk, a curious smile set to her lips. For a woman of sixty-two, and a committed smoker, she looks amazing. There are laugh lines around her mouth and eyes and her chestnut-brown gaze sears straight through to my soul.

"What?" I bug out my eyes and sigh.

"You had dinner with Mr. Chavis. The man with the incredible deep voice."

I press my lips together and glance out the window, nodding. "Mmm-hmm."

"And what did you discuss?" she pries.

"None of your business," I shoot off, and then clamp my mouth closed. Telling a woman like Regina that something is none of her business is like waving a red flag at an angry bull. Guaranteed to pique her interest.

She's a major gossip, an incredibly dedicated busybody, and she uses my life and the lives of her blood relations as her personal playground. Living vicariously through everyone else as she claims to have the life she loves. One with her children, her small home, her God and her smokes.

Regina's eyes light up and she sits in the chair opposite my desk, crosses her legs and grins.

Crap.

Regina has been my assistant since I started my business a decade ago. When Suda Kaye was off traveling the world, I was attending holiday meals and spending my birthday with Regina and her family. And there is nothing my very nosy, well-meaning, motherly assistant likes more than juicy news involving a man. When I dated Stanley for those two years, she constantly badgered me about how she didn't feel he was the right man for me. Said he was too boring. In the end, she was right, though I'm not sure how I fare any better to the opposite sex. I'm admittedly married to my job.

"Oh, *really*... None of my business. Hmm." She taps a pale-pink-painted nail to her lips. "In the past ten years, just about everything has been my business when it pertains to you. And since your mother, God rest her soul—" she makes the sign of the cross before continuing "—is no longer here to take care of you, God saw it fit to put you in my path. So that means it is my job. To worry, to be there and most specifically to hear all the tawdry details of dinner with deep-voice Milo Chavis. Now give!" Her tone brooks no argument.

I cross my arms over my desk and let my head plummet on top of them in defeat. "He's my childhood crush. I've been in love with him since I was eight years old. And all of a sudden he's decided that he wants to not only do business with me but date me. And I'm losing my mind and I just realized I have to tell my therapist about you, and that you and your girls count as things that make me happy so she doesn't think I'm a huge loser!" I brain-dump all my current problems, sucking in a huge breath.

Regina doesn't blink. "Let's go back to dinner with Milo. What happened?"

I frown and rest my chin to my forearms while staring at her kind, loving face. "I got drunk. He took me home. I woke up in his shirt not remembering anything..." This time her eyes widen to the size of beach umbrellas.

"And..."

"Apparently nothing happened. He made me breakfast. We kissed twice and he said he'd call me."

Regina leaps out of her chair like a jaguar jumping from a tree branch.

"Happy days are here again!" she sings while dancing around my office, shimmying her small rounded hips from side to side.

"Ugh! No. Not happy days. Did you miss the part about how I'm freaked out? I don't understand why he wants me.

He never paid me any interest growing up beyond saving me from a bunch of bullies. I haven't seen him since Suda Kaye's store opening."

"He was there? Dammit, I'm so mad I missed that! If my girls hadn't bought me and my sisters a cruise to the Bahamas, you know I wouldn't have missed it."

"I know, I know." I sit up and ease back in my chair. "But listen, just before Suda Kaye's opening, I bumped into him having lunch with his wife!"

She gasps and places her hand to her chest, covering her heart. "He's *married*," she says, positively scandalized.

I shrug. "According to Suda Kaye he's not anymore, but I don't know the details. All I know is when I met her, she was blonde and beautiful."

She smiles wide. "Then he has a type. One you fit perfectly."

Running my hands through my hair, I close my eyes. "I don't know, Reggie. The timing is off, and the repeated mention of doing business together has me uncertain of his true intentions."

"You think he's using your crush on him as a way to get in the pants of your business?"

"Honestly…" I sigh. "I'm so confused. I don't know what to think."

"What does your heart say?"

"He's everything I ever dreamed of," I answer honestly.

"And your head?"

"He scares the living heck out of me." Also true.

She frowns, comes around the desk and holds out her arms. I push my chair forward, wrap my arms around her waist and cuddle against her chest.

Regina runs her fingers through my hair and keeps me

close for a full five minutes. Then when my mind and heart feel a little more at peace, she pulls away and cups my face.

"Evie, you are a kind, successful, intelligent, beautiful young woman. Any man in his right mind would be falling over himself to make you part of his life. It's not strange that a successful and attractive man would want you in his world. I've cherished having you in mine and will continue to do so for many years to come."

Tears prick at the backs of my eyes as the only motherly figure I've had in the past decade lays out her truth.

"Maybe it's time you take a chance on a dream outside of work. You deserve more. I want more for you, as does your sister, as does your mother in heaven. You are worthy of a good man. A family of your own. Never doubt that."

"I love you, Reggie."

She smiles and kisses my forehead. "I love you, too, my darling one. Now take a few deep breaths, give yourself one of your pep talks you think I don't hear and get to work. And when Milo calls you later, give yourself a gift and answer it. Give the man a chance to prove himself."

After imparting her wisdom, she sashays toward the door. "I'm going for a smoke break."

"Cigarettes will kill you!" I holler.

"Probably. At least I'll die doing what I love! Isn't free will great?"

Free will is great.

Now if I can only apply it to my personal life I'd be set. I decide to call and update Suda Kaye on everything that happened. Maybe she'll have different advice.

The bell on the door chimes as I enter Gypsy Soul, my sister's boutique.

The place has at least fifteen customers milling about. I

spy my sister literally dancing to Abba's "Mamma Mia" behind the cash register. She's hand in hand with Addy, her sixteen-year-old sales associate, spinning her around while the customer waiting to pay watches and claps along.

"Looks like I'm late to the party." I set my purse on top of the long counter.

"Sissy!" Suda Kaye lets go of Addy's hands and rushes the few feet to me as Addy turns her attention to the customer. Suda Kaye flings the top half of her body over the barrier to pull me into a hug. "Oooh, I missed you." She kisses me on the lips in a sisterly peck and smiles. "I know we talked earlier but are you still mad at me?"

I slump over the counter. "No. Though I do feel like I need a little retail therapy. It's been a weird couple of days."

She tunnels her hands into her wild brown locks and gives the entire thing a good fluffing. The bazillion gold and silver bracelets she has on both wrists trail up her forearm and tinkle prettily. She's wearing a crop top and a flowy maxi-skirt. I can't see her feet but, knowing her, they are clad in some wild tall wedges, beaded sandals or a pair of cowboy boots if she's feeling a little honky-tonk.

"You told me about the Milo debacle on the call earlier, but have you decided what you're going to do?"

I shake my head. "Heck, no. That's why I'm here. Getting loved up by my sister and giving my credit card a workout."

"You know family discount applies to everything. You pay my costs and we're solid." She smiles and rests her arms over the counter.

"Kaye, you're never going to make money if you keep giving everyone the family discount."

She frowns. "Pish posh! I'm doing awesome thanks to my man, and consistent financial advice from the world's greatest planner ever!" She shimmies and spins around so her skirt twirls in a wide circle. I spy her red sandals that tie all the way up to her knees.

God, sometimes I wish I could be as sassy and free as my sister. "Thanks, *Huutsuu*. I'm gonna shop."

She snaps her fingers. "Oooh, I have a stunning dress I want you to try on."

I squint. "Try on or model for you?" Last time she asked me to try on a dress, she got out her phone and took pictures, which she later put up on her brand-new Gypsy Soul website.

"I can't have Addy and her friends be in all the pictures. I need women to wear these clothes, too! And you promised you'd help me in any way you could. Now come with me."

"Gahhh, you already owe me for the setup with Milo." I grumble and plod toward the dressing room.

Suda Kaye jolts her head back as if smacked. "Say what? How you figure?" She sets her hand on her hip and narrows her caramel-colored gaze my way. "The way I see it, you've had two full-on, fantasy-driven kisses and saw your man for the first time without a shirt. By my count, you owe *me*!" She points to her chest and smiles.

I open my mouth and glare. "Now you're claiming that I should be thanking you for what you did!"

She grins wide. "Yep! I'll expect my payment in the form of modeling at least four outfits."

"Did everyone take insanity pills? You, Milo, Regina."

"Oh, how is Regina?"

"Good. Wants to see you for a Sunday brunch with the girls soon. Says she wants to gather up all her babies. And she's adopted you as her sixth child."

Suda shrugs. "Works for me. I love that woman. I owe her a great deal for looking after the most important person in my world for all those years."

"Camden?" I joke even though there is a lot of truth

in my response. It's just easier to keep the peace and those thoughts to myself.

She bumps her shoulder with mine. "No, silly. My sissy. Hmm, maybe I'll pick her out a nice scarf or a bracelet and bring it to you. Ooh, and some for the girls, too. Get them hooked on my wares early on. Score me a few more customers."

I smile and focus on my sister's stunning face. She's really incredibly pretty. Long dark brown hair, caramel-colored eyes, high wide cheekbones and full lips. "I'm impressed, sis. Marketing in the form of gifts. Very business savvy."

"Right! Cam's got me taking an online marketing class with the local community college."

That has me stopping at the foot of the dressing room. "No kidding? You said you'd never step foot in a college. Claimed higher education wasn't for you."

"And I'm not. I said I'm taking a single online class. I have no desire to get a degree, just learn a few things that could help me along the way. If I flunk out, I flunk out."

"If you pass that class with a C or better, I'll let you take photos of me anywhere you want for a full weekend and fill in for another belly dancing spot when needed."

Her mouth drops open and she holds out her hand. I take her warm one into mine.

"Deal! Boy, are you going to regret that. I have a whole new line of summer bikinis coming in!"

I hold on to my sister's hand and don't let go. "Have I told you lately how proud of you I am?" My throat clogs and my voice is reed-thin as I push down the emotion filling my veins.

She pulls me into her arms for another hug. "Thank you. From you specifically it means more."

I hug her tight and then sniff while wiping at my suddenly wet eyes. "You know Mom would be screaming her pride from the rooftops."

Her smile is adorable. "I hope so. This is all such a very different world for me, but one I really feel settled in. You, Cam, his family, Gypsy Soul, *Toko*...it all feels right. I'm where my heart and soul want me to be. I've never been happier."

"Wanting what you have is an incredible feeling, I'm sure." I offer her the wisdom I wish I could apply to myself.

"And what about you? Do you want what you have?"

I think long and hard about her question, knowing the answer instantly but trying to find a way to truly come to terms with it. "Some of it, yes."

She nods solemnly. "Then it looks like we're going to need to find what you need to fill in the gaps!"

Always the positive one. Silver linings for days. The good thing is when it comes from her, I almost believe it. At least I want to. That's gotta be worth something.

My phone rings as the fabric of the third slinky dress my sister put me in falls to midthigh. I study myself in the mirror while digging through my purse. Without looking at the number, I accept the call and push the device to my ear while stepping into the silver platform heels she gave me that go with the dress.

"Evie Ross," I answer a little breathlessly.

"*Nizhoni*, you answered. I am very pleased."

Shoot! I did not plan on him calling this soon. I pull the phone back and realize the time reads six on the dot.

"Um, hi, Milo. How are you?" I try for small talk.

"Better hearing your voice. Have you eaten dinner?"

"No, uh, I haven't," I answer stupidly while pushing my foot into the other heel. They're a little tight but it doesn't

TO CATCH A DREAM • 71

matter since she just wants to take a picture of me in the getup for the website.

"Excellent. I'll pick you up in an hour."

"Wait, what? I can't." I push the hair off my face and squeal when my sister yanks open the curtain.

"Holy smokes. You look so freakin' hot, Evie! Yowzers! This dress is going to sell out the second I put your picture on the website."

"Kaye, I'm on the phone. Give me a sec," I grumble, and focus on the phone.

"What are you wearing, Evie?" comes Milo's warm tone.

"Excuse me?" His words roll around my scattered brain and connect. "Oh, right, I'm trying on dresses for Suda Kaye. Sometimes she has me model them for her, so she has new images on her website."

"And according to your sister, you look hot."

I can feel the flush of heat rushing up my neck and over my cheeks. "Her words. Not mine."

"You're a gorgeous woman, Evie. And since you're already wearing the dress, why not keep it on so I can see it. I'm already in my car and on my way."

"No!" I screech. "I'm not in Colorado Springs. I'm in Pueblo at Suda Kaye's shop."

"I gathered that, *adinidiin*. I'm close to Pueblo. I've just finished up with a client in Wigwam."

"Hurry up. I want to get a picture of you. Cam wants to take me out to dinner tonight," Suda Kaye blurts.

I wave off my sister. "I have to do this for Suda Kaye. And we're supposed to have dinner with her husband," I lie.

Suda Kaye's brows furrow as she tips her head and mouths, *Milo?*

I nod as she grins.

"Of course Milo can come to dinner with us, too!" she says so loudly the entire store can hear her.

Milo laughs heartily. "I see your sister is as eager to have us together as I am. I must thank her in person. I'll be there in twenty minutes. And, Evie?" His voice dips lower and just the timbre has my heart pounding and arousal slicking between my now-clenched thighs. "Wear the dress for me." He hangs up and I press the off button and toss the phone into my bag.

"I cannot believe you did it to me *again*!" I grate through clenched teeth.

"What? You didn't want to have dinner with us? It's what you said on the phone." She pouts and then follows up her sweetness with a snarky evil grin.

Then I hear another phone go off. Suda Kaye digs into the side of her cleavage and pulls out her phone. She answers it while holding up a finger to me in a "hold that thought" gesture.

"Why, hello there, Milo... Yes, Evie is still in the hot-as-Hades dress... Mmm-hmm. Of course you can. Family discount!" She blathers on happily while walking over to the counter. "With the discount the dress is seventy-nine dollars. The shoes another eighty... The real price, oh, the dress is priced at eighty-nine and the shoes ninety-nine... Mmm-hmm... Aw, really, I'm happy to discount you. Just like Evie. She never lets me give her the discount, either. You money people." She shakes her head and writes something down before saying, "A hundred and eighty-eight. And no, I refuse to charge you sales tax... Okay, deal. Drinks on you tonight." She stands in front of the credit card machine and starts pressing buttons.

"What are you doing?" I gasp-whisper, and wince as the too-tight shoes pinch my toes and the backs of my heels.

"Ouch, ouch." I teeter-totter after her, eventually making it up to the counter.

"Evie, those don't fit. Let me get you a half size up," Addy says helpfully, dashing to the back where they keep the extra stock.

"Not a problem," Suda Kaye says to Milo, and then looks at me. "Smokin' hot. You won't be able to keep your hands off her." Her lips press together before she bites into the bottom one, clearly holding back her laughter.

My mouth falls wide open and I gape like a fish. "You're dead meat!" I whisper, and try to move but am forced to stop as the too-tight shoes cut into my heels.

"Karma," she fires back with her hand over the receiver so Milo can't hear, then goes back to the call. "Looking forward to it. See you soon! Bye!"

"I cannot believe you. My own sister. A traitor of the worst kind!"

Suda Kaye flounces her way around the counter and stands in front of me. She puts both of her hands on her hips. "I did this for your own good. Milo is into you. You are into Milo."

"But—"

She shakes her head and swipes at the air. "Enough buts. Life is too short to worry about the what-ifs. For once in your damn life, leap toward something you've always wanted. Stop weighing all the pros, cons and risks. Just jump. Please. I really feel like he's going to give you a safe place to fall. And if he doesn't, I'll be here with open arms ready to take the *I-told-you-so*'s until you're blue in the face."

"And if I'm a blubbering brokenhearted mess?" I fire off.

"Then I'll hold you close, tell you repeatedly how much it's his loss and cry with you. Sissy, you don't know what you're missing out on in life if you don't take the chance when it comes along. I did, and look what happened. I've got the only man I've ever loved back in my life. His ring on my finger. My own store. You in my life every day. A family. I'm not traveling the world anymore looking for something I already had. Though I don't regret leaving. I wouldn't know how important what I have is if I hadn't experienced losing it and gaining it back. This is your chance to go for something you've always wanted. You'll never know unless you try. Really try."

My shoulders fall and I glance down at the shoes that are killing my feet. Just then Addy pops back with the new shoes in my size. I slip out of the old painful ones and into the correctly sized pair. They fit perfectly and suddenly they look gorgeous. There's no pain and they are stunning. My heart patters against my chest and I can't help but see a correlation between the first pair of shoes and the second. I tried the first pair and they didn't work. They hurt. Felt terrible and wounded me with every step. The same exact pair, in the right size, are suddenly amazing. Fit great, look sexy as heck and actually feel rather comfortable.

Is this the universe's way of telling me Suda Kaye is right?

"Fine. We'll all have dinner together. I make no promises."

"Oh, and he bought the dress and shoes for you. He says he'd pay any price to see you in something that's smokin' hot." She smiles so big her mouth is all bright white teeth and chipmunk cheeks.

I shake my head and sigh. "Can you take your photos so I can at least freshen up before dinner?"

"Go stand over there against the gallery wall."

I do as she says, and place my hand where she tells me on my hip, making the dark purple with sparkly iridescent shimmers glisten in the last of the sun's rays. I stare out the window and wonder if I'm capable of taking the risk on Milo. He has the power to not only devastate me but ruin me for all other men. Just the two kisses we had were already better than any other I've experienced before him.

How will I survive if I let myself have him and he leaves me? Because he will. Everyone does. Mom. Dad. Suda Kaye. Eventually work will become too much. Or maybe another woman will catch his eye. Then again, he could just lose interest. Like my therapist made me see, I'm a rather boring workaholic with little to no hobbies.

Yeah, he has too much integrity to cheat or leave me hanging. He'll simply lose interest and break it off.

Will a small amount of happiness with Milo be enough to carry me through the rest of my life? Is it possible that Milo could really be the man of my dreams?

I just don't know if it's worth the risk to find out.

5

The sound of two car engines has me looking out the window to see Camden's blond head exiting his car. Right behind him is Milo's truck. His large form folds out of the cab. He's still in his suit. The long hair I love so much is pulled back, this time in a braid, which instantly makes me jealous of whoever got to put their hands in his hair and braid it for him.

"Crapola!" Suda Kaye groans while looking out the front window display and dashing off. "Cam dressed up. Need to throw on a dress. Be right back," she says while grabbing a black-and-gold number off a rack and sprinting into the dressing room. "Addy," she hollers. "You're gonna need to close up and do the credit card run for the day."

"You got it, boss lady!" Addy moves around the counter and finishes ringing up the last of the patrons.

Suda Kaye giggles from behind the partitioned-off dressing rooms. "Boss lady. I love it!"

I watch as Milo and Camden shake hands on the sidewalk in front of the store. My own hands tremble as I take in their masculine forms. The two men couldn't be more different in build and coloring. Camden is tall with shoulder-length dirty-blond hair, and an athletic muscular body in a gray suit that I'm certain was tailored to fit him. He has hazel eyes and a mustache-goatee combo that suits him very well.

Milo is a dark horse. A couple inches taller, and much broader, with a hard chiseled jaw and striking bone structure. His brown skin is clean-shaven at the jaw and the part in his hair is a perfect line down the center of his head that flows back into a long, ropelike braid. His suit is dark, as is the shirt underneath, which calls attention to the turquoise bolo tie I've seen him wear before. At his waist is a matching belt buckle with additional turquoise stones in a shape I can't see from this distance.

The men are equals in the eye-candy department but there's something about Milo that sets a thousand bees buzzing in my stomach.

As if he can sense me, his head turns and his gaze zeros in on me through the window. His lips tip up into a slight smile, but his eyes rove over me from top to toe. Even from this distance and with a wall of glass between us, I can feel the power and heat pumping off him as he takes in my attire.

I blush at his blatant perusal before the moment is cut as he says something to Camden and moves to enter the store.

He walks right up to me and stops only a couple feet away.

"*Nizhoni*, you are more stunning than the stars and moon on a clear night."

I tip my head and swish the dress a little, feeling suddenly shy. "Thank you."

"No, thank *you*." He curls a beefy hand around my hip and tugs me forward. I rest my hands flat against his chest and he dips his head. "I'm going to kiss you, Evie. Are you ready?"

I shake my head and mutter, "No." Because I'm not. His kisses make me lose myself.

He gifts me the most precious smile. I lift up onto my tiptoes, wrap my arms around his neck and take his mouth.

He groans into my kiss, plunging his tongue deep, leaving no room for subtle, timid swipes. I moan and flick my own against his. One of his hands slides up my back and into my hair to control my head. The other eases down my body until he cups my bum and squeezes. Lifting me up and more firmly against him. I sigh into his kiss, allowing him to take his time, enjoying every sweep and nibble of his talented mouth.

When he's done taking my mouth, he kisses my cheek, my jaw and then the side of my neck. It's the neck kiss that has me squeezing my thighs together and trembling with desire. If he keeps this up, I can't be held responsible for what my reaction will be.

Straight up, I'm sex-starved. Suda Kaye is right. I need to get laid. This intense heat that hits me every time I'm near him, the arousal currently wetting my panties, it's all because I need a good roll between the sheets.

Maybe I should just let it all go and let him have me. It will likely be the best sex of my life, but then what? I'll be left with only the memory of great sex to live off. Which technically is better than nothing.

"Now that's a greeting, my *adinidiin*." He wraps me in his massive arms and for the first time all day I feel safe and at peace.

I shiver and sigh at him calling me "his light" and rest my head against his warm chest. My brain is fried. After the day I've had and the night before, I don't know which way is up or down any longer.

For now, it's time to just let it go. Have some fun with my sister and her husband. Enjoy the night to the fullest.

My therapist will be so proud.

"Woo-hoo! Look at you two all snuggled up like bugs in a rug," Suda Kaye teases as she struts up wearing a sexy super-short number that molds perfectly to her curves. Way shorter than anything I'd wear, but with her skin tone and the shine she's got on her legs, she looks out-of-this-world gorgeous.

"Sweets, you are a vision. An *unholy* vision. Does that even cover your ass?" Camden chuckles.

"I don't know, why don't you check?" she asks in a coy tone, and then spins around slowly in gold four-inch wedges. My sister doesn't usually do stilettos. Says it hinders her ability to run. Where she needs to go fast enough that she'll be running in four-inch heels is beyond me, but Suda Kaye dances to the beat of her own drum. I admire that in her, even when I equally hate the effect of her ability to run off just as much.

Camden swings an arm out and catches my sister by the waist, pressing her backside to his hips. He cants his head to the curve of her neck and layers the side of her face and jaw with a series of loud kisses. "You look utterly fuckable, so we better head out, or the only place we're going tonight is the studio above the store." His gaze lifts to mine and he winks.

I cover my mouth with my hand, chuckling at his blatant display.

"Oh, yeah, forgot to mention we're having Milo and Evie for dinner. Is that cool, baby?" She turns in his arms, cups his cheeks and stares into his face. He only has eyes for her.

"Absolutely. Love to spend time with our Sunshine." He grins and kisses my sister soundly on the mouth.

I look up at Milo.

"Seems to me that my Evie is shining her *adinidiin* on more than just me. Hmm, *Sunshine*," he repeats. I don't know if it's a compliment or a hint of jealousy I hear in his tone. Maybe a little of both. One can only hope.

Either way my stomach rumbles and I cover it with my hand, embarrassment filling the air around me.

"Have you eaten anything since breakfast?" he asks, a stern tone in his voice.

"Uh..." I purse my lips together.

"That would be a no. Well, come. Let's get you fed. Camden?"

"I'll call the restaurant on the way to make it for four. Just follow me. Unless you want to ride together?" he asks almost as a throwaway.

Milo wraps an arm around my waist. "We'll take my truck. Thank you, though."

"Sure thing. Come on, Sweets. Your chariot awaits."

"Bye, Addy! Thanks!" Suda Kaye says over her shoulder.

I turn and wave to the teenager to find her chasing after us. "Wait! Moments like this should be captured!" She says a little breathlessly when she meets us outside with her phone. "Get together."

"Righteous!" Suda Kaye saunters to her husband and wraps her arms around his middle. I step to her side, turn the other way and stand stiffly for a second, not sure what I should do.

"What is this?" Milo murmurs, pulling me against his side, taking the guesswork out of it for me.

"Just follow along. It won't take but a few seconds. And *smile*," I warn as Addy puts the phone up in front of her face.

"This is going to be awesome for the website with you two in those dresses and shoes." She clamps her mouth shut and focuses on the phone she's got held aloft. "Okay, now a funny one!" she demands.

I look up at Milo and he frowns.

"She means be silly."

"No," he deadpans.

I sigh and watch while Suda Kaye goes behind her husband and he crouches so she can jump on his back. Good thing the supertall truck is behind her or she'd be giving the world a booty shot.

Milo watches the two avidly. Just as I think he's not going to do anything, he loops one muscular arm around my back, dips down and locks the other under my knees and lifts me in the air. My legs go flying to the side. I cry out laughing and look at his face. All smiles.

Good Lord, he's brilliant when he smiles.

"Yes! So cool!" Addy squeals, and the four of us laugh.

It's the first time in a long time I felt free as a bird to just laugh and let go. Being silly with my sister and my new beau. At least I think he is.

I push those thoughts of worry aside and mentally chastise myself for letting them in. Tonight is about fun, and I'm determined to have it.

"Thanks, Addy. Send those to me. Sissy, I'll forward them to you," Suda Kaye offers.

"Thanks, sweet girl," I praise, more excited about getting those photos of me and the hunky man at my side than I have been about much of anything in recent months.

"Have a blast, guys! Don't drink and drive." Addy waves and shimmies through the door of Gypsy Soul and locks it behind her.

I look up at Milo, smiling wide. His gaze is focused on my mouth.

"I love to see you smile, Evie. It's why I've always found you so beautiful. Ever since you were a little girl, always such an enchanting smile. A smile like yours can change the world. It's already changing mine."

My throat dries up and I stare at the truth evident in his expression.

Before I can say anything or respond at all, he kisses me softly.

"Come, my woman is hungry," he reminds me.

"Your woman?"

He smirks and I can't help but wish I could kiss that sexy grin right off his face. "Yes."

"There is still much to be discussed," I state for his benefit and my own. We both need a little reality check to remind us of the complex nature of our new relationship.

"Not about that. You're mine, Evie Ross, and I'll spend all the time needed proving it to you." He opens the door for me and helps me into the cab.

"I suspect this will be an entertaining experience." I try for sexy, but he ramps it up to scalding hot when he steps toward me in the open doorway of the car and puts his face right in front of mine.

He cups my cheek and traces my jaw. "There is nothing that will prevent me from making you mine. No mountain I won't climb. No hill too steep. No distance too far. Age and circumstance prevented us from being together years ago. I will no longer allow anything to get in the way of my destiny. And you, *Nizhoni*, my Evie, are my destiny."

"We are having all the booze!" Suda Kaye notifies the waitress the second we sit down.

"Food. Evie needs something now," comes the rumbling voice seated next to me.

Milo has me sit on the inside of the booth, and he places his long arm around my form and rests it on the back of the tall seat.

"I'm fine. I can wait until we order. I'd like a cosmopolitan, though."

Milo waits until both Suda Kaye and Camden order their drinks before adding his own. "Whiskey, neat. We'd like an appetizer. Whatever you recommend."

"Ohh, I love surprise food." Suda Kaye dances in her seat.

"You love surprise everything, Sweets," Camden adds.

She shrugs. "Guilty."

The waitress hands us our menus before leaving to fill our drinks.

I scan the food before choosing the blackened grilled chicken sans the starch on the side with double the veggies. Camden orders a pasta dish and he and Suda Kaye discuss the merits of sharing their plates. Camden, of course, gives my sister anything she wants.

"My girl loves options." Camden grins.

Milo surprisingly orders the same as me but with a baked potato. I frown.

His dark gaze focuses on my mouth. "What has stolen your happiness?"

I shrug. "Now I kinda wish I ordered the baked potato."

He nudges my temple and places a soft kiss there. "What's mine is yours, Evie. I will share."

"Aw, that's so nice. Isn't that sooooooo nice, Evie?" my sister gushes.

I inhale long and slow before letting it out. "Yes, Suda Kaye, that's very chivalrous of Milo to offer to share."

"Milo, tell me how goes it in the financial sector?" Camden asks, and the two of them start talking shop. Of course, since I also work in the business, I could have answered but I want the two men to get to know one another. Until Milo says my name, which has me perking up.

"Excuse me? I missed what you said."

"I explained to Camden my idea of the two of us coming together to join our businesses. Be the one-and-only go-to for all the tribes' financial advising needs."

"Most of my clients aren't Native American. Well, I'm sure some of them are but it's not information I keep track of."

"I know, but I do. And all my clientele are of our people. Right now, I'm in the position to grow much larger but I need more sway. Proof that my company can handle more clients and, most importantly, businesses. Which is where you come in."

"And how's that?"

"Half your portfolio is made up of businesses, correct?" he asks.

"Yes, my commercial accounts have grown exponentially."

He gifts me a small smile, grabs my hand and brings my knuckles up to his lips. "That's why I need your expertise and why I'm proposing a merger."

Suda Kaye gasps. "Merger. Meaning everything my sister has worked for would be yours, too?" Her tone is circumspect to say the least.

"Yes. And everything I have built would be added to hers. Together, the growth potential would be astronomical. And I already have a plan in place. Part of why I need you, Evie."

"Wait a minute." My sister's voice rises and is tinged with concern. "Are you here to schmooze my sister into doing business with you or because you want a relationship with her?" Suda Kaye's eyes narrow on Milo, putting words to at least one of my biggest fears.

"Sweets, his interests—romantic or otherwise—are none of your business. It's between him and Evie." Camden nudges her shoulder.

"The hell it isn't! I'm her sister. We look out for one another. Now answer the question, Milo. Which is it?"

"Suda Kaye!" I say heatedly, though still low enough to be considered a whisper. I want to know but it is rather abrupt and rude coming from my sister and not me directly.

This has Milo curving his arm around me and bringing me close to his side. "Suda Kaye, I have every intention of having a private and personal romantic relationship with Evie." He kisses my bare shoulder as though he were proving his point. "However, that is not the only relationship I want."

Her brows furrow and her expression shows one of distrust. "Or is it that you're willing to throw in a romantic relationship if she agrees to do business with you," she challenges, sitting back in her seat and crossing her arms over her chest. "I'll not have my sister be used or put in a crummy position. She's had enough of that in her life helping to take care of me while Mom was traveling. Not to mention all the years of taking care of me and Mom when she got sick."

"I agree and I don't intend to harm but to expand her life in all things. Love, work, marriage, children and everything in between."

Both Suda Kaye and I sit up straight and stare at Milo. Mirror images of shock blazes across our faces.

"Well, all right, brother." Camden holds out a hand for Milo to shake. "Awesome. Welcome to the family." He laughs good-naturedly.

I turn in my seat and focus just on Milo. "I can't believe you just said that," I hiss.

"Why not? I've made my intentions very clear the past few days."

"But I… You." I try to shake my head of the craziness he's just stated. Love, marriage, babies…what!

"Evie, you are finally a part of my adult life and were a very important part of my childhood. Soon you will be my entire life, and I yours."

"Oh my word." Suda Kaye presses her hands together in a prayer position. "Sorry for giving you the third degree. I had no idea you were so serious about my sister." Her words come out rushed and in a whoosh of instant happiness.

Milo smiles softly. "It's okay. I understand all of this is sudden—"

"Sudden!" I snap, cutting him off. "You're going from zero to a hundred at the speed of light! We've only kissed a few times and you're talking marriage, children." I shake my head again as my heart starts to pound so hard I lose my ability to breathe. I gasp air in and wave at my face to get more.

"Breathe, Evie. In for four, out for four. Man, I've seen this before with Suda Kaye. She's having a panic attack," Camden explains.

Visions of my mother coming and going from my life bring tears to my eyes. New images of Milo giving me everything I could ever dream of and then snatching it away race through my mind. I shake my head over and over.

My entire body is flaming hot as though I've stood too close to an open firepit. I open my mouth and can't seem to take in any air or catch my breath. Everything seems to blast me at once and my vision starts to weave in and out from black to color.

Suda Kaye presses my drink toward me but I can't even find the energy or ability to lift my arm to reach for it.

"Evie." Milo is holding my arms. His black eyes liquid pools of worry. "Breathe with me."

I do as he says, but it's too fast. In and out. Each breath on top of the last. His handsome face blurs and then suddenly I'm swimming in and out of consciousness.

What must be a minute later I blink away the fuzz to a cool wet cloth napkin pressed to my forehead and one behind my neck.

"She's coming out of it," Suda Kaye says, sounding far off in the distance.

"What's happening?" I pull the cloth around my neck and drop it on the table.

"You fainted, *Nizhoni*." He removes the cloth from my forehead and kisses me there. His tone is low and concerned.

"Are you okay?" Suda Kaye reaches across the table and I take her hand, all the lights and sounds of the restaurant coming back to me.

I take in her pretty face and watch as her eyes fill with worry. "I'm so sorry. I shouldn't have been grilling him, and if I hadn't you wouldn't have freaked out and then—oh my God, are you okay?" She sniffs and I squeeze her hand.

"Fine, fine. I just… I don't know what went wrong. That has never happened to me before. Fainted?" I glance at Milo, whose jaw is firm and unrelenting. "Um, maybe it was the alcohol before the food or the—"

"I pushed too hard, too fast. I'm sorry, Evie. Deeply." Milo cups my cheek again and stares into my eyes. His fear is plain as day as I cup my hand over his and nuzzle into his warmth.

"I'm okay. I promise. Just, um, need to eat and get some water."

"Oh, thank goodness," the waitress says, setting down a glass of ice water. "I was worried we'd have to call the paramedics."

Milo stands up. "We're leaving."

I tug on his hand and glance around the restaurant hoping no one is watching the show. "No, I want to stay. Enjoy dinner. Let's just take it easy." He sits back down by my side. "Perhaps you can bring me some bread? My blood sugar must have been too low or something," I ask the waitress.

"Absolutely! Right away!" She scampers off and literally is gone not even thirty seconds before she puts a bowl of warm rolls in front of us. "I'll go get your appetizer and your entrees will be out shortly."

"Thank you." I smile.

"We should get you home. Maybe take you to the hospital," Milo suggests.

"No, you guys. I'm fine." I grab a roll and take a huge bite. Instantly my mouth salivates, and I realize I'm famished. Maybe it was just the need to eat. "See? Already feeling better."

Milo pushes the pretty red cosmo away from me and eases the water closer. Suda Kaye grabs my drink and pounds the entire thing in one go. "You scared the crap out of me!" She slams the now empty glass onto the tabletop.

"I'm not sure why that happened but I'm already starting to feel more like myself. Let's just enjoy dinner. Camden, tell me about your family. How is everyone doing? And Kaye tells me that you've been working like a demon. What has your focus these days?"

Camden takes on the role of distractor and tells us about his job and then launches into tales about his three brothers. CJ, the eldest, has been taken with a photographer that he admired from one of the images from Suda Kaye's grand opening a while back. Porter is a nonstop workaholic but I already knew that. And Preston has a woman from the IRS giving him a run for his money doing an audit of his business for the last five years. Apparently she's a real ballbuster but Camden thinks he's secretly got the hots for her. A personal trainer gym owner and an IRS auditor?

"Huh. I guess stranger things have happened," I add to the bit about Preston.

"And he's such a good guy. He deserves a smart woman who will whip him into shape and keep him on his toes!" Suda Kaye adds with a beaming smile. All worry about the fainting spell forgotten, my sister is ever the glass-half-full girl. She'll find the good and spin a bad situation into something bearable every time. It's one of her superpowers.

When the waitress brings the bill at the end of our meal, Milo hands her his credit card.

"No way, brother. At the very least we go halves." Camden eyes up Milo.

"How about the next dinner is on you? And I'd like that dinner to be very soon. Evie's family is important to her. We should make this a regular occurrence."

Suda Kaye positively swoons in her seat, her hands holding on to Camden's bicep, her face resting on her husband's shoulder. "I love you, Milo."

That has Camden shaking his head and laughing. "Oh, dear. Now you've done it."

Milo chuckles, pays the bill and reaches for my hand.

Me, I just sit there stupidly, not sure how to respond to anything anymore. It's as if everything I ever wanted is standing before me, hand held out, ready for me to take hold. Only it has thorns, sharp knives and snakes slithering all around it.

I can't trust the safety of reaching out and grabbing what I want. At least not yet. Worse, I'm not sure if I'll ever be able to. If I could truly believe that once I take hold it will be mine forever, nothing could stop me, but in my experience nothing in life is easy or just handed to you. Most specifically not love or trust.

How am I supposed to handle being given everything I could ever want with the knowledge that it can so easily be taken away?

6

It takes me a full thirty minutes to realize we are not headed to my condo in Colorado Springs. We pass my exit off Highway 25 and head out toward a mountainous area. Honestly, I am too wiped to even comment. I scan the dark landscape, enjoying how it becomes more rural, until he takes the exit for Lake Avenue.

Turning my head, I study Milo's profile. With his hair back, the moonlight kisses his strong features. High cheekbones, chiseled square jaw, a tall brow. When at rest his features soften a bit, and he looks more peaceful. Normally I find Milo not only strikingly handsome but quiet, stern and stoic in appearance. He commands an audience not only with his size but his ability to stay calm, direct and forthright. He doesn't smile unless he means it. If he smiles at you, you have his time, and often his admiration. And what a thing to behold. Being admired by this man.

"We're almost here, *Nizhoni*."

I blink a few times, slowly easing out of my Milo stupor, and look out the windows.

"Where is here?"

"My land, my home."

A spear of panic shoots through my system. "Um, why are

we at your house instead of you dropping me off at mine?" I swallow against my suddenly dry throat and push a lock of hair from my face.

He drives up a long gravel driveway and parks his truck in front of what looks like a real-life cabin in the woods.

"You live here?" I tip my head to see the sprawling two-story cabin, complete with a wraparound veranda.

"Yes." He doesn't explain further in answer to my question.

I get out of the car and scan what I can see of the land before me. "You live in a cabin?"

He comes around the truck, grabs my hand and tugs me toward the front door. "I do."

"And all of this is yours? You own it?" I'm not able to hide the shock in my tone.

"Three hundred acres of it, yeah."

"This is part of Emerald Valley, right?"

He nods and ushers me up the steps.

"There's a lake." I point over my shoulder to where I can see the moonlight glistening off the top of the water. A lone pier juts out into the open water with a small rowboat bobbing next to it.

"I like water."

He likes water.

I stop when he releases my hand, removes his keys and opens the door. I ignore him completely and walk the veranda. "You have a mountain as your front yard."

"I do."

I shake my head. "How? This is right out of a fairy tale."

His lips twitch, but instead of responding he comes up behind where I stand with my hands curled around the edges of the railing. He cages me in, shifts my hair to one side and rests his chin on my shoulder. His body presses up against my back and he wraps his arms around me, holding me close.

"I'm good with money. When the housing market took a fall a decade ago, I sold what I had in stocks and bought this place."

"Wow, it's incredible. Beautiful," I whisper, taking in the dark pine trees surrounding the lake, the mountain, the moon. It's incredibly soothing, standing here with this view, even at night. The warmth of the man behind me lulls me into a peaceful, dreamy state. Reminds me of the reservation at night.

He squeezes me tighter. "It is. Almost as beautiful as you."

I close my eyes. "Milo...why am I here?" I sigh, once more feeling uncertain and confused.

"I think you were always meant to be here," he murmurs against the skin of my cheek before placing a kiss to my temple. "Come, I'll make you some tea."

Tea.

The man brought me all the way from Pueblo, didn't take me to my own home and is now going to make me tea. It's official, I've entered a parallel universe.

Milo takes my hand, opens the front door and flicks on the lights. I follow him down a large hallway that opens into a huge open living room and kitchen. My entire apartment could fit into this one room. The kitchen is off to the right with cabinets that seem to disappear into the knotty pine wood paneling covering every wall. A giant hearth made of large stones covers the middle of one wall. Floor-to-ceiling bookcases hug the sides of the hearth beautifully. To the left is nothing but windows with views of the lake and the mountain vista beyond. Right now it's dark and I can only see what the moon is highlighting, but I'll bet during the daylight hours it's breathtaking. Directly to the left of the kitchen is a twelve-seater wood dining table. Would be perfect for a big, happy Thanksgiving dinner.

In the center of the room is a huge U-shaped sectional couch that faces the fireplace, anchored by a stunning Native American rug in orange, black, brown and teal tones. In front of the couch sits a table with magazines; *Forbes*, *Native Peoples*, *National Geographic*, *Entrepreneur* and a few others I can't quite discern from this distance are splayed out in a fan shape. There isn't a TV in sight.

Milo allows me the quiet time to walk around as he grabs a teakettle off the stove and fills it with water.

"You never answered my question before. Why am I here?" I interlace my fingers and place them on the dark gray granite countertop.

"You fainted tonight. You won't go to a hospital. Therefore, I need you close so I can ensure your health and safety." He lights the stove and I watch as the blue flames flicker against the kettle.

"I told you I was fine."

His lips flatten and he walks over to the opposite side of the counter and presses his palms flat to the surface. "With you here, I'll know you're fine."

"Milo, what are we doing?" My voice is small, that of an uncertain child.

"I'm taking care of you."

I shake my head. "I don't need to be taken care of. I've been doing it all on my own for a helluva long time."

A sadness flashes across his dark gaze. "Not anymore."

I let my head fall forward and sigh before looking back at him. "Why now?"

"Perhaps it was always meant to be now," is his unusual response.

"And what about Kimberly?"

His brows pinch together. "She is not your concern."

I jolt back a step. "Is she still your wife?"

He shakes his head. "Not for a long time. Longer than when our divorce became official months ago."

My heart sinks and my stomach twists. "But I saw you at lunch…"

"That was when she came to say goodbye. The divorce was final that day."

I allow the shock of his response to register while I stay as outwardly calm as possible. It's a trick I learned through years of disappointment when Mom would announce she was going on another one of her adventures.

"I'm sorry to hear that." Am I really, though? I'll have to discuss that with my therapist.

"In my heart, I'm not." His voice is low and steady. "In my mind and what I believe of divorce, I am torn."

"Because divorce is frowned upon in our culture, I was raised that you married for life. Part of why my mother stayed married to Adam even after they separated and she'd had an affair with the unknown man that fathered my sister."

He nods.

"How long were you married?" I trace one of the veins in the granite with my fingertip.

"Ten long, lonely years."

I frown. "Lonely?"

"Kimberly is an actress. She was away more than she was ever home. I didn't want that life. Glitz and glamour. She did what she did. I stayed here."

"So, it was the distance that came between you?" I nudge, wanting to know what happened.

His lips twist into a scowl as the kettle starts to whistle. He turns around abruptly and pulls it off the heat, and then sets it on a nearby pot holder. I study his body as he pulls down two black mugs. Everything he does is calculated and smooth.

"Distance can make love stronger," is his obscure reply.

I wait while he scoops fresh tea leaves from a jar into a tea diffuser and sets it into one cup. Then does the same with another.

"Like your sister. She was gone many years, yes?" he asks. I nod.

"And did you fall out of love for her?"

I shake my head. "No, I think maybe I loved her more because I missed her so much."

That has him gifting me a small smile, as though he is proud of my answer. "It was like that for me. It was not for Kimberly."

"How so?"

"She invited another man to her bed. Many men." His shoulders slump and that simple movement has my feet moving as if on autopilot.

Before I know what I am doing, I place both of my palms to his back, my forehead resting against the bunches of his hair. "I'm sorry she hurt you."

I slide my hands to his sides. He grabs them both and pulls them up his chest. He takes a huge breath that I feel shimmer through my own body. I close my eyes and rest my cheek against his strong back, wanting to give him as much strength as I have to offer.

"My Evie, your presence has given me clarity. I now understand the hurt. I had to feel it in order to be here. With you at my back. You are the beauty I earned."

He turns around and cups my cheeks with both hands. Tears prick at my eyes and I lick my lips. I can't help but rub my cheek against his warm hand.

"Don't you see, Evie. The gift of you is the light at the

end of a dark tunnel, my treasure beyond all the pain and sacrifice."

A tear falls and he leans forward and kisses it away. "You weep for me." His voice is filled with emotion and a twinge of awe. "Never have I wanted another the way I want you. The want, it lives inside me. A living, breathing thing that grows every day. Can you feel it?" He grabs my hand and puts it against his heart.

I gasp at the sensation of his heart beating against my palm and nod as more tears fall down my cheeks. What feels like a lightning bolt strikes my hand and zaps me, sizzling with an electrical undercurrent that can't be contained.

"I endeavor to make those tears of joy, my *adinidiin*."

He dips his head once more, pressing his lips to each tear, and then takes my mouth in a soft kiss. The desire to take it deeper moves through me so intensely I'm a slave to it. I wrap my arms around his neck, slant my head and kiss him for all I'm worth. I give him everything I can in this kiss.

My need.

My fear.

My heart.

He takes the offering, cupping the back of my head and plunging his tongue inside. Nothing in my entire life has felt this good, this all-encompassing, this *right*.

Milo presses me up against the counter and takes his time, sipping from my mouth. Licking deep, swirling his tongue against mine, flicking it against my teeth, nibbling on my bottom lip and sucking hard against my top one. I mewl and sigh into each new exploration, doing a little of my own.

Just as I think he's going to take our coupling to a more intense phase, say, by lifting me up and taking me to his bed where he could spend the night ravishing me whole, he pulls away.

His eyes are pure black and glittering with heat.

"I knew together we'd catch fire." He traces the sides of my face as if he's memorizing my features.

"Um, maybe we should take this somewhere more comfortable?" I offer boldly, my cheeks flushing red hot.

He grins wide and my knees wobble at the sight.

"Not tonight. Soon."

I frown. "Why not? We're both willing…"

"No, we're going to do this right. My last marriage started with what was supposed to be a single night." The heat and desire leave his eyes. It's as if he pulled the shutters down over his feelings. "I will not risk you to that."

"Risk me? What are you risking?"

"Our future."

I'm certain I look like a bug-eyed clown right about now. Here I'm talking sex—hopefully amazing, wicked-hot, mind-melting sex—and he's talking about the future.

I run my hand up and down his rock-hard chest. "Aren't you getting a little ahead of yourself? Besides, sex is part of getting to know one another." I step closer, pressing my body against his, feeling the steel length of him pushing against my belly. I look up at him and bite into my bottom lip as I let my hand slide down the sizable erection he's sporting.

He hisses and steps back, holding me at arm's length, which might as well be a football field because his arms are so long.

"I don't get it. You want me. Told me you wanted me in your bed. Now I'm willing and you're saying no?" My voice shakes and I try to get hold of the chaos of emotions flooding my cerebrum as I step farther away from him. I look around to see where I can go, how I can escape.

He takes a few quick steps and presses me back up against the counter, caging me in. "I had one night with Kimberly. Six weeks later she found me. Told me she was pregnant. I did the right thing. Married her a couple weeks later. We lost the baby a month after that. I was twenty-two and married to a woman I didn't love. Committed to a woman and a life I didn't want, but I tried to make it work and honor my commitment."

"Milo," I choke out, feeling the weight of what that must have been like so young. At that time I was living on my own, focusing on schooling, and he was dealing with losing a child, married to someone he didn't know. "I'm so sorry, I didn't know."

He presses his forehead to mine. "Thank you. You need to see and accept what this is for me, Evie."

I swallow down the fear and anxiety and push ahead against my better judgment. "What is this?"

"My second chance for a real life."

Oh my.

"But you don't know that. We don't really know each other, either."

His breath is hot against my face when he speaks. "I've known you since you were a child. The day those boys hurt you was the day I saw my light. Shining like the sun over the desert. When I got them off you, and you looked at me with those sky-blue eyes, I was lost and found in that single moment."

I grip his biceps. "Milo, no."

"Yes. I watched you grow into a beautiful young lady, then a teenager. I'd always planned to come home. Sweep you off your feet and make you mine. My light. My sky. My beauty. All mine. And then it all changed. Gone the day Kimberly told me she was pregnant. All the sacrifice I went through with her, the lying and cheating all made sense when I came to *Toko*'s home that day."

I remember that day clearly. Suda Kaye had come home

from her decade of travel about nine months earlier. I'd taken her to visit our grandfather at the reservation. Milo drove up to visit *Toko* as my sister and I were sitting outside having a morning cup of coffee.

"You were wearing a white dress. Your golden hair down around your shoulders. Seeing you made my knees weak. You smiled and my heart pounded. Your blue eyes shone, reflecting the sun and sky, so blue it was as if I'd been hit by a wave of clarity. There you were, my Evie, now a woman. I knew in that moment I would do what it took to make you mine."

"I don't know what to say to that."

"Just promise to be with me, to explore this between us. Give us a chance."

I close my eyes and suck in a full breath, which doesn't help because all it does is soak my senses with his smoke-and-leather essence.

My mind becomes hazy as all the things he's said swirl in dizzying circles. "I think I need sleep. Time to understand all of this."

He kisses my forehead. "Time you can have. Come." He takes my hand, leaving the tea cooling on the countertop, and leads me through his vast home. There are open doors, but he brings me to a set of stairs. "Master bedroom is up here, as is my home office, a bathroom and a spare room. Downstairs are three additional bedrooms, a gym and a TV room."

He's using more words tonight than I think I've ever heard him say all the years I've known him. Why he's telling me all these things about his home, I don't know.

"I wanted a big home for a big family one day." He answers the question I didn't ask out loud. Though his reasoning has me trembling as I imagine little feet running up and down the wooden floors and up the stairs to jump on Mom and Dad's bed. It's something I've always wanted but never thought could be mine.

He opens the double doors to a huge master bedroom. A king-size four-poster bed dominates the room, set on a raised platform and flanked by two matching bedside tables, with a series of skylights in the ceiling above. Across the room is a seating area with another fireplace. Over the fireplace is a large TV, which makes sense because if you wanted to watch it from the bed, it would need to be big enough to see. The cream-colored couch looks plush, accented with an afghan draped across it in soft hues of mint green, cream, pink and black.

For the most part the room is quite spare, nothing on the walls at all, but there are spots where pictures might have been. I don't say anything, mostly because I don't want to know and I'm so tired I can hardly keep my eyes open.

Milo leaves me standing in the center of the room as he opens a door and flicks on the light. I can see it's a closet. I walk over to find him in a space that's easily twenty feet long and ten feet wide. One side of the closet is completely empty, nothing but a few straggling hangers. Kimberly's side. He riffles through a built-in dresser drawer on his side and hands me a black T-shirt.

"My pants will not fit you."

I smile softly. "This is fine. Bathroom?"

He closes the closet door and opens another one. Inside is nothing but cream-colored marble and wrought-iron fixtures. The ceiling has two skylights, one above the double-sink area; like the closet, one side has men's toiletries lying out, the other side spick-and-span with not so much as a soap dispenser. The other skylight is over a massive sunken tub with jets. Next to that is a giant stand-up rain shower that's separated by a single piece of glass like you see in European bathrooms.

"That's an awesome tub."

"You enjoy baths?"

I nod. "Very much."

His lips twitch as I turn back and stare at the gorgeous tub. "This is good."

"How so?"

He gives me a small smile. "There is plenty of room for two."

"Okay! I'm gonna get ready for bed," I blurt, my voice rising. "Do you have an extra toothbrush?"

"Top drawer on the left. I believe it has my dentist's name and number on the package."

My cheeks heat. At least he doesn't have a drawer full of toiletries for all the many women he brings up here.

"Thank you," I murmur, and wait until he takes his leave and shuts the door behind him.

I rush through my nighttime routine hating that I have to wash my face with hand soap, but it's better than nothing. Though I do find a facial lotion next to his shaving cream, so I use it, figuring he won't mind.

Once I've got my clothes folded in a neat pile on the counter, I pull on his shirt, which falls to midthigh and covers all the goods. I brush out the tangles in my hair using his brush and note how the strands of my golden hair mix with the black of his in the bristles. Light and dark.

Taking a deep breath, I exit the bathroom expecting him to be in bed waiting for me. I'm surprised to find he's set up a bed on the sofa in the sitting area and has taken half the pillows from the bed. He's leaning against the pillows barechested with his hair spread out over his shoulders.

He's the hottest thing I've ever seen in my life. All compacted large pecs, no hair to speak of across his chest aside from the little black trail at his abdomen that I can see dipping into his plain gray pajama pants. His chest is a masterpiece. His abdominals not only swoonworthy but lickable.

I gulp and twiddle my thumbs, feeling shy and awkward. "You, um, don't have to sleep there."

He stretches an arm out over the back of the couch. "Where would you have me sleep?"

I lick my lips and flick my gaze to the bed, then gesture with a tip of my head toward the same.

The smile he gives me is panty-melting. "Soon we will share a bed, *Nizhoni*. When the time is right."

I frown and grip my hands into fists, stomping over to the bed, feeling weird and out of place like an ugly duckling. I rip the covers back, slide into the bed and punch the pillows, flattening them down just so before dropping my upper body back dramatically.

Milo chuckles and claps three times. All the lights in the room go out. I'm left with only the moonlight coming from the skylights. I stare at the stars through the glass. It's shockingly clear. If only I could feel the relationship budding between Milo and me was as clear as the night sky.

Clenching down on my teeth, I run through what I know. First, he tells me he wants me in his bed. Then he brings me to his home but won't have sex with me when I offer myself up on a platter. All because he wants to give us a real chance.

What does that even mean?

I get the part about being gun-shy after having bitch-face Kimberly cheat on him, which in and of itself is the definition of insanity. Who on God's green earth would cheat on a hunk like Milo? No one smart, that's for sure. Good riddance, Kimberly.

And why would he stay married to someone who he didn't love, who he says lied and cheated on him?

No one is that much of a saint.

And now I'm lying in his bed, not my own, because he wants to keep an eye on me. But he won't share the bed.

I sigh loudly and turn over, pulling my knees into my chest.

Everything about Milo Chavis is confusing. One minute I feel like I'm drowning in it all, the next he's lifting me up, keeping my head above water.

I can't begin to imagine what tomorrow will bring.

7

They're after me again. Anakin, Dakota and Maquilla. I shouldn't have gone to the bluffs alone. Toko has warned me a thousand times but I love the view and enjoy taking my schoolbooks with me to do my homework and read. It's my special place but Toko told me not to stray too far from his watchful eyes. Toko knows everything. I wish I'd listened to him.

My chest burns like fire as I run and run and run across the desert plains. I can just see the tops of the buildings on the reservation and the fence I climbed over to get to the bluffs. I aim for them with all my might, holding my now heavy schoolbooks tight to my body. Tears drip down my face as I run, the wind whipping my hair all over the place, the strands like little needles sticking to my wet cheeks.

"Get back here, bilagáana!*" Anakin screams the Navajo word for "white person."*

"Yeah! Keep running, whitey!" Dakota hollers.

"Get her!" Maquilla adds.

I can hear the sound of their feet against the desert floor. Harsh, angry sounds that rachet up my fear. My skin is blazing and sweat beads against the crooks in my arms, behind my neck and at my hairline. The books in my hands are becoming slick and impossible to hold but I grit my teeth and dig my fingers around them until the spines bite into my palms. It's too much. I hit a rock and my foot slips, my ankle twisting painfully. I go down.

"Ha haaaaa!" one of the boys crows, but I can't tell which as I'm facing the other way. Then pain roars through my head as one of the boys fists my long hair and tugs my head back. Another pinches my butt hard and laughs when I scream.

I curl on my side and lift my knees to my chest. "No, no! Stop it! You're hurting me!"

"Stupid bilagáana," one of them growls. "You don't belong here."

"Look how ugly you are with your white skin and yellow hair. You're gross!" Maquilla says, and spits on me. The wetness lands on my arm as I tremble in fear.

"Please stop. Please, please," I beg through my tears.

Anakin straddles my body. His weight forces all the air from my lungs. He brutally yanks my hair, ripping it at the roots. I scream as he forces me to stretch and arch back against the nasty tugs.

"Cry, little whitey. Cry, cry, cry until you die, die, die." He yanks again and laughs.

"Get off her. Right now," comes a new voice. Powerful and strong.

His voice.

"Back off, Milo. This is between us and the ugly white slug invading our reservation." Anakin sneers and pulls me back again.

I moan in pain, my vision coming in and out.

Then out of nowhere, one of them kicks my thigh and I convulse, the pain rippling up my leg so strong that my stomach clenches and I retch and vomit on the ground in front of me.

"Ew, sick!" I hear right as the weight of Anakin on top of me disappears and I can gasp for air.

I curl around myself again. Praying for it to end.

"Get up, Evie!" Milo yells right as I hear one of the boys cry out.

I scramble up to my knees. My ankle hurts so bad as does the leg where I was kicked. My scalp is sore and throbbing. I wipe the dirt and grit from my eyes and mouth and see through the strands of my hair as Milo Chavis, the nicest boy, and the biggest for his age, punches Anakin in his nose. Blood pours out and Anakin screeches and covers his face.

Maquilla rushes Milo off his feet and they both tumble to the ground. Dirt and rocks go flying. Milo gets the upper hand and straddles the boy and punches him in the face, too. Maquilla covers his face with his arms as Milo gets in another one.

Eventually Milo jumps off him and stares down Dakota, the youngest of the evil brothers. "You like spitting on people?" Milo sucks in air through his mouth, making an icky sound in his throat and then spits right in Dakota's face.

Dakota stands there shaking. He's only one year older than me and likely knows when he's been beaten. The other brothers are ten and twelve.

"Any of you ever touch her again, I'll find you. There won't be a place you can hide that I won't go. Now run home to your nimá." He screams the last word. "Your mother" in Navajo. And stomps his foot and jerks his upper half as though he's going to come after them again.

The three boys scramble and dash off toward their home.

"I'll find you!" he hollers the warning once more. None of the three so much as look back.

Milo turns to me where I stand awkwardly, one foot resting on my toe because I can't put any weight on it. His chest is falling and lifting with his breath. He's wearing a white T-shirt that's smeared with blood and dirt. In my little-girl mind, he looks like a warrior just come home from battle.

"I need Elder Tahsuda. He's my toko," I mumble softly, and glance down and away.

"Are you okay?" The boy is so tall for his twelve years. He's twice my size but only four years older.

Tears fall down my cheeks and my body starts to quake. I nod but keep my head down.

He moves in front of me, blocking out the sun, and lifts my chin with two of his knuckles. I can see they are ripped and bleeding a little.

"Evie, right?"

I nod, surprised he knows my name. We've seen each other around the reservation, of course, but I'd never talked to him.

"You're as bright as the sun," he says warmly, taking in my features, wiping away my dust-coated cheeks and tears.

I look up into his ebony eyes. They are kind like my grandfather's. He has black hair parted down the center and pushed behind his ears. It falls just to the top of his shoulders. His skin is a bronzed brown, much darker than my barely toasted superlight brown skin.

He's so cute. The cutest boy I've ever seen.

He pushes the wild lengths of my long hair behind my ear but holds a lock and rubs his thumb and finger together. "Pretty, like you."

I frown and shake my head. "I'm ugly. Everyone thinks so." I swallow but it hurts at the back of my throat from the vomiting.

"I don't." And that's when Milo Chavis smiles at me for the first time. I'd never seen him smile. He was always so serious. Doing his homework outside on the picnic bench in front of his house. Working with his father on the reservation. Exercising the horses. Cleaning out the stalls. What Toko called men's work, even though he was only in seventh grade.

"Do you think the sun is ugly?" he asked me.

"No."

"And you are bright like it. I hear your family call you Taabe. That means 'sun.' So you are like the sun. And the sun gives us warmth and light. That means you give the world your warmth and light, no?"

I press my lips together and think about what he said. "Why are you so nice to me?"

"Why wouldn't I be?"

I shrug. "Because I'm different."

He tips his head and his black eyebrows pinch together as he looks around the vast plains. He points to a series of bushes. "See those two butterflies?"

Squinting, I zero in on what he's pointing at. One is pure white, almost glowing. The other is bright orange and black.

"Yes."

"Do you think that both of those butterflies are pretty?"

I watch as the two flutter along the leaves and tiny desert flowers. "Yes, they are lovely."

"Different is beautiful," *he says simply.*

I stare at him for a long time, my little heart filling with a love I can't comprehend for a twelve-year-old boy that believes I am beautiful.

Milo glances around and sees my books. He picks them up, curling them in one arm while I stand there not sure how to respond.

"Come. I will get you to Elder Tahsuda." *He wraps an arm around my back and waist. Together we hobble back toward the reservation.*

Tahsuda, having that sixth sense all the elders have, is waiting for me. He sees us coming and is by my side faster than I thought the old man could move. Within a second, he has me lifted into his arms.

Within his safe hold, the tears come in full force, spilling down and over my cheeks like a waterfall.

"Taabe, what hurt you?" *His voice is soft and sincere.*

"I found her outside of the fence a ways out. Anakin, Dakota and Maquilla were bullying her. Hurting her."

Toko's kind black eyes flashed with venom. "The Chee boys?" *he confirms.*

Milo nods.

"What did you do?"

"I punched Anakin in the nose until he bled. I punched Maquilla in the face until his lip bled. And I spit on Dakota. One of them kicked her and pinched her bottom. Another pulled her hair many times while sitting on her and one spit on her. All after chasing her until she twisted her ankle. I should have done more."

Toko's lips flatten into a thin angry line. *"You have done well, young man. Thank you for protecting my granddaughter."* Toko dips his head, a sign of gratitude you don't often see from an elder.

Milo straightens to his full height, chin in the air, my proud savior. *"They will not hurt her again. I warned them."*

That has Toko smiling and petting my hair. *"Looks like you have a guardian beyond your Kaku in the great beyond."* He references my grandmother who died of cancer a couple years ago.

"Leave us, son. I will handle this."

Milo nods at Toko and then looks at me softly before turning around.

I cuddle into my grandfather's arms and then realize I never thanked the boy who saved me. *"Milo!"*

"Nizhoni, I'm right here." His voice is much older-sounding.

It also isn't what he said.

I take in all that was Milo as a boy; he stands proudly and strong, waiting for me to say what I need to say.

"Thank you!" I put as much effort and gratitude into those two words as I can.

"Thank you for what?" I hear him say, but Milo's mouth doesn't move.

"Thank you for saving me!" I try again.

"Evie, wake up, you're scaring me." His words and the strain in his voice have me shaking my head. The desert and the reservation shimmer and warp as I blink open my eyes into a mostly dark room.

Milo the man is sitting on the bed at my side. One of his hands is wrapped around my neck warmly.

"Evie?"

I blink a few times and just stare at the man I've worshipped since I was eight years old. His long hair is hanging down like a curtain on both sides of his chiseled face. His onyx-colored eyes are swirling with concern. His lips are pursed and his intense brow is furrowed.

I reach up and cup his cheek. "You saved me. You're my hero, Milo."

"When did I save you? In your dream?"

I smile and run my thumb along the bottom of his lip. "Yes, and no." I continue to pet his beautiful lips, this time tracing the top one.

"I don't understand," he murmurs, and I can feel the sensation of his words rumbling against the pad of my thumb.

"When I was little. You saved me from those bullies."

"Ah, you are dreaming of the past. Why?" He squeezes my neck lightly.

"It is a part of me."

He nods. "It is not who you are now, though."

"Isn't it? Aren't we defined by how we were raised, by the things we've done and experienced, good and bad?"

He runs his hand down over my shoulder, along my arm to my hand. He laces our fingers together and brings my hand to rest on his bare chest. I can feel his heartbeat through our clasped hands.

"I do not think it defines us. Every day we grow and change. Make choices on who and what we will be today, and in the future."

"You don't think it's predetermined?"

"Fate?"

I shrug and press my lips together.

"Some things, yes. Was I meant to be there that day those bullies attacked you? Yes, I think so."

"Why?"

"Because I was meant to be important to you. And you to me. We're tied to one another by our past and now in this moment." He brings our hands to his lips and kisses my fingertips one at a time.

"And the future?" I whisper.

"Is ours to define. It hasn't been written in the stars yet, *Nizhoni.*"

"I don't think it's that simple." I tug on my hand until he lets it go.

He stands and places his hands on his hips. The moonlight gleams off his skin, making him look cast in stone.

"Move over." His voice is a low, deep rumble. A command, not a request.

"But I thought…"

"Evie," he warns.

I shift across the bed and take one of the two pillows there to the new side. The cold side.

Milo eases his large body into the bed, turns to his side, curls an arm around my waist and spoons me to him. The sense of warmth and protection of his large frame steals my breath. Using the arm wrapped around me, he trails his hands along my forearm until he reaches his target and grips my hand before bringing it to my chest.

"Let your light rest, my Evie," he murmurs sweetly against my ear. "Tomorrow is a new day."

I can't help but snuggle further into his form. He only seems to hold me closer, tighter, as if there is no way he's going to let me go.

It's not an experience I've ever had with a man in my life. That feeling of stability. It's definitely not something I can trust, but I'll soak up as much of the feeling as I can, enough that when he tires of me, or moves on to another woman, I'll still have this memory for me. A time in my life where I was held, felt loved and was safe in the arms of Milo Chavis.

"Sleep, *Nizhoni*," are the last words I hear before sleep claims me.

I am awakened not by the sun, but by the sound of banging on a wooden surface.

Milo sits up and pushes his hair back away from his face. Instantly awake. His dark gaze taking in everything as he sits perfectly still. I lift up onto my forearms and attempt to take in my surroundings, sleep coating my eyes.

The banging happens again.

"*Yázhí*," I hear yelled from somewhere downstairs. *Inside* the house.

"*Shimá* is here. Which means *Azhé'é* is, too." Milo jumps out of bed and goes into the closet.

His mother and father. Oh. My. God.

Oh my God, oh my God, oh my God.

I get out of bed and look around. The only thing I have to wear is the sexy, flirty cocktail dress and heels from last night.

Oh my God, they're going to think...

I push my hands into my hair, holding the heavy lengths back away from my face, and freak the heck out.

Milo exits the closet wearing a T-shirt with his pajama pants. He has a pair of sweats in his hand and has just handed them to me when the bedroom door opens with a flourish.

"*Yázhí*..." Milo's mother announces as if she enters her adult son's bedroom regularly. Her eyes widen and then narrow on me. Her dark gaze taking in my messy bedhead, down my T-shirt-covered form to my bare legs.

Her lips twist into a scowl and she lets off a string of

rapid-fire Navajo. Far too involved for me to pick up every word, but the words *bilagáana* and *kiiya' sizíní*. The first being "white person"; the second I distinctly remember learning when I was about thirteen means "whore."

I look down at my feet. Devastation and embarrassment crawl all over my skin like hissing snakes.

Milo blasts his mother with his own fury and reaches for my hand. I try to pull away, but he holds it tight. Then he tugs me close and wraps his arm around my waist, bringing me flush against his side. I put my hand to his abs because I don't have anywhere else to put it.

That's when the party gets worse and an older gentleman with black hair looking almost exactly like Milo but twenty-five years older steps into the room.

"What is going on?" He speaks in Navajo, addressing his wife before he looks up to see his son with a woman he doesn't know in his arms.

Kill me now.

Milo switches to mostly English. "*Má*, this is Evie," he starts.

"I do not care who this *bilagáana* is. Haven't you learned your lesson after Kimberly! They are all *kiiya' sizíní*'s out for your money and land!" The hate in her gaze sears my flesh as though she'd branded me with a white-hot iron.

"*Shi'áád.*" His father uses the word for "woman" and sets a hand to his wife's shoulder. "Let my son speak."

"*Shimá, Azhé'é*, this is Evie Ross. Elder Tahsuda Tahsuda's granddaughter. She is of our people."

His mother's expression is accusing as she asks, "Catori's daughter?"

He nods and I bite down on my lip, trying to deep breathe through my nose.

"A horrible mother. Leaving her *bilagáana* children for the tribes to care for every time she left."

If cutting me straight to the bone was what she was after, her words couldn't have hit their target harder. I stiffen in Milo's arms as though I've been struck.

"*Má...*" Milo growls, fury filling that single word and spilling all over the room in angry toxic waves.

I turn to look at Milo and put my hand to his heart. "Don't. She's right. I didn't have a very solid upbringing. My mother did leave to travel the world and fulfill her own needs, selfishly leaving me and Suda Kaye behind for *Toko* and the tribes to raise. She's not wrong."

Not being like everyone else has been part of my life for as long as I can remember. Being half–Native American and half-Caucasian of European descent on my father's side, I've always had a foot in one world and a foot in another. No true home. And looking like I do, the only blond-haired, blue-eyed, mostly white girl on a reservation that spanned dark hair, dark eyes and perfect brown skin as far as a person could see, I was noticeably an outcast.

On that thought I press my lips together, take in a full breath and turn to address Milo's parents, pushing the old prejudices and feelings of not belonging far enough behind me that I can get myself out of this embarrassing scenario.

"Mr. and Mrs. Chavis, it was nice seeing you, though the circumstances are understandably unfortunate. If you will excuse me."

I pull out of Milo's hold and head into the bathroom where I've left my clothes and my purse. I quickly dial up an Uber and one is luckily only a few miles away.

I change out of Milo's shirt and fold it into a pristine square. Once I've got my dress and shoes on, I brush my teeth and plait my hair into a braid. It falls all the way down my back to my bra strap.

A car horn blares from outside. My ride.

I exit the room and Milo is sitting on the bed.

"They've left…" he starts to say, but I wave him off and make my way quickly out of his room and down the stairs.

"Evie," he calls, but I head straight for the front door.

He reaches me before I can open it and presses his hand to the door, keeping it closed.

"Don't leave." He presses his chest up against my back, his presence almost making me change my mind.

I shake my head. "I have to."

"Don't let this come between us," he whispers against my ear.

I swallow down the emotion that's threatening to overtake me and remember what his mother called me.

Bilagáana. White person.

Kiiya' sizini. Whore.

Those words cauterize any warm feelings I woke with after Milo joined me in bed last night.

"It already has."

The car horn blares three more times in succession, and I yank the door. He allows me to open it. I push through and run down the stairs to the gray Honda in the driveway.

"Nizhoni," he calls out.

I spin around with the back door of the car open, my hand curled around the frame.

"This isn't over." It's not even a warning, more of a promise.

I close my eyes, trying to fight back the sudden wave of tears wishing to fall and pull out my standard Evie defense, building a huge wall in front of me that no man can climb. Not even my dream man, Milo Chavis.

"For me it is. Goodbye, Milo." I get in the car and slam the door shut. "Go, please go now!" I blurt to the driver.

I can't help but look out the window as the driver flips a U-turn.

Milo is standing on the top step of his porch, his feet shoulder-width apart, his arms crossed. His gray pajamas stretch against the muscle in his quads. The thin T-shirt highlighting the shadow of every one of his abdominal muscles and his large pecs. The hair I adore so much is long and straight, parted down the center and shining like black oil framing his angry face.

He's a god readying for battle.

A warrior.

A hunter.

And I've just become his prey.

8

The sun slowly glides over the desert horizon, creeping just past the bluffs. The reservation is quiet and peaceful. I inhale, allowing the scent of the earth to fill my lungs, bringing with it that sense of serenity I need right now. Usually I do some deep breathing techniques at home and calm myself of any niggling anxieties or discomfort I'm feeling. This time, I need the safety of my true home. Regardless of whether or not some of the tribe considers me an outsider due to my white skin and mixed ethnicity. Even though many of the kids bullied me endlessly for being different.

Home is where *Toko* is. Where my mother would return after her travels. Where my sister and I learned to speak Comanche, Navajo and bits and pieces of other tribes' native tongues.

Last night I showed up, suitcase large enough for a full week. I debated getting out of town, traveling somewhere tropical, but that's more Suda Kaye's method to the madness. Mine is to ground myself in what I know, what feels safe. *Toko* is the only safe place I know.

When I arrive, he is standing on the porch, his black hair moving in the breeze, his hand curled around a cup of his favorite Native American wine.

He doesn't speak when I pull the suitcase out of my trunk and carry it over, setting it next to the step.

He doesn't speak when he puts his long arm out wide and I dip my head, the tears filling and falling as I curl my body around his barrel chest as he holds me.

He doesn't speak when I cry until my eyes are so heavy I need sleep.

He brings me into my childhood home, down to the room my sister and I shared, and ushers me to sit on the bed. He crouches and removes my slip-on shoes. Then he pulls the blanket my grandmother, known to us as *Kaku*, made for my mother that she put on our shared bed to wrap us in love at night. Then he tucks me in. On all sides.

When he is done, he presses his lips to my forehead and kisses me. Then he brushes my hair off my face and cups my chin.

That is when he finally speaks. "Welcome home, *Taabe*," he murmurs low in Comanche. "Whatever it is that brought you to me, I shall take unto myself. Give it to me. I will fight your demons this night. You sleep. Tomorrow we will mend what hurts."

I reach out and hold his weathered hand against my face. "I love you, *Toko*."

He dips forward and kisses me again on my forehead. "And I you. Rest now."

I close my eyes. It feels like a hundred years have passed since I left Milo's under a cloud of hurt and shame. Taking the Uber to my sisters' boutique to pick up my car. Driving back to Colorado Springs to pack a bag and then the several-hour journey here. I barely remember the drive. All I remember are Milo's mother's biting words. Proving what I already knew.

Milo and I were never meant to be.

★ ★ ★

I lift my coffee cup and let the steam warm my face and the ceramic do the same against my palms. I've got another one of *Kaku*'s homemade blankets wrapped around me as I sit in one of the chairs on the porch. I just finished emailing Regina about my unplanned absence. She was all too thrilled to reschedule clients and shore up any concerns while I'm out since I haven't taken any real vacation time in years.

The door behind where I'm sitting creaks and *Toko* ambles out. He's wearing his lounge clothes and a Native American–inspired robe I bought him for Christmas a couple years ago. It's a bright teal with black triangles, mixed with white lines. His hair is swept out of his face in a ponytail at the nape of his neck. Like Milo often does, his hair is secured with a single thin strip of leather.

"You woke with the sun." He sets his own cup of coffee on the wooden railing and stands looking out over the horizon.

"I'm sorry I showed up out of the blue late last night. I should have called." I press my lips together and focus on the sun lifting higher over the desert. Never ceases to amaze me with its beauty.

"This is your home. No call needed." He sips on his coffee.

Toko is quiet. Content to let me stew until I'm ready to speak. It's his way. He has never been one to pry.

"Do you think I'm different?" My voice cracks with the emotion I'm holding back.

This has his black gaze sliding to me as he nods.

That nod rips through my heart.

"We are all different. You. Me. That tree. That cactus. That flower." He lifts his chin to gesture to each new thing. "Special for our differences, not our similarities."

I swallow and inhale a shaky breath, trying to formulate what I need to know. "No, I mean, different from our people."

He leans against one of the pillars. "Explain."

I lift up a lock of my golden hair. "This?" I fling the tresses back and point to my eyes. "This?" Then my lips tremble as I slide my hand down my arm gesturing to my skin. "This?" My entire life I'd have given any amount to look like my mother and grandfather.

His body tenses and he frowns.

"I don't look like you." I shrug one shoulder even though the traitorous tears start up again. "I don't look like our people." My voice is hoarse and raw. "I don't belong. I don't belong *anywhere.*"

Toko doesn't say anything. He moves to a chair next to mine and reaches over to where his whittling tools are. He grabs one of the small knifelike instruments.

"Give me your hand," he says cryptically.

I hold out my hand toward him. He takes my index finger and presses the tip of the blade, making a tiny wound. A small bubble of red blood oozes at the tip. He then takes the tool and does the same to his wrinkled one. Another drop of blood seeps out. He then puts his finger by mine and stares down at them both.

"Do we not bleed the same color?"

"*Toko...*" He doesn't get it.

He shakes his head and his voice turns into a growl. "Do we not have a beating heart?"

I try to pull my hand away, but he doesn't allow it and holds me firmly.

"You are my blood. This blood." He shows me his finger. "My blood helped create you. My ancestors fought in wars and battles, bleeding this same blood across the land to give you this life." His hand shakes as the drop of blood slides down his finger. "Hair, eye and skin does not define where you belong, because it is me who you belong to. Understand?"

I grip my hand into a fist and dip my head toward his chest. "Thank you."

He holds me tight as I breathe deeply and take in the stunning natural view around me.

"Who made you question who you belong to?" His tone is rigid and severe.

I shake my head. "It doesn't matter."

"Tell me," he urges.

Not being able to hold back any longer, I tell *Toko* the entire story about Milo. How he plans to woo me and make me his woman. How he helped me after I passed out at the restaurant. How I slept in his bed while he slept on the couch. I don't mention that we shared the bed after my nightmare. I tell him about Milo's parents, that his mother said some mean things about my mom, even though she wasn't wrong, and that she hates me because I am white and look like Milo's ex-wife, who cheated on him. I leave out the part when she called me a whore because I couldn't even comprehend telling my beloved grandfather that someone called me such a name.

Toko listens to it all without interrupting.

"So, I decided I needed a break from my life. I need to reassess everything. My business, my crummy love life, or lack thereof, and figure out what makes me happy."

"I will discuss this issue with the Chavis people and the Navajo elder."

I think my head is going to explode at his statement. "No, *Toko*!" I breathe. "You can't! Don't you see? I'm so embarrassed as it is. I can't have my grandfather fighting my battles for me. I'm an adult. A grown woman."

"You are my child."

My shoulders sink.

"Racism is unacceptable," he continues.

Which, in truth, is accurate. Racism is unacceptable. I just didn't want to be a martyr for *Toko* to take to the elders and make a huge deal out of this.

"*Toko*, I have to figure this out on my own."

His lip flatten into a thin, rather angry-looking line. "You are not alone, *Taabe*. You have family. A tribe. You are Co-manche." His voice lifts with such pride, on any other day I would have been clapping. Today is not that day and this is not the right circumstance.

"Well, it wasn't the Comanche part they had a problem with, and you can't change the fact that my father is a big, blond, white military man of European descent. That isn't ever going to change."

"Nor should it. It also doesn't change your Native American heritage, which is rich and vast and should be respected by all of our people."

I slump back into the lounge chair. "It's not that simple." I sigh and note I missed the sun separating from the horizon line. That's always my favorite part. Oh, well, perhaps tomorrow.

Toko lifts his hand and puts it on my shoulder. "It is that simple." And on that note, he stands up and leaves me to my peace, going back inside, probably to make breakfast.

He's going to say something. Involve the elders. Chat with Milo's parents and raise hell in his own quiet yet demonstrative way.

I'm so screwed.

I sip my now lukewarm coffee and sigh, finding I can't bring myself to care too much about what *Toko* will do. Honestly, things couldn't get any worse.

Boy, was I wrong.

★ ★ ★

The next day I'm sitting on the porch again, working a deburring blade into a chunk of wood. *Toko* claims it helps still the mind when you have something specific to focus your attention on. I'm not sure I buy it since my whittling skills are clearly lacking.

"Why are you at the rez?" Suda Kaye prattles on in my ear as I hold the phone with my shoulder. I can hear she's doing something at her store, as there's Bob Marley music playing in the background and Addy's voice comes in and out through the line now and again.

I cross my legs and focus on the piece of wood *Toko* gave me to whittle. It looks like a misshapen, scary owl-type monster. "I just needed to get away."

"That's not like you. You never need to 'get away,' especially from work. And you're also avoiding what happened after Milo took you home the other night."

"Nothing happened. He let me sleep in his bed. Then I picked my car up and decided I needed to visit *Toko*, suck in some desert air. You know, do some earthing." I scrounge up a rather lame excuse.

"Bull. You don't *earth*," she snaps, calling me out.

"You know I love the desert." Which is true. Always have, always will. I love nature. Like Milo's cabin in the woods— my God, it's beautiful. I could sit on his porch for days just staring at the view and soaking up the scent of pine trees.

"You love work more," she answers astutely.

"Yeah, well, I needed a break. From everything."

"You needed to *escape* Milo and his demonstrative ways. There's no fooling me, Sissy. I got your number."

I grind down on my teeth. She is not wrong. He's sent me a text each day with the very straightforward **Call Me** as the message. Then he left a voice mail saying the same.

According to Regina, he's also called the office the last two days and left messages. I'm avoiding him like the plague. If anything is muddling up my mind, it's Milo Chavis.

"Whatever. Then I needed a break from Milo." I admit it so she'll let it go.

She hums. "I don't get it. You've been in love with him since you were a child. He finally shows you he's interested, and when I say interested I mean 'knock you over the head, drag you by the hair caveman-style and install you in his home' interested, and yet you run away from him."

I purse my lips and imagine Milo doing that very thing. The caveman Neanderthal nature of that man is not far off from the real thing.

"Can we just drop it? I came here for some peace. Bringing up my issues with Milo is not helping."

Suda Kaye sighs loudly. "Fine. And how is *Toko*?"

"He'd like to see you more than once every month or two."

That has her sighing. "I know, I know. It's just hard with the store to get away. I only have Addy right now and she's part-time and a teenager. She can't open *and* close."

"Do you think maybe it's time to hire more staff? Someone to help you with the hours. Give you a weekend off once in a while?" Suda Kaye has been working herself ragged even though you wouldn't know it by her endless exuberance for the shop.

"Cam and I discussed the very same thing recently. He wants to take me out hiking and camping on the weekends. Also said he wants me in a bikini on a beach. I want that more than I want just about anything right now, but I don't know…" Her voice trails off.

"You don't know what?"

"It just seems irresponsible and I've been irresponsible

enough in my lifetime. Heck, I've been irresponsible enough for ten people's lifetimes."

That has me chuckling. "True."

"And I want to prove to you, to Cam and most importantly *myself* that I can keep Gypsy Soul successful and profiting. If I bail and take off every time I want to, it could fail, and I'm committed to this."

Her concerns are valid. If she wasn't happily married to Camden I'd be worried, too. Ever since settling back in Pueblo and starting her business, her entire outlook on life has changed. She's more content, happy where she is and definitely more responsible.

It's funny. I spent my entire adult life trying to get Suda Kaye to settle down. Now that she has it's as if my whole world is twisting and turning sideways and upside down. I'm a mess and she's content.

"You don't have to prove anything to me, Kaye. I believe in you and you're doing an amazing job with the store. There's nothing wrong with wanting to take some time for yourself or time with your new husband to be newlyweds. Just keep one foot on the ground, Sissy, and you'll be fine."

"And what about you? Pot meet kettle, kettle, pot. How do you do, ya sexy *thang.*" She dips her voice in a silly timbre.

I smile and realize how good it is to talk to Suda Kaye. To be her sounding board. Fill that role as big sister. Even though my own life is all over the place, it helps to settle something deep inside me. Like cuddling up in a warm, comfortable blanket on a cold day.

"I'm good, just needed a little time back home. I'm gonna walk the bluffs today, get some perspective. Miss me," I tell her.

"Miss me more!" she fires off.

I grin. "Always. Send my love to Cam."

"Will do. Love you," she says, and ends the call.

I set the phone down and stand by the railing, allowing my brain to filter through the rampant thoughts until I see two figures far off in the distance striding this way.

Toko's house is set off to one side of the acres and acres of the rez. He has an unimpeded view of the desert hills and the bluffs beyond. Closest to the houses and community buildings, there are acres of land that all of us use to walk, exercise the horses and commune with nature. However, the bluffs are my favorite. It's where my mother always took us to view the stars and make our wishes. It's where *Toko* took me and Suda Kaye walking to learn about our heritage over the years.

Whoever was coming this way, they meant to visit *Toko*.

"*Toko!*" I call out, squinting to see who it is. A man and a woman, I think. "You have visitors heading this way," I holler.

My grandfather comes out onto the porch with two plates in hand filled with his scrumptious homemade succotash, which consists of ham, corn, onion, okra instead of the standard lima beans and a variety of spices and other homegrown veggies *Toko* tosses in for flavor. Next to the hot dish are some succulent fried green tomatoes. My mouth waters at the sight and I take one of the plates, immediately reaching for a fried morsel and biting into the juicy, salty, fried bit of heaven.

"Mmm, the best," I mumble around one of my favorite comfort foods of all time, second only to *Toko*'s fry bread.

Toko's lips twitch in approval and humor at my grabbing hands.

I sit down and dig into the food, forgetting about the visitors on the horizon until I realize that *Toko* is glaring. He's set his plate down on the table, and his arms are now crossed in front of his chest, making him look like a pissed-off warden.

I glance up with a bite of food held aloft on my fork. The succotash falls off the tines and plops onto my plate as I see Mr. and Mrs. Chavis, Milo's parents, making their approach.

"Shoot!" I grumble, and wipe at my mouth and make sure nothing has spilled on my sundress, quickly setting aside my plate and clenching my hands as a nervous energy fills the air around me and my grandfather.

We watch in silence as they approach. They stop at the bottom of the porch stairs once they reach the front of the house.

Both of them duck their heads in deference to his status. *Toko* doesn't speak.

"Elder Tahsuda, we have come to speak with you and your granddaughter," Milo's father announces.

My body starts to tremble, but I walk over and stand behind my grandfather, feeling like a small child instead of a thirty-year-old woman who can fight her own battles.

Toko's eyes flash to me in warning. Meaning, do not speak. Do not say anything right now. This is between him and them, even if it's definitely about me.

I would never consider disrespecting my grandfather by butting into something he clearly decided was his issue, but it grates on my nerves. Still, I withhold my opinion in order to keep the peace. Something I'm an expert at.

"Elder Tahsuda, we have come to apologize to you and Evie," Sani Chavis says.

Tahsuda narrows his gaze at Milo's father but still doesn't speak.

"Lina spoke out of turn." He gestures to his wife, who also isn't saying much. Her head is cast down, her eyes on her sandaled feet.

"Lina, you have something to say?" *Toko* asks, his voice a booming force that would likely scare the daylights out of anyone if they didn't know he rarely uses that tone.

The woman looks up and her eyes meet mine and a flash of sadness pierces her dark eyes. She nods and focuses on my grandfather.

"I was surprised to find your granddaughter with my son. Her coloring reminds me of his wife. A woman who hurt him deeply. I said some very harsh things that weren't meant for Evie but meant for Kimberly." Her eyes come back to mine and I shiver at the loss and sadness I see there.

"Evie, dear, I'm sorry. Truly. Please forgive me." Her voice shakes and she looks away. Sani places his hand on her back.

"Elder Tahsuda, can you forgive us?"

My grandfather looks at me and I squeeze his arm, my heart in my throat. "*Toko*, I forgive them," I whisper loud enough that all three people can hear.

Tahsuda nods once and I watch in fascination as the couple's shoulders sag in relief. I guess pissing off one of the elders is more than frowned upon.

"Do you accept Milo courting my granddaughter, descendant of my lineage, half–Native American, half-European?" *Toko* asks rather bluntly. His jaw seems to tighten in front of my eyes, and I take in all that is my angered grandfather.

Sani lifts his head sharply and looks directly at *Toko*. "I do. She seems lovely," he says as his coal-black eyes, so like Milo's, slide to focus on me. "I know her not, other than what my son has spoken and that of what you shared yesterday. He is taken with her."

I clench my jaw once more. *Toko* gave the smackdown yesterday as I suspected. While I was whittling away wood and getting my head together, sulking mostly, he was out raising Cain.

"The world has changed. As have our people. We are not tribes scattered among the land. We are one in many ways. Sharing a common interest. Native Americans as a whole. It would do good for you and your wife to remember that." He lays down some *Toko* wisdom.

Sani nods and puts his arm around his wife. "Come, let us leave them to their lunch."

"Evie," Lina calls out, and I hook my arm around Tahsuda's elbow and lean my head against his shoulder and wait for her to continue.

"Don't hurt him. He's been through so much."

After her parting shot, she nods to her husband and they turn and leave us where we're standing, watching them walk away.

I wait until they're far enough away to turn around and cross my arms over my chest.

"Kee." He says "no" in Comanche and holds his hand up as though he isn't going to hear anything I have to say about what just went down.

"Toko, I told you not to get involved."

"I am your grandfather. I'm always involved. When wrong is done, it needs to be made right. It is now right."

"Is it? Now they probably hate me even more because they had to kowtow to one of the elders on my behalf!" I just barely prevent myself from stomping, which is my initial knee-jerk reaction.

"Eat your lunch." He picks up his plate and sits in his favorite chair.

"This isn't over."

"It is," he states firmly. "When an apology is accepted, you move on. It is done."

I suck in a quick breath and let it out sharply. "That's not the way of the modern world."

"It is our way. The way of our people."

I groan and pick up my plate. "*Toko*, you have a lot to learn about the world outside the reservation."

"Nothing but you and *Huutsuu* interest me outside of the reservation." He offers me a smile—which from him is almost like he handed me a gift.

Regardless of how it all went down, I do feel a little better.

And, of course, the second I start feeling better, my phone buzzes on the table next to my plate. I sit down, set my plate in my lap and pick up my phone. It's a text message from Milo.

Where are you?

I sigh and pick up a fried tomato and eat it, looking out over the land once more. The food is a bit cold now but still wonderful.

What in the world am I going to do about Milo?

9

The sky is just starting to lighten as I peek out the window of my childhood bedroom on the reservation. I grab *Kaku*'s blanket and wrap it around my shoulders. I'm wearing only a camisole and light cotton sleep pants. They're supercute. White with tiny peach roses all over them with just a hint of green leaves. The half-inch lace trim around the bodice matches the green satin tie at the waist. Slipping into a pair of house shoes, I pad down the hallway, skipping the boards in the floor that would likely wake the sleeping giant. Over the years, I got really good at walking the hall without making a noise.

I don't know what it is, but when I'm home, I wake with the sun. It's my favorite part of daily life on the reservation. Seeing the sun crest over the hills and set the day on fire. Mom always said it's why they called me *Taabe*. She said when I was a baby, I'd wake in the wee hours. I'd cry until she brought me outside and, together, we'd watch the sun rise. Later, when she traveled more, *Toko* would take on the chore of allowing me my quiet time with the light of day. Sit me on his big knee with a warm cup of milk. I'd lean back against his loving hold and watch the day start.

Wrapping the blanket around me, I ease open the front

door and step out onto the porch. A dark shadow at my right has the back of my neck tingling with unease.

"Good morning, *Nizhoni*."

I stifle a gasp and jump back, until I realize it's Milo's hulking form sitting in the chair my grandfather normally uses.

"Jesus, Milo!" I whisper-snap. "You scared the heck out of me. What are you doing here? It's barely six in the morning."

He eases forward and leans his elbows on his knees. He's wearing a pair of faded jeans, a forest-green Henley and a pair of black cowboy boots. His beautiful hair is pulled back into a single braid.

"I've been told my woman rises with the sun."

I hold the blanket tighter around me and stiffen my spine. "Milo, I'm not your woman. Why are you here?"

He adjusts his jaw and in the low light of the morning it looks like he's chewing rocks. A long sigh escapes his mouth. "Sit. We need to talk."

Gripping my blanket like a lifeline, I shuffle to the empty seat farthest away from him. His lips twitch at the not-so-subtle move.

We sit for a full minute before I start to get uncomfortable under his intense gaze.

"Well?" I ask.

His entire face changes and he smiles softly. "I didn't get to enjoy a sleepy, just-awake Evie in the morning when I had you in my bed. I'm enjoying the view."

I can feel the heat infuse my cheeks. "Why are you here?"

"You're here," he says simply.

"So?"

"Haven't you figured it out yet?"

I shake my head.

"Evie, wherever you are is where I want to be."

I close my eyes and let his words fill my head with all kinds of beautiful thoughts, but it won't work. We've already established that his family will never accept me, regardless of what they said to make amends with my grandfather.

"Milo, you shouldn't have come."

"Evie, when are you going to realize that I'm never going to stop chasing after you? Never going to stop seeing you as my future."

"It won't work," I state firmly.

"What won't? Love. Family. A relationship?" His words are soft yet stern, just like the man using them.

I shrug and hide a bit behind my blanket shield. "All of those things. Any of them."

"Why not? Give me one good reason and I'll walk right now."

"Your family hates me." My voice is but a whisper flying on the breeze of discontent.

He shakes his head and pierces me with his dark gaze. "They don't know you."

"Do you? You think because we knew one another as kids and spent a little time together you have it all figured out. I'm the one and that's it?"

"Yes. You're the one." He states those words so matter-of-fact it's like a vice around my heart.

I grind down on my teeth so hard they might turn to dust. "And how do you know that? We are not the same people we were as children. I'm not the scared little girl you need to save anymore." Though lately I sure feel like her.

"Aren't you? Scared, that is? Otherwise, why would you have ignored me? Avoided my calls and messages. Fled to your childhood home."

He has me there.

I take a deep breath and push my hair out of my face, finding my backbone for the first time. "I needed some space to get my head together."

"That's the last thing you need. With this, you need to lead with your heart."

"See. Right there. You think you know me so well. I never let my heart lead the way. Dragons lie in wait when you do that. I think with my head because it keeps me safe."

"Safe from what?" He tips his head as if he finds me immensely interesting.

"From going off half-cocked. From making bad decisions."

"From taking chances, you mean."

I sit up straight and the blanket falls back off my shoulders, the chill of the morning not only settling on my flesh, making goose bumps rise to the surface, but making my nipples erect against the thin cotton of the camisole.

His gaze falls to my neck, then down over my chest.

He curses under his breath in his native tongue and his mouth tightens. His hands fist against his thighs.

"I'll have you know, I assess a situation and make a calculated risk assessment. Then I determine what's best for me. It's protected me from a lot of crummy situations in the past and made me very successful in business."

"And what about your personal life?"

"I'm happy in my personal life," I lie.

That has his lips twitching. "You are happy in my arms."

I gasp and lean back.

"You are happy when I take your mouth."

I bite down on my bottom lip and try my best to look away from his handsome face, but I can't bring myself to do so.

"You were happy with my body keeping yours warm as you slept."

"That isn't fair. I was unconscious," I grouch.

He continues undaunted. "Let me show you what happy can be like. Take a risk on me. I promise the end result will be far better than you can ever imagine."

I close my eyes and look away. "I'll never be what your family wants." Not to mention I'd most likely get my heart broken, anyway, when he found something better.

"I spent the evening with my family last night. They apologized to me and explained how they came to you and Elder Tahsuda. It is my understanding that you have accepted their apology."

I groan. "And I have. I'm sure they didn't mean to hurt my feelings, but it doesn't change the fact that I'm not who they want for you. I'm Kimberly 2.0 in their minds. Every time they see me, they are going to relate me to her."

His head jerks back. "You want a life of materialism and camera flashes?" he asks cryptically.

"Huh?"

"You want to be worshipped and have your face in every magazine and on every screen?" His words carry a hint of boiling frustration.

"Well, no. But—"

"You want a variety of men in your bed, men who are not your husband, to make you feel beautiful and wanted?" That has a muscle in his jaw ticking right alongside the angry fire blazing in his eyes.

"Gross, no!" I scrunch up my nose and a sour taste hits the back of my throat as I learn how truly depraved the situation with his ex was.

"You want to make promises and vows, and break every last one of them?" This is said with a low rolling timbre that cannot be denied. His disgust is no longer hidden—it's right there spilling out all over him, the floor and me.

"Milo." I can't help but reach out and take his hand, the years of hurt still so close to the surface.

He tugs my hand so swiftly I'm up and tumbling into his lap.

Milo cups the side of my head, keeping my face close to his. "You are *not* her. Nothing like her. I never wanted her or the things she wanted out of life, but I did what I thought was right at the time. Supported her dreams and desires and tried to love her in my own way. She did not feel the same commitment."

"I'm sorry you had to live that life." I run my thumb against his bottom lip, then trace the side of his face with my fingertips. "That must have hurt a great deal."

"That life ultimately brought me to this moment. To you. I am not sorry for it. I learned and lived. Now I understand exactly what I want. A kind, intelligent, loving woman who would put her family and mate above all. A woman who enjoys the quiet, loves nature, understands our people and is content with her lot in life."

"Milo, you don't—"

He presses his thumb to both of my lips.

"I want *you*, Evie Ross. My golden sun. My light."

Tears prick at my eyes and I stare for a long time into his coal-black gaze. The truth can easily be seen there. He hides nothing from me.

I press my forehead to his. "You're right. I am scared."

This has him wrapping his other arm around my form and holding me against his warm chest. I feel so small and secure in his arms.

"Just give us a chance. Let me show you how good it can be. Don't run. Don't hide. Be strong. For me. For you. For what we could be together."

I tremble and close my eyes as the wind picks up and blows my hair away from my face.

"What are you afraid of, *Nizhoni*? Tell me. Give me your fear."

"If I let you in, you'll eventually leave." I admit my deepest, darkest fear.

"No," he whispers against my lips, and kisses me softly there, just a featherlight touch of skin on skin.

I nod. "You will. Everyone does."

He shakes his head and cups my cheeks with both his hands.

"Evie, I have no intention of ever letting you go. Trust me."

I close my eyes and press my lips to his.

Allowing myself to fall.

Giving in to a dream.

Hoping I don't end up shattered in the process.

Milo holds my hand as we walk the dirt path to the stable where the horses are kept on the reservation. I haven't been to the stalls in decades since *Toko* doesn't have any horses of his own. Stall after stall line each side of the huge barn. Each one is manned by their own family, but everyone on the reservation chips in to keep up the stables, pay their portion for the feed and either hires one of the ranch hands to muck the stalls or does it themselves. They negotiate for breeding and other equine-related items.

After our talk and a bit of making out, Milo encouraged me to change into jeans, boots and a long-sleeve shirt. Thankfully I lived on the rez most of my childhood, so I knew to bring the appropriate clothes. I even had a cowgirl hat that I plopped on my head before we left *Toko*'s. I left my hair long to protect my neck from the sun in case we ended up outside for a long time.

When I realize he is taking me to the barn, I get excited, a tingle of energy zapping through my veins. I know his family has a bunch of horses. They do a lot of breeding for the area and I'm hoping we'll get to pet some of them.

"Hey, Dakota," Milo greets the man going into the stables ahead of us. My entire body goes stiff as a board. Dakota Chee was one of the bullies that I grew up with. He wasn't as bad as his two brothers, but he was never nice to me. Over the years I'd done my best to avoid the Chee brothers, spending my visits mostly at *Toko*'s house and the land nearest his home. As someone who looked and felt like an outcast, the communal areas were not my go-to.

I look down and away, tugging at Milo's arm. "Maybe a walk, uh, that way instead." I tip my head in the opposite direction.

He frowns and tugs me closer, wrapping an arm around my waist. "I want to show you something in here," he murmurs low and sweet. Just his voice at that decibel makes me shiver.

"Hiya, Milo. How goes it?" Dakota asks, making polite conversation.

I keep my head down and don't make eye contact.

"Good. Business is busy as usual," he offers the man.

"Hey, thanks for last quarter. The extra rise in the stocks you chose really helped us get out of a bind. Was able to buy the new saddles we needed."

"Good news. It should continue to rise. We're gonna stick with it awhile but I've got my eye on it."

"I trust ya," Dakota says jovially. "You here to see your girl?"

That comment has me dragging my feet and snapping my head to look at Milo.

His body language doesn't change a bit. "Yeah, want to show Evie. She loves horses."

I do love horses but how the heck did he know that?

"Evie, Evie Ross? Tahsuda's girl?" Dakota guesses correctly. I mean, it's not that hard. Evie is not a common name and mine isn't short for Evelyn or Evangeline. It's just plain ole Evie.

"Yeah." Milo lifts his chin.

"Wow, Evie Ross. Prettiest girl on the rez growing up." Dakota chuckles.

I jerk to a stop. "Excuse me?"

Milo stifles a laugh.

"How the heck are ya, Evie? Still absolutely gorgeous, I see," Dakota notes, as if he is shooting the breeze with an old friend or acquaintance. Not someone he and his brothers bullied mercilessly.

I open and close my mouth a couple of times not knowing the first thing to say.

"Knew you came around to visit Elder Tahsuda, but you don't ever commune with the rest of us," he continues. "Damn, now I wish you would have. I'd have asked you out ages ago."

"Dakota, mind yourself. You miss that she's on my arm?" Milo's statement is a command, not a suggestion.

Dakota grins and waves his hand as if it's all the same to him. "Whatever. You always had a thing for Evie Ross. Everyone knew it."

I'm pretty certain my head just lifted on my neck and floated away like a child's party balloon. "You really did have a thing for me?" I ask, flabbergasted. I didn't believe it when he said it before.

That has Milo giving me one of his sexy side grins. "Told you I always intended to make my move after college."

"I... I... I don't even know what to do with this information."

He hugs me closer to his side. "Enjoy the fact that I've been as gone for you as you were for me?"

Again, my body turns to stone. "I was not *gone* for you, Milo Chavis," I grumble, and squint. "I may have had a healthy childhood crush."

"Wish that crush was on me. Damn, but you grew up nice," Dakota gushes, his dark gaze taking me in as though he were undressing me with his eyes. If I wasn't gone for Milo, I'd have given him more than a second look—had he not tormented me as a child, of course.

"You hated me. Bullied me relentlessly," I fire off, finding my backbone.

"Yeah, of course. You were so pretty. All yellow hair and big blue eyes. Every boy had a crush on you."

"Your brothers beat me up and you spit on me," I sneer.

He sucks in a hiss. "Sorry about that, Evie. That was a long time ago and I was a young hoodlum following along with whatever my brothers did. Trying to be a big man."

"A big man picking on a little girl," I remind helpfully lest he forget how bad it was.

Dakota rubs his hand behind his neck. "Again, I'm sorry about that, Evie. I'd be happy to make up for it but, uh, looks like Milo might wring my neck if I so much as tried. How's about I get the saddles ready for the two of you? You came to ride, right?"

Milo nods and Dakota disappears into the barn, effectively ending the conversation where it stops.

"What was that!" I blurt, and spread my hands out and then slap them against my thighs.

"That was a hot-blooded male who got a good look at you and saw a tasty meal and he was *hungry*. That will not happen again as the only person that will be feasting on you is me." Milo hooks a thumb toward his own chest.

I smack his bicep. "Not him hitting on me. Jeez. He said I was the prettiest girl on the rez, and he liked me?"

"Yeah."

"That's impossible. They were so mean!" I clench my teeth and glare at the barn where Dakota entered.

"Stupid boys often are mean to pretty girls because they don't know how to behave and haven't been raised right. Dakota has since learned his lessons. Mostly the hard way and by getting turned down by the women he's chased."

I shake my head. "I have no idea what to do with this information, either. Everything is confusing the hell out of me today."

"Take it with a grain of salt. Besides, I want to show you something."

"Your *girl*." I purse my lips and cock a jaunty brow.

That has him smiling a blinding-white smile. It's so beautiful it hurts my eyes, but I don't close them for fear I might miss the miraculous and beautiful sight.

He dips his head forward and steals a hard and fast kiss. "Love when you look at me like the world has just stopped spinning."

I hold on to his biceps, trying to keep my footing. "Milo, I never know what I'm going to get with you. Can't you see how that would be unsettling?"

"Life is full of surprises," he offers sagely.

"You were going to show me something?" I change the subject.

He nabs my hand and leads me into the barn. We mosey down the long center strip until we're closer to the middle.

He makes his way to a stall that has a placard on it that reads *Adinidiin* next to it.

I trace the Navajo letters. "My light." I smile as my heart starts to pound.

He gestures to the stall.

I walk up, curl my hands over the wood and peer inside.

Standing next to a beautiful light chestnut mare is a palomino foal nursing. The baby isn't pure white but more a golden light blond.

"Your family's?"

"Mine. The filly was born a couple weeks ago. I named her after you."

Shot. Right through the heart.

The pounding in my heart picks up and I have to breathe through my mouth because there doesn't seem to be enough air suddenly. I swallow and take a deep breath. "She's amazing," I say in awe as I watch the baby nurse. "Mama seems content, as well."

Right as I say that, the foal unlatches from Mama and the mare moves forward and puts her nose to Milo's face and nudges him.

He rubs his head along hers and lifts his hand and pets her face, then down her long neck. "Chenoa. How's our girl doing?"

The horse whinnies and nudges his hair.

"You want to pet her?" he asks me.

"Oh my, yes." I ease my hand toward her shoulder as I was taught to do when I was younger by *Toko*, and press my hands to her silky hide. I pet her in long strokes and speak to her. "Hi, Mama Chenoa. You are beautiful and your baby is lovely."

The horse nickers and then puts her face near mine. I rub

her nose and brow and behind her ear. She seems to like that best. Then she playfully nudges my hat and knocks it off.

I chuckle, loving interacting with such a magnificent animal.

"Do you have stables on your property?" I ask Milo.

He nods. "I do but I wanted Chenoa to be with her foal and the filly to be with her dam until she's done nursing. Maybe in six months. Then I'll bring mother and baby home."

"Thank you for introducing me to them."

He curls an arm around my shoulders. "You're welcome. Now it's time to ride."

I bite into my bottom lip and know I'm dithering. I love horses but I haven't ridden in ages, which makes me a bit nervous. "I haven't ridden in a long time..." I frown. "Not sure if it's a good idea."

"Then you will ride with me. My stallion, Dezba, will handle us both. He is also Adinidiin's sire."

"Cool!" I follow Milo down to where they have the stallions separated from the mares.

Dakota exits the stall leading a ginormous horse. The thing is huge. Strong, well-built and absolutely stunning.

"Wow," I breathe, and approach the horse.

Instantly the horse comes right up to me and puts his face near mine. Milo stands close but doesn't interfere. The horse nuzzles my hair and nibbles playfully.

"Flirt," Milo scowls. "That's my woman, Dezba. Mouth off," he chastises, and I can't help but giggle.

I raise my hands and pet his long, muscular neck. "He's incredible."

"And choosy. He likes women far more than men."

I grin and run my hand down his body. "Can you blame him?"

The horse ushers his body closer to mine for more loving pets.

"No. I can't. Besides, he has perfect taste." His eyes blaze with an unkempt fire as he sizes me up.

"Do you need the other horse?" Dakota asks.

Milo shakes his head. "Evie will ride with me."

"Do you need helping to saddle up, little lady?" Dakota offers.

"Don't you have a job to do?" Milo cocks an eyebrow.

"Yeah, I'm doing it. Making sure pretty women get safely on a horse is part of it." Dakota grins.

"Not this time." Milo's voice is low and warning.

"I can do it myself," I huff, and speak to the horse. "I'm going to ride you now, okay? No bucking me off and I'll find an apple and sneak it to you later."

The horse neighs and clops to the side to get closer to me. "See? He likes me."

"There's a lot to like." Milo tips his head to the side but his gaze is firmly on my bum.

I mock glare and grab ahold of the saddle, put my boot in the stirrup and attempt to haul my body up onto the massive being.

Instantly I start to sway and fall backward but Milo's hands curl around my hips and he lifts me up and onto the horse. Then without any trouble at all, he jockeys his form up and onto the beast without issue. Like a modern-day cowboy.

"Show-off," I mumble to the horse, and pet his long mane. I wonder if Milo would let me braid it. Or maybe I could braid Chenoa's.

"For you, I'll take any advantage I can get," Milo rumbles into my neck. "Can you make sure her hat is safe?" He points where the hat fell off my head when I greeted the horse. I already forgot about it.

"Sure. Have fun, you two."

Milo clicks his tongue and we start to mosey toward the horse trails riders use. The second Milo gets us away from the hubbub of the reservation, he urges the horse to a trot, then a full gallop. My hair flies in the breeze and my body moves with the horse. Milo has his arm wrapped around my body and one hand on the reins. He leans us both forward and says something in Navajo to the horse.

Dezba hears it and shoots off like a rocket, galloping full speed.

It's the most freeing thing I've ever felt in my life.

10

Milo steers Dezba back to the stables. He walks the horse right into the barn and catapults off as though he were a gymnast and did this feat every single day. Then I am flying through the air, Milo's big hands curling around my hips as he lifts me up and off the massive beast and sets me on my shaky feet.

I push the wild strands of hair out of my face and smile huge. "That was *awesome*," I whisper-gasp, my entire being from head to toe reeling with tingling excitement and sizzling euphoria.

Before I can filter my reaction, I wrap my arms around Milo's hulking frame and smash my lips to his. His hand comes up and curls around the back of my head, holding me close, his mouth opening and tongue sliding inside.

Deep. Wet. Soul-searching.

He steals control of the kiss, wrapping his arms around me tight, lifting me up against his chest and taking the kiss to a new plane of existence. I follow his lead and give as much if not more, letting go of any fear, any niggling anxiety. I'm living free and fast in the moment.

Before I know it, he's pressed me fully against one of the stalls. He's everywhere at once. His hand sliding down and cupping my bum, squeezing and pressing his manhood into my belly. I up the ante, curling a leg around his hip and thigh, pressing myself close. Wanting more. Needing him surrounding me, showing me how amazing this could be between us.

I moan and pull my mouth away from his in order to breathe but that does not deter him. His mouth goes to my neck and he sucks and nibbles a line down the column, sinking his teeth into the muscle where neck meets shoulder. My lady bits respond with glee, heating, throbbing and swelling with intent.

"Milo," I sigh, closing my eyes. One of his hands cups my breast over my clothes. He lifts it enough that he can run his tongue along the plump flesh peeking out from the scoop neck of my top. Once again, he bites down, only this time on the weighted globe—hard enough I know I'll have a hidden bruise there.

"Son." I hear a deep voice rumble from somewhere behind our clench.

We both turn our heads to see Milo's father, Sani, holding the reins for Dezba.

"Think you, uh, forgot something after you dismounted." His lips twitch and I can see he's holding back a smile.

Milo eases his hand away from my breast and hooks me around the waist, tugging me against his side. He lifts his chin to his father but stands there unspeaking.

"Came to see if you and your Evie would like to come to dinner tonight. Lina has a spread planned. Think it's part of her apology, especially after yesterday and our talk last night."

I stiffen in Milo's arms.

He looks down at me. "Remember what I said about giving me your fear? Trusting me?"

I lick my lips and can still taste Milo's rich male essence on my tongue from his kiss.

Fear of being rejected a second time wars with concern that once Milo sees his parents' response to me in their home, he'll realize the error in his ways. There's also the possibility that I will ultimately ruin the little we have gained today by not trusting him as I said I would.

"Uh, I'm not sure what *Toko* is up to." I try a different approach.

"He is most welcome, too," Sani offers in rebuttal.

I grind my teeth together and squeeze Milo's waist in the hope that he can feel my unease.

"We'll discuss privately, *Azhé'é*." He addresses him as "father" in their native tongue.

"Nimá—" "your mother" he says in Navajo "—wants to make amends, *Yázhí*." Sani calls his son "little one," which I can't help but snicker about under my breath because Milo is anything but little. I press my face to his warm shoulder to prevent the laughter building from bubbling out.

Milo's black eyes focus on me and his lips twitch. "Understood, *Azhé'é*, but Evie has been through a lot. We will discuss and get back to you."

"It's important to *Nimá* that she mends this rift. She couldn't sleep last night." His father tips his head to the side as if he's trying to reach his son's sympathetic side.

That has Milo standing up taller and holding me closer. "Penance for being cruel. If I hurt someone, that would take time to accept even if they forgave. It will take time for *Má*, too. Until then, Evie and I will discuss and get back to you. Thank you for rounding up Dezba."

His father nods and hands the reins to Milo.

"Lina used to distract me from the world, too. Now she is all I see." Those parting words help me realize how very much like his father Milo is. Milo is making a statement and putting me first as is his father with his wife.

Sani goes to another stall and disappears behind it. I can still hear him murmuring something but likely just talking to the horse in the stall with him.

"Come, I'll take you home but I'm staying for lunch." He takes care of unsaddling and tucking his horse back into his stall, then he comes back and wraps his arms around me again.

After he stuck up for me and my feelings with his dad, I'll accept a little bossing. "Okay." I rub my cheek against his chest. As we pass a table, I see my hat and grab it, but I don't put it on because I rather like having my face resting against Milo's sun-warm chest as we walk.

"What are your thoughts on dinner with my parents?" he asks conversationally. There is no pushing one way or the other, just genuine curiosity.

I shrug a shoulder. "I don't know. Normally I don't put myself into uncomfortable situations willy-nilly."

He curls his fingers around my shoulder. "Willy-nilly?" He laughs and I nudge him back playfully.

"On one hand I want to make you happy and pretend everything is fine, but I know better. That never works for one of the parties and usually that means me. I did it my whole life."

"Did what?"

"Pretended everything was okay."

He lifts his chin, which apparently is bossy hot-guy speak for, "Explain."

"My mother had extreme wanderlust. She traveled the entire world, and Suda Kaye followed in her footsteps a couple decades later. Mom was gone more than she was ever here. And the longest stint she was home was when I was fourteen and we moved to Pueblo so we could go to public secondary school."

"I knew Catori was gone a lot. Saw you and your sister with Tahsuda alone, more often than not. I assumed she had a job that had her traveling. Until *Má* started mumbling about it through the years."

I laugh dryly. "Yeah, a job. If only. My father has a job that kept him away. He's military. Very high up, which necessitates his primary residence be on one base or another, depending on where he is needed."

"And your mother?"

"Dancer, artist, waitress, bartender—whatever job she could get she took on. As long as it gave her money to live off while she was living her best life away from us. Mostly, though, she was dreamer. Always trying to catch a dream she could never quite grasp."

"And what dream was that?"

"Happiness."

For a while we walk quietly until eventually he stops.

"You do not think you were enough to make her happy?" He curls his arms around my waist loosely and brings me closer into his hold.

I shake my head. "No. If we were, she would have never left."

"You needed a mother."

"We managed. *Toko* raised us until she came back and moved us to Pueblo suddenly."

"And why did she do that?"

"At first she didn't tell us. She didn't travel for a year, and she was losing weight and not feeling well, then she could no longer hide it. She was sick. Cancer. For the next several years I took care of her and Suda Kaye. Made all the meals. Did the shopping. Paid the bills with money my father put in her account regularly. She did what she could, but with little to no strength, it wasn't easy for her."

"You cared for your ailing mother for five years after she spent the first fourteen years in and out of your life like a revolving door."

I try to push out of his arms, not wanting him to see how much his words cut me to the core. Milo doesn't let me move an inch. Instead, he cups my cheek and lifts my chin with his thumb. "Evie, look at me."

I frown and lift my gaze. His expression is rigid, his cheeks high and brow furrowed as he focuses on nothing but me. The entire world could be crumbling around him and all he would see is me. It's magnetic, moving and heart-melting.

He runs his thumb over my cheekbone and brings his face close enough to mine until I'm unable to see anything more than his eyes.

"I'm not going to disappear, Evie. I *want you* in my life. I'm willing to work for it until you believe it's real."

"Why?" I choke on a sharp inhale, as so many feelings I don't know how to control swirl around me like a tornado.

"Because I know the sweetness I'm going to receive will be better than anything I've ever known."

"Milo." I sigh, pressing my forehead to his. This man can't possibly be real.

"Believe in this, Evie. Believe in us. Stick with me. Live in the present. Right here, you in my arms, exactly where you should be."

"I want to…" God, how I want to. I'm just not sure if it's smart.

"That's all I need to know."

"But I'm so messed up." I admit what we both know. I have some serious demons I'm fighting. Years and years of hurts I'm trying to catch up with and battle one at a time, but it's scary. And having something as good as Milo, someone so beautiful wanting to stand by my side and fight them with me, is hard to believe in. More than that, it's hard to accept at face value because the only person who ever had my back from the day I was born until now was *Toko*.

"We all have wounds. Scabs we can't help but scratch. Eventually, *Nizhoni*, they'll just be scars. A reminder of what came before. Of what we don't want in our lives. The rest is up to us to face head-on. Let's do that together, yeah?" He pushes my hair off my shoulders and keeps me there with the power of his words and the light hold on the sides of my neck.

I close my eyes, lift my head and move the few inches in order to press my lips to his. He kisses me hard and fast in return. All too soon he lets me go and we continue our walk back home. This time, we're hand in hand. Neither one leading the other, but both of us moving forward at the same pace. Together.

I chose not to have dinner with Milo and his family. He understood but I could tell by the way his eyes closed, by the weighted nod and the fisting of his hands, that he was unhappy with my decision. He didn't attempt to convince me otherwise or guilt me into it. He accepted my decision. Mine. Proved I truly do have the power. There was something beautiful about having a person, a *man* that I was quickly becoming enamored with, in my life that disagreed with my decision but let me have it and didn't berate me for it. Almost made me change my mind.

Almost.

Instead, I spent the evening with *Toko*. Cooking, drinking his favorite wine and playing cards. All in all, it was a good night.

Now as I sit here with my stack of pink letters tied with a ribbon, I wonder if I made the right choice. Should I have pushed myself outside of my comfort zone to make another person happy? Would my mom have? Suda Kaye?

One thing I know for certain is that Suda Kaye would have gone off on Milo's parents. She wouldn't have taken the outrage lightly and would have probably lost her ever-loving mind. Sometimes I wish I could be as strong and confident as Suda Kaye when it comes to matters of the heart. It's just not who I am. Never has been.

Every person in a family has their role. Mine is peace-keeper. Which doesn't mean I don't feel things deeply, or can't be passionate about an issue; it's just I don't spout it off to the entire world and spread my opinions widely. It also doesn't mean I will sit back and take it when someone has wronged me. However, I *will* move on. Leave hateful people in the dust. This has the often-negative effect of making me seem cold or detached. Unfortunately, in this situation, if I truly want a relationship with Milo, a real one, something long-lasting, I'm going to have to face his parents.

Pulling the ribbon on Mom's letters and filing through the top handful, I pull out the one I want, needing her strong advice right now. I always take Mom's letters with me when I travel, even if it's only to *Toko*'s. I don't want to ever be in the position of losing the only physical connection I still have to her.

This particular letter is from when I turned twenty-five.

Evie, my Taabe,
I'll bet by now my golden girl has graduated college and is running the world! You always knew your own mind and stuck to a decision once you made it. Your confidence and commitment are things I have always admired. I think you got those gifts from your father.
Strong, solid and loyal.

Since the day you could walk you had your path mapped out. Always looking to the future, constantly focused on where your feet were gonna land next. Just because I didn't share that same trait doesn't mean I wasn't enchanted by it, my darling.

Honestly, I wish I had more of it in me. Then perhaps I would have been more content with my feet staying in one place. Still, there is something to be said for taking a chance, making waves and fighting for what you want outta life, and I adore that in you.

Even when I was diagnosed, I didn't worry about you. I knew you could take care of yourself. You had been for years, helping me, being there for Toko and your sister. My Evie, the strongest, most compassionate and tenacious young woman I've ever known.

Regardless of what you may have thought, you have always been a beacon, Taabe. A light that shined so bright I always knew my way back home.

Continue being that light. Don't ever let anyone dim it.

I know the man you choose one day will see that light and be forever warmed by it.

Don't settle for anything less, and once you find it don't ever let it go.

Be better than I was. Stick up for what you want. Fight for it. Shine your light on it and I swear to you, Taabe, you will never be cold.

With all the love I have within me,
Mom

Knowing my mother believes I could take care of myself is incredibly uplifting, especially now when I feel like everything is unsettled and uncertain in my world. Though what she says in the letter is true. I have taken care of myself. In spades. In fact, I've done extremely well getting my degrees and setting up my businesses.

And now, at thirty years old, I have the man of my dreams choosing *me*. Fighting for me. What kind of person would I be if I didn't fight for him in return?

It's like Mom said in the letter—don't settle.

If I had married my ex, I would have been settling. Milo had settled for a life with a woman he didn't love. One who hurt him. Repeatedly. He's free of that and he's fighting for a life with me. The woman he says he wants.

And by God he absolutely is the man I want. He always has been. Sure, he's bossy. But on the other hand, he's well-meaning. Doesn't speak unless it's necessary, which can be trying, but also nice to have the quiet, too. A person who you can just sit and enjoy the silence with. The quiet of the morning.

I shiver in my robe as I fold up Mom's letter and put it back in the stack. Then I stare out at the sun rising over the bluffs.

A tall, dark figure is coming this way.

I can't help but smile.

Milo.

He knows I rise with the sun. I also figured out how he found out this information—including where I was. One person. Three syllables.

Suda Kaye.

Apparently when he didn't hear from me and my office kept saying I was out until further notice, he visited Suda Kaye at Gypsy Soul. She had no problem telling him exactly where I was.

Traitor.

When will she learn?

I seriously am gonna have to sit my little sister down and

tell her to stop meddling in my love life. It seems like it's that way with every newlywed you come into contact with. The second they get married some switch inside of them flips and suddenly *everyone* should be married and in the same place in their life as they are.

If you're not married, they want to know why. If you're not currently in a relationship, they want to set you up.

Only my sister is worse because she genuinely wants me to be happy. Maybe even more than she wants happiness for herself. Her love is that big and all-encompassing. She simply cannot help herself. It would be sweet if she had it directed at anyone else.

While I ruminate on this, Milo has gotten closer, his long legs eating up the desert floor with every long-legged stride.

My…he's beautiful. Black jeans and cowboy boots. A white linen shirt that the wind whips around his body like a waving flag. His hair is loose and flying in the breeze, looking like black strands of silk gliding through the air. There's a choker at his neck with a series of three stacked ivory beads mixed with small round teal and silver ones. Hanging down from the center are a few hammered metal medallions, but I can't see what they are. Though that leather and those beads sitting at the base of his throat like that makes my mouth water with the desire to kiss him there.

He strides up the wooden stairs and smiles softly.

"I see I have sleepy, thoughtful Evie this morning." He holds out a hand and I take it. He pulls me up and against his form, dipping his head down to press his lips to mine.

The leather-and-smoke scent wafts around his body as if he's been sitting in front of a fire. His skin is far warmer than mine. So much so, I wrap myself and the blanket I have around us both.

He tastes of mint and man, just like he did the first time we kissed in my apartment.

I tunnel my fingers into the long strands of his hair, cupping the side of his head while I flick my tongue against his in teasing, probing little jabs. He growls, cups my bum with both hands and kisses me deeper, harder. I whimper and mewl like a kitten trying to get at her cream as I chase his tongue, suck on his succulent bottom lip and get lost in him.

All too soon he pulls away and rests his forehead on mine.

"Good morning, *adinidiin*. Sleep well?"

I smile and nod. "You?"

He shakes his head. "No, which is why I'm here."

I frown and pull away, but he doesn't let me get far.

"Oh?"

Milo shuffles us to the love-seat-style rocker for two and holds my hands. "My mother is on a tear. She feels like she's ruined any hope for a relationship with you and fears this will put a wedge between us all."

This news has me frowning deeper.

"She wants me to invite you to breakfast this morning. I have to go back to Colorado Springs tonight for a meeting with a big business prospect tomorrow. It's actually one I had hoped we could do together as it relates to the expansion plans I have."

I lick my lips and hold on to his hands. "Okay, there's a lot there. One being you wanting me to have breakfast with your parents. Two being this work venture we have yet to discuss."

He brings my hands to his lips and kisses each of my fingertips. "I do not want you to attend breakfast if you are not ready. I am a man of my word. My mother asked me to see if you'd reconsider a meal together. Whichever way you decide I will support. I have no fear that eventually you and my family will be one. If it takes a day or a year, I am happy to wait."

I squeeze his hand and cup his cheek, appreciating how he is putting my comfort above that of his mother's. It says a lot. More than a lot. It says it all.

I love you.

The words are on the tip of my tongue, but I hold them back. It doesn't, however, change how defining this moment is for me. I'm in love with Milo Chavis. Real love. Adult love. Not just the crush of a lifetime. And I know with him putting me first, he has to be on that path.

He's made it very clear how much he wants me in his life, his bed and his future. But right then he proved it.

Instantly I make a decision for him and for our future that I hope against all odds I won't regret.

"I'll have breakfast with your family."

One of his hands cups my cheek. "Are you sure?"

He's such a good man.

"Yes. For you, for us, I will." And like Mom said in her letter, once I make a decision it's final.

"Evie, you have pleased and surprised me." His expression is soft and soulful.

I grin wide, wanting to please him. "Then I've done my job. What time?"

"Eight. I'll let you get ready and come back and pick you up."

"You know I can just walk over. It would only take ten minutes."

He puts his arm around my shoulders and tucks me to his side. "As I said, I will pick you up and walk by your side."

I snuggle into his warmth. I focus on the horizon as the sky starts to lighten. "Oooh, we didn't miss the best part."

"Which is?" His eyebrows rise up on his forehead with the question.

"When the sun separates from the horizon and shines its full light on us." I beam, loving having this moment with him. A first, watching the day arrive with a man.

It seems to happen in slow motion. The sun just cresting up and over the bluffs, kissing the sky with its endless beauty and powerful rays of light. As I take it in, I look at Milo to see his eyes are not on the horizon but on me.

"Baby, you're missing it." I pout and look back at the sun in all its glory.

"No, I'm not," he says with reverence, his gaze focused.

"You are." I close my eyes and let the sun's golden rays warm my face.

"No, I'm not. Seeing the sun light your face first thing in the morning, *Nizhoni*...there is nothing more magnificent."

11

"You are calm, *Nizhoni*." Milo addresses me for the first time since we started our walk to his parents.

I look out over the reservation and take in the sun shining, people riding horses along the trails up near the bluffs I so adore and the many kids running around, squealing and screaming in glee as only children are capable of.

"I feel calm." I squeeze his hand and smile at him.

His face is set. His expression looks thoughtful, which on any other man might seem stoic or stern. I've come to understand the many subtle changes in his expressions.

"This pleases me."

I nudge his shoulder as we walk. "And you please me. Not nearly as much as it pleases me when you kiss me, though," I taunt and tease.

Our make-out session earlier this morning ended abruptly when *Toko* surprised us by coming out to the patio and clearing his throat. Of course, my grandfather has too much class to say anything to embarrass Milo, but he made his feelings known in his quiet way by offering him a cup of coffee. This showed that he welcomed Milo's presence at his home. Milo demurred, giving me time with my grandfather, and he left, promising to come get me for breakfast.

"You are not playing fair, *adinidiin*."

I grin and swing his hand as we approach his parents' home. It looks similar to *Toko*'s. Nothing huge or ostentatious. A one-story house, simple, fitting in with the environment so it doesn't take away from the desert around it but instead flowing with it. A pair of rocking chairs sit on the porch that is dotted with many colored pots bursting with every variety of rich succulent.

"Your mom's work?" I gesture to the pots.

He nods. "She has a way with plants."

"They're beautiful." I crouch down and run just the tip of my fingers along one of the succulent petals. It's lavender in color with a burst of bright pink at the tip.

"You may have that. A peace offering," Lina says behind me.

I shake my head and pop up, my simple yellow sundress flowing in the breeze. "Oh, I couldn't. But thank you."

Lina stands at the door, twisting her fingers together in front of her. "Welcome, Evie." She gestures for us to come in. "We're happy you came."

I smile and take in her appearance. She's wearing a simple blue wrap skirt and a loose white tank. There are brown leather sandals on her feet and her long black hair is twisted in a bun at the base of her neck. She's wearing a single silver chain around her neck with a big turquoise pendant.

"Your necklace is stunning!" I stare at it because it reminds me of one of the bolo ties that Milo wears.

This compliment has his mother gifting me a beaming white smile as she places her fingers to her neck. "I made this myself. Thank you."

"Wow, really? It's awesome. Do you make the pieces Milo wears?"

Talk about doubling up on the smile. Lina's eyes positively

light with excitement. *"Aoo' Aoo.'"* She says "yes, yes," in Navajo. "I have a little booth at the local craft fair and Aiyana, Milo's sister, has made me a new website. I could show you!"

"I'd love to see it."

Lina bites into her bottom lip, looking pleased. "Come, come. The food will be served shortly."

"Thank you for having me. I'm sorry I couldn't make dinner last night. I had other things to attend to." I offer an apology to pave the way for us to move past that particular discomfort.

Lina waves her hand as if it's all the same to her and moves forward.

Milo curls an arm around my waist from behind, stopping me in my tracks, and presses his mouth to my ear. "You are making me happy, *Nizhoni*. How will I reward you?" His voice is a low rumbling whisper that shoots straight down my body to settle hotly between my thighs. It doesn't help my sudden arousal when he places a warm kiss on the side of my neck.

A shiver rushes through my body and I take in a sharp breath. "I'm sure you'll think of something," I whisper back.

He hums against my neck and I feel that hum through every nerve ending I possess.

Milo kisses my neck once more and then, with his knuckles at the base of my spine just above my bum, nudges me forward.

When we reach the kitchen, the dining table is already set. A gorgeous Lina doppelgänger is sitting with a cup of coffee held to her lips and the other hand plucking at a laptop keyboard.

Lina hollers something at the woman in Navajo but I don't catch all the words.

Aiyana looks up and smiles wide. She's the spitting image

of her mother and has the exact same coloring as Milo, only her style is obviously far more modern. Her black hair is cut to her shoulders and there are layers and flicky wisps here and there in the contemporary cut. She even has a swooping, thick layer of bangs running across her forehead. She stands and holds out her hand.

"You must be Evie! I'm Aiyana but everyone calls me Yana."

I take her hand and shake it. "Hi."

Lina says another rapid-fire bit of Navajo.

"*Má*. English, please," Milo warns, but Lina just huffs and makes a pfft sound with her lips.

Yana's eyes light up. "Oooh, come here." Yana gestures toward the seat next to her. "She wants me to show you her website. I was just adding some new products. *Má* makes everything by hand. Cuts and rolls the stones into the shapes she wants and everything."

"I'd love to see." I smile at Milo and make my way around the table to sit beside his sister.

Yana brings up the site and shows me the products that are currently available. Each piece is spectacular and priced well below what she should be asking.

"You know, my sister owns Gypsy Soul, a boutique in Pueblo. I'm going to have her look at the site. Though if she buys your pieces, she would mark them up so she can make a considerable profit."

"Awesome," Yana says. "I told *Má* she's selling her jewelry way too cheap, but she's always thought of this as a hobby, not a business. Her job is to take care of her family, help with the reservation and keep the home. But I keep telling her…" She raises her voice so Lina can hear from the twenty or so feet away where she is working in the kitchen. "This could give them the extra money they need to put away for retirement. Dad can't work the rez, cattle, horses and everything in between forever."

"It's a really good idea."

Lina's dark gaze, so like Milo's, glances up and focuses on me. "You think so, Evie?" she asks, as if my opinion somehow matters.

I nod and smile. "You're really talented."

"And she has tons she's made over the years. I'm upping the prices! Though we'll give your sister a good deal on anything. Would love to see my mom's art being displayed in a real store." Yana shimmies excitedly in her chair, reminding me of my own sister. Suda Kaye is a bundle of energy and it seems she and Yana would be birds of a feather.

Milo enters the kitchen and gets a cup of coffee for himself, and then lifts the mug, offering me a cup.

I shake my head. "Already had coffee. Water would be great, though."

He nods and moves around the kitchen, sidestepping his mother as if this dance is well practiced. I imagine it was over the years. I didn't exactly have that as I was the only one in the kitchen when Suda Kaye and I lived alone with Mom in Pueblo, but I did a little of that with *Toko*. Mostly, though, he wanted us kids out of the kitchen unless he was teaching us how to cook something specific. I always figured it was because he was sneaking veggies into other tastier dishes so the two children under his charge would have the good stuff their bodies needed along with all the rest.

Sani enters from the hallway and smiles at seeing me. "Hello, Evie. I'm glad to see you this morning."

I nod. "You, too, Sani. Did you ride yesterday?"

"Yes. I exercised a few of the horses but could use some help if you, Milo and Aiyana each want to take one out today."

"Evie rides with me until she's comfortable riding again."

Sani nods and doesn't question this as he enters the kitchen and wraps an arm around his wife from behind the same way Milo did to me not fifteen minutes ago. He kisses Lina on her bare shoulder and then on her neck. Her shoulders fall and she sighs with contentment.

"Looks good, *shi'áád*." He murmurs "my woman" affectionately to his wife.

"Wash up. It's time to eat." She tips her head back and he kisses her softly and nods before moving to the sink.

Milo brings his coffee cup around the table and sits at the opposite end kitty-corner to where I'm sitting next to Yana.

"Aiyana, computer," Sani says in a warning tone.

She slaps the lid closed and grins. *"Aoo', Azhé'é."* "Yes, Father."

"We are speaking English, Yana," Milo says softly, and glances at me.

I shrug. "It's okay. *Toko* mostly speaks to me in Comanche. It's natural and I do know a lot of Navajo."

"You do?" Lina says with what I think is hope in her tone as she sets down a warm plate of fry bread.

"Aoo'." I grin. *"Toko* and my mother believed in learning as many of the Native American languages as we could out of respect to our bloodlines. My great-grandmother was Navajo, and my grandmother was half. My grandfather and his line are Comanche. My mom was fluent in Comanche, Navajo and English."

Lina stares at me as her eyes start to shimmer, then she looks to Milo. "This is very good, *Yázhí*," she says with pure joy.

Milo nods. "It is an unexpected pleasant surprise but my Evie having Navajo blood or not would not matter."

Lina nods and hums. "It is still good for your offspring,"

she says casually, as if she didn't just basically state that she is happy I have Navajo blood running through my veins since she believes I'll be bearing her grandchildren.

I reach out and grab Milo's strong thigh and squeeze the holy heck out of it.

He covers my hand, dips his head and chuckles under his breath.

"Relax, *Nizhoni*."

Sani brings a cup of steaming coffee and sits at the head of the table as his wife lays plate after plate of food on the center of the dining table.

My senses are assaulted with the mixture of eggs, beef, blackened spices, fry bread and scrumptious potatoes. As my mouth waters at the heavenly feast of traditional Navajo recipes in front of us, my stomach growls.

Yana next to me starts cracking up. Milo is not far behind her.

"Hey! I can't help it. I'm starved and this food looks so good!" I snap at Milo, and then prod Yana with my shoulder next to me.

That has her laughing harder. "I'm sorry, girlie, but seriously. Your belly just spoke to all of us and it said, 'Feed me now!'"

I can't help but giggle even as my cheeks heat with embarrassment.

Milo reaches out and cups my face, running his thumb across the rosiness of my cheek. "I like this color," he says on a wink.

"Dig in, Evie. Lina has been cooking up a storm to impress you," Sani admits, reaching for the potatoes mixed with black beans, corn and other vegetables.

Lina smacks his chest with the towel she has hanging over

her shoulder. "You're not supposed to tell her that!" she snaps, and glares at her husband.

He plops a mound of potatoes and beans on his plate. "It's true, *shi'ááád*."

"I'm trying to make a good impression and win her back after my bad behavior."

Her comment has Yana's attention.

"Oh, no. What did *Má* do this time?" She reaches for the fry bread and adds a piece to her plate as Milo adds what looks like an egg taco onto my plate and then places two on his own.

"Well, I..." His mother twists the towel in front of her and looks down and then back at me. "I was rude and mean to Evie. We apologized and she forgave me. I hope."

"Yes, absolutely. It's fine." I smile at her, wanting her to believe me.

Milo shakes his head. "Not fine. She compared Evie to Kimberly—made assumptions about her. Very wrong ones." His words are low and heated, making it clear that he, however, has not forgiven his mother yet.

"Yikes. No one should be compared to that witch. She was horrible. Never loved my brother and showed it in all her devilish glory. I'm surprised that woman doesn't have horns. Speaking of, do you know any witches? There are some tribes back in the day that believed in that. Know anyone?"

I shake my head. "Uh, no."

"Bet Elder Tahsuda would!" Her eyes light up. "Maybe after breakfast we should go talk to him. I would happily pay someone to hex that evil woman."

Laughter bubbles up and out of my mouth at the image of Yana asking *Toko* if he could hook her up with a witch doctor or the equivalent. *Toko* would lose his mind.

"Yana!" Milo snaps.

I put my hand out and pat his arm. "No worries. That's really funny, Yana, but *Toko* would never participate in anything that would harm another in any way. It goes against every value he has."

She pouts. "Bummer. I'll do more research," she says while chomping down on a hunk of fry bread.

"Anyway, Evie, tell us about you," Sani interjects.

I reach for the potato-bean mixture and add it to my plate. The steaming dish has the scent of curry and fennel wafting up and my mouth salivates.

"I'm a financial planner, like Milo. I currently have two offices. One in Colorado Springs where I live and one in Pueblo where my sister lives."

"And you like this business?"

"I do, and I'm good at it."

"She's being modest, *Azhé'é*. She's one of the best in the area and has built an impressive business. I hope to one day merge our businesses into one and expand across the plains." He gifts me a small smile that I return.

"Interesting. And what of your family?"

"Well, my father is in Europe. High-ranking military. My mother passed, as I'm sure you know." He nods and Milo puts his hand to my shoulder to give it a comforting squeeze. "My sister is married and settled in Pueblo and you know *Toko*. That's pretty much it."

"Small family."

"Yes, but with big hearts," I respond, instantly proud of the little family I have.

"Yes, that I can see," he compliments me, and my cheeks heat once again but this time with happiness.

I find out that Aiyana is a graphic designer and web developer who is also visiting from Colorado Springs. Our offices are actually really close to one another. She suggests having lunch some time and I tell her that I'd like that very much.

When we're done with brunch, I help clean the dishes—something that Lina obviously approves of because she thanks me several times but does so smiling and carrying on.

The weirdness between us has totally abated until right before we decide we're going to change clothes and exercise the horses. Lina asks for a moment with me alone.

Lina leads me to a room that is clearly devoted to her crafts. Metal jewelry and boxes of multicolored stones are spread out across one table. A second table holds a variety of beads, and colorful strips of leather and metal chains in silver, gold, rose gold and black in wide spools hang off the wall for ease of uncoiling.

I scan the items. "This is really cool." I hold up a metal silver wrist cuff. In the center it is missing a stone, but I assume she'll put one in it. Turquoise would be amazing.

"It's a work in progress," she says softly.

"You wanted to speak with me?"

She nods and takes both of my hands in hers. "I want to say I am truly sorry for how I behaved. I said hateful things about you and your mother that I shouldn't have. I don't believe them. Your mother…she loved you and your sister. Everyone on the reservation knew that."

"It's okay, really."

She shakes her head. "It's not. I liked Catori. We were friends in school. She was nice to me. Always. Though all the men liked her, she never had eyes for a man of our people." Her dark gaze takes in my hair and eyes. "Catori was partial to the fair-haired and fair-skinned boys that were not on the reservation."

I smile. "Makes sense why my father is blond and blue-eyed."

Lina presses her lips together. "My Sani asked your mother out many times during high school. She would never go. I fear that she was the one that got away."

Whoa.

"Um, Lina this is news to me. She never spoke—"

Lina shakes her head and drops my hands. "She wouldn't. Catori knew I loved Sani since the day we met in school. Followed him around like a puppy. When I found out he liked her most of all, I ended our friendship. I was mad and foolish. Eventually I got Sani, but lost Catori, and then she was away so often. Never gave me a chance to be her friend again."

"I'm sure that wasn't her intent. Mom was just a free spirit. Just like her name. Catori means 'spirit.'"

Lina nods, her face solemn. "I think I took out the fear of my son being treated badly by Kimberly and my own regrets of losing Catori out on you. I have much to pray about."

"I'm sorry that you lost Mom but I'm not sure she was a person any of us could hold on to. She went the way of the wind."

"And you? Do you not feel the desire to fly?"

I shake my head and smile softly. "No. My feet are firmly planted on the ground."

"And what is it you want in life?"

"Family. Love. Happiness. I think it's what everyone wants."

She shakes her head. "I do not agree. Your mother wanted freedom, friendship and adventure. I think she loved easily and did it often."

"You're right. She did. My mother never disliked a soul. Found beauty in everything, which leads me to believe she probably loved you very much and respected what you wanted. Removing herself from the situation with Sani to give you the ability to shine on your own. That was also her way."

Lina closes her eyes and dips her head. "You are so much like her."

I laugh out loud. "Actually, my sister, Suda Kaye, is exactly the same."

"Maybe more in looks and spirit, but you have her ease, her gratitude and her ability to see into people's hearts. That is a gift she has left you. A beautiful one at that."

Her words wrap around my heart and squeeze until I have to take a breath. Only *Toko* has ever compared me to my mother in a positive light.

"You really see all of that?" I ask, my voice wobbling.

"Catori knew how to speak to people. Could see into their hearts and souls. She was very profound and thoughtful. Forgiving above all. I definitely see you in her."

"Thank you, that's kind to say."

"Not kind. Honest."

"Be that as it may, it was sweet. And thank you for breakfast." I rub my stomach.

"Need to get more bread in you. The Chavis men do not make small babies." She wags her index finger.

"Uh, well, since we're just starting out, I don't think we have to worry about that just yet."

Lina smiles wide. "Milo will not wait long to make you his."

Heart pounding.

Mouth going dry.

Stunned stupid.

Yep, that's where I'm at right now.

"*Má*, you done with my Evie?" Milo appears in the doorway.

"Your Evie. Yes, *Yázhí*. We are done talking. Have fun riding the horses."

Milo curls a hand around mine. "Come, let's get you changed," he murmurs, bringing me through his parents' home and back outside.

"You going to help me get changed?" I tease with a hint of innuendo.

"Don't try me, *Nizhoni*. I'm hanging on by a thread."

"How so?" I frown and he hooks me around the waist.

He dips his head toward my ear. "Because I want you naked, in my bed, at my cabin, as soon as you're ready…"

"I'm ready," I fire off without hesitation. It's true. I am more than ready.

He stops fast, dust billowing out around our feet.

"Evie," he says through clenched teeth.

I press both my palms to his chest. "Don't *Evie* or *Nizhoni* me. I say when I'm ready and I am. Ready to take that step with you. We're moving forward in this relationship, remember. Not backward."

He closes his eyes and his chest rises and falls as he takes silent large breaths through his nose, likely calming the fire I see in him every time he looks at me that way. The way a man looks at a woman he wants to bed immediately.

"Will you leave later tonight? I want to make us a picnic and take you somewhere special to me."

"I will do anything for you." He opens his eyes and they are dark pools of black onyx.

I lift up on my toes, wrap my arms around his neck and smile-kiss him. Meaning, I'm smiling as I press my mouth to his. He does the same until he's done smiling and takes the kiss further, deeper. Our tongues dance and mingle, sipping from one another for a long time before I pull back. One of his arms is slanted and cut across my back, holding me up and taking my weight. His other is cupping the back of my head keeping me close.

"You are an incredible woman, Evie Ross. I'm happy we are here."

"Me, too. Now walk me home so I can change. I'm looking forward to riding the reservation with my man."

"Your wish, my command, *Nizhoni*."

12

The light over the bluffs is a stunning fiery orange mixed with hues of purple and pink. I'm back in my sundress, a shawl over my bare shoulders. Milo is in dark jeans, brown cowboy boots and a beige linen shirt. The choker I admired yesterday is around his strong throat. He's carrying the picnic basket I filled with goodies after our ride. Since breakfast was a big meal and he needs to get on the road, I thought a late lunch-hybrid-supper would be best. Besides, the view of the light as the sun sets over the land from the bluffs is almost as magical as the sunrise.

"Did your mother make that necklace?" I point to his neck.

"Yes. She gives me pieces regularly. It honors her when I wear them, so I do."

"That's really sweet."

He tips his head to the side. His hair is back in a perfect French braid.

"Who braids your hair?" I shoot for sounding light and aloof, but it comes out strained because it drives me crazy to think about someone else braiding his hair, having their fingers in his gorgeous mane. It feels personal.

Intimate.

His lips twitch and he grins. "Are you asking because you are curious or jealous, *adinidiin?*"

I stop and try to tug my hand away as we trek up the incline I've traversed many times in my lifetime.

"Curious!" I lie.

He knows I'm lying. I can tell by the huge smile that suddenly blinds me with its awesome light.

"This style braid from the top of my head is not one I can do on my own."

"French braid is what it's called," I state with a haughtiness that even sounds know-it-all to me.

"I asked Aiyana to do it. Though when it's braided low, that is my own hand."

"Oh."

"Yes, oh." He smirks. "I will love for you to tend to my hair when you come to live at the cabin with me."

I pull my hand away so fast it's as if I was torn from him. "Excuse me?" I narrow my gaze.

"Do you not wish to share a home?"

I slap the side of my thigh.

"Oh, I don't know. How's about we date for a while first? Get to know each other, and besides, why would I automatically move into your home? I have a home, too, you know."

"If that is as you wish, we can discuss it. Though yours is an apartment and rather small for a couple and a growing family."

"Whoa, whoa, whoa. You skipped right over moving in, marriage, and now you're talking about having children?"

He smiles and grabs my hand and we keep walking. "You want children, yes?"

"Sure. Yeah. I mean, when the time is right with the right man…"

"Am I not the right man?" He frowns and his entire expression flits from gentle giant to stoic warrior about ready to fight a battle he intends to win.

"Uh, I mean, maybe. Probably. Why are you moving so fast?" My throat goes dry and I realize I really need that bottle of wine I stole from *Toko*'s stash.

"I'm not. It's you who are moving too slow."

"We haven't even slept together and you're planning our future." I sigh and pick up the pace until we're just about there.

"When I know what I want, Evie, I chase after it until I catch it. Once I do, it becomes mine. And when it's mine, I take care of it."

My shoulders fall. What I wouldn't give to have him take care of me. Show me what a life could be like if I didn't have to make all the decisions. If I didn't have to be the reasonable, responsible one in the mix all the time. Having a man to share life's burdens and help weave the right path through them. A path I didn't have to walk alone...sounds too good to be true.

And yet, he's offering a shared path up on a silver platter. It's me who's scared to accept it.

I think about all of this as we hit the crest of the bluff. The sun shines its golden light on me, and I inhale, scenting the breeze, the desert, the cacti, the earth. Everything that makes this place special.

"It's unreal. I've never been here," Milo says, setting down the picnic basket. He grabs the blanket that was woven through the handles and settles it on a flat section of the ground. He sits and spreads his legs out, knees up at a ninety-degree angle. "Share this with me," he encourages.

You don't have to tell me twice. Having him seated in my very favorite spot in the entire world is the stuff dreams are made of. No. It's a dream come true.

I crawl on my knees between his legs, turn around and sit on my booty. He loops an arm around my waist and chest and eases me until I'm resting fully against him.

I cover his hands with mine and rest my head against his strong shoulder.

"This is my favorite place."

"It's almost as breathtaking as you are."

His honesty and the sincere way in which he shares his feelings and thoughts is overfilling my cup, making me believe this could really work the way he sees it. Even if our relationship continues at record speed.

"I'm falling for you, Milo."

He rubs his chin against my shoulder and kisses my neck. "I know. I have already fallen for you."

Tears prick the backs of my eyes. Not tears of sadness but those of joy, promise and, yes…love.

I tip my head back at the same time he brings his down.

Our lips touch and I can not only feel how this kiss is different, I can taste it. I'm breathing it. Milo is becoming part of me. We're becoming an *us*. Building a bond that I've never felt before. He flicks his tongue against mine and I tremble. He doesn't stop. In fact, he takes the kiss further, growling into my mouth. I suck it down and follow it with a moan of my own.

And that's when things change.

Suddenly I feel a slight breeze on my thighs.

Then a warm touch against my bare knee.

He pulls away from my mouth and says one word. "Open."

Instinctively my body responds, my legs falling wide open, resting against his.

His palm continues its journey down my inner thigh.

My center responds, arousal making the space between my thighs hot and slick.

When he reaches my panties, he cups me possessively.

His nostrils flare as I bite down on my bottom lip and look into his handsome face.

Then his hand trails up to the hem of my simple cotton panties. He doesn't take his eyes off me as he touches my bare flesh with his fingers.

His gaze swirls with heat and desire as he finds the target and uses his fingers to manipulate it in dizzying circles.

I mewl and jerk my hips.

He watches my face.

I lick my lips and then gasp when he plunges two fingers deep inside.

"Milo!" I moan, and pant.

"My Evie, so beautiful. I want to watch you let go. Right here. So, every time you come to your special place, you'll remember how you felt with me in this moment." He slides his fingers in and out, swirling an adept thumb around and around until I'm pressing my hips up against the movement and gasping for air.

"Milo, please," I beg. For what I don't know.

He dips his head and arcs me back farther. I lean back harder against his chest. My legs are wide open. The cotton band is constricting his movements, making the scene more graphic and deliciously erotic as he pulls and pushes against it, adding an intense friction that's mind-melting.

In this moment, I don't care. He could do anything he wants to me.

I'm a wanton hussy chasing after my fix. I open my eyes and watch the sun glimmer its early-evening rays, streaking the sky with a burst of watercolors Monet himself would swoon over.

Powerful pleasure ripples up from between my thighs until

I'm riding his hand like I rode the horse earlier. Needing just that tiny bit more to push me over the edge.

"*Nizhoni*, give me your pleasure," Milo murmurs against my neck as he kisses and bites there, never stopping his agile hand spinning me into a vortex of unexpected bliss.

"I'm gonna…" is all I get out before I'm gone.

The second the orgasm rolls through my body, I cry out, arching into the man I've fallen in love with. I thrust my hips up wildly, seeking more. I open my eyes and see the beauty of my favorite place as life-changing pleasure rips through me. The euphoria I feel mingles with the innocent beauty and it's almost too much to take in. Until my head is turned toward him, and it's his eyes that are all I see.

He greedily watches me as I peak, then takes my mouth and plunges his tongue inside while his large, blunt fingers hook me deep. Milo works me through the release, kissing me softly as I come down.

Except I don't want to come down. I don't *ever* want to come down from this plane of existence.

The moment he removes his fingers, I turn around so fast he has no clue what's happening. And that's when I pounce. Pushing him onto his back and going for his belt.

"Evie…we can go slow."

"Screw slow! I want fast and hard." I fumble with his pants and practically cheer when I get the belt undone, the button out of its loop and the zipper down his bulging package.

"Evie," he warns, but I don't listen. The only thing I want to hear is *yes* and *more*.

I stand and lift my dress over my head, then stand still in my panties, backlit by the view.

His eyes burn with lust as he takes in my body. His jaw grinding to a halt.

I look my fill and want him with a lot less clothes in my

way. "Pants. Off. Now." I'm so love-drunk I'm down to one syllable words.

He kicks off his boots and shoves his jeans and boxer briefs down and off his legs. His thick, large erection points up, almost touching his naval. Goodness me. I'm not surprised to find it's just as big as the rest of him. I lick my lips, wanting to take him into my mouth, taste him completely, but I need him inside me more.

I flick the back of my bra and let it drop, then shimmy out of my panties as he unbuttons his shirt. My gaze is zeroed in on every inch of male skin that is revealed. The shirt falls open and his beautiful muscular chest becomes visible. He shrugs off his shirt and I'm gifted golden, toasted brown, succulent skin. With him sitting naked on a blanket, the sun cresting over the mountains, the sky shooting colors of blue and purple and pink, I straddle him, center the wide knobbed head where I need him and slide home.

He groans and runs his hands up my bare back, the strands of my long hair tangling with his fingers as I arc and take him deeper.

"My God…" I lose my breath the second he wraps his mouth around one pale pink tip.

Heat. Belonging. Desire. Love.

So many things run through my mind as we become one.

It's more than I expected.

Better than I could have ever fantasized, and I had a million fantasies of being with this man.

He pulls away from one breast and focuses on the other one. He swirls his tongue and blows warm air against the wet tip. Both nipples bead tight for him. He cups the mounds and runs his thumbs across each peak. His gaze following every movement. Then he lifts my breasts and squeezes them as though he's memorizing their weight and heft, the way they fill his palms perfectly. I sigh and lift up to my knees just a touch and ease back down. He sucks in a sharp breath but doesn't take over like I expect him to. He's content to run his hands over my skin reverently as I sit in his lap, his large cock embedded fully inside.

"My Evie. My *Nizhoni*. My *adinidiin*. You are my life now," he says low and deep in his throat as if he's coming to terms with it on another level. He gathers my hair in his hands, twists it into a rope and sweeps it over one shoulder.

"Milo, baby, please," I whisper, and rest my hands on his shoulders. "I need to move."

"As you wish." He lifts me up, one hand trailing up my back to lock me in place, the other lifting my breast to his mouth.

His strong arm comes up, taking my body weight with it, and then slams me back down, impaling me on his stiff length. I moan, allowing the luxurious feeling of being connected to Milo filter through my body and brain. It starts with a sizzling deep in my lower spine, which flows up my back in flickering electric bolts as though the two of us finally connected is magnetic, creating energy by simply becoming one.

I clench around his length and glide up and then back down. It's so good. I tip my head back and moan. That's all it takes. Without a word, he wraps his arms around me, spins me to the side and comes up and over me. I spread my legs, raise them high up his rib cage, and he settles deep.

So deep inside I can't think straight. He's huge, filling me so completely I can hardly breathe.

"Milo." I close my eyes.

His lips fall to mine as he adjusts his arm up and around my shoulder and uses it for leverage to thrust harder, join-

182 • AUDREY CARLAN

ing us so there is no separation between our bodies. It's only Milo and me. Connected.

Absolute nirvana fills my soul and my body. Through it all he whispers beautiful Navajo words of love against my skin, into my ear and over my lips.

My thighs stretch wide around his powerful frame as he plunges in and retreats. Over and over he takes me higher and higher. Time slips away, the desert disappears and there's nothing but Milo making love to me for the first time.

I run my hands down his broad back and grip a handful of his tight rear end. He growls and thrusts harder.

"Baby," I whisper, my body heating, my heart pounding, sweat prickling against my skin as our bodies mate.

"I want all of your pleasure, *Nizhoni*." He lifts up and onto his knees. His body is insane, hovering over me. Nothing but sinew and muscle, boxed abdominals that make you want to run your tongue over them and play connect the dots. Square toned pecs that are nothing short of miraculous.

"Your hair, I want your hair." I gasp on a particularly delicious thrust.

He stills inside me, reaches up and pulls the tie holding it. He shakes his head and the black strands fall in a sheet until the breeze picks them up and off his shoulders. His face is chiseled stone and he looks like a deity. A mythical creature from another time.

"You're a god," I sigh when he puts his thumb between my thighs and spins it in merciless circles.

My body jolts, another orgasm building, this one far more powerful than the first, about to roar its way through my form.

"Then I shall show you a miracle." He grates through his teeth, comes down over me, hooks my thigh up and over his forearm and splits me in half by pounding inside.

It's beyond exceptional. It's exquisite. The pleasure so acute my toes curl.

With him this deep, farther than any other man, stars shoot across my vision. He crushes that sensitive spot between us, and I soar. My body detonating, locking around his so tightly, he arches his colossal frame and rides me hard and deep. His body is a machine, giving and receiving pleasure so intensely the veins in his biceps and forearms are popping out. He sucks air through his teeth and bellows out an animalistic cry that sizzles through my veins as he plunges and stills for a moment.

I wrap my arms around his entire body and hold on as wave after wave rolls through him, his essence spilling hotly inside of me. He tucks his face against my neck and holds me tight, his body twitching with the aftershocks of a damn impressive earthquake. Which is what this is. The earth separating and shattering as we come together.

"I'll never be the same," I say out loud, not realizing right away that I vocalized the concern instead of just thinking it.

Milo lifts his head from my neck and his black gaze swirls with mirth. "Good." He then presses his head right back to my neck where he kisses me.

For a while I lie with Milo inside me, him supporting most of his weight with the power of his forearms yet still keeping me warm and protected.

Eventually he pulls out and shifts to the side. Instantly he wraps a thick leg and arm over me, turns me to the side and tucks my back to his front.

The sun is barely visible on the horizon as the sky is darkening. I can just see a sliver of it left at the tippy-top of the mountain beyond the bluffs.

"You are stunning in the morning when the sun rises, but I think I prefer you in the evening when the sun has set." He tucks his chin in the curve of my shoulder and neck while we watch as the sun disappears.

For a long time we lie entangled with one another. Milo holding me close, running his hands down my bare hip and thigh and back up to my waist, ribs and over my shoulder, and down my arm to start the cycle again. It's soothing and magical.

"I would stay here forever with you," I whisper.

He kisses my shoulder and rests his cheek there. "We have not seen the sun rise or set from my land. You may change your mind," he teases.

"I guess it only matters that we're together. Making beauty while seeing beauty."

"Yes, that is all that matters," he agrees.

"I know you have to go soon."

"Does it help that I don't want to?"

I chuckle and turn in his arms so I can kiss him. We kiss for a bit longer, dragging out the inevitable parting. He'll be off to his cabin, while I'll go to *Toko*'s for another day.

"Come home with me," he whispers against my lips, pressing his forehead to mine.

I press my palm to his beating heart, enjoying how much heat the man radiates even naked.

"You know what? I think I will."

He jerks his head back and I smile. Apparently he wasn't expecting me to acquiesce.

Milo jumps up and I laugh as his still half-hard cock bobs with his movements.

"*Nizhoni*, you do not look at my manhood and laugh." His voice is a low warning but laced with amusement.

That has me bursting into laugher. "I can't help it. You jumped up and it was bouncing all over the place. Sorry. I promise not to laugh at your *manhood*. And who says *man-*

hood anymore, anyway? Jump into the twenty-first century, honey."

He makes a face that I decide is him moving on with my silliness and grabs his briefs, and then slips them on. I watch him dress, absolutely fascinated. He's so efficient with his movements. Looks perfectly comfortable in his nudity as he is in his clothes. Me on the other hand, I cover my bare breasts and scramble to turn away while putting on my bra and then undies.

"I have seen it all," Milo taunts, running a finger down my bare spine from my neck down to the top of my underwear. I shiver as even that small touch excites and ignites the fire he had burning twice already tonight.

"I know but it's only been once and now that we're not in the heat of the moment I feel like a teenager hurrying to dress to get back to *Toko*'s house." I grab my dress and pull it over my head, instantly feeling better when I'm covered.

This time Milo is the one chuckling.

Together we pick up the food and wine we never had a chance to eat or drink, but I don't care. Making love with Milo for the first time in my most favorite place on earth is something I'll never forget. Not ever.

"We'll stop to eat halfway," he promises.

"Works for me."

Hand in hand we take the twenty-minute walk back to *Toko*'s.

When we arrive, two men wearing military uniforms are shaking my grandfather's hand. They turn and nod in our direction and then get into a black sedan.

"*Taabe*, come to me," *Toko* demands. His voice is strangely raspy.

I hook a thumb toward the sedan that's backing up. "Who were they?"

"I said come to me, my girl." *Toko's* voice shakes enough that I stop. Milo squeezes my hand and gooseflesh rises on my skin.

"Were they friends of Dad's?" I frown.

Toko nods but opens his arms. "*Taabe.* Come."

"Why?" I shiver and let go of Milo's hand, lifting my arms to rub against my suddenly cold shoulders and biceps. All the heat of my time with Milo on the bluffs gone.

"Go to him." Milo presses a hand to my lower back, his voice soft and low.

"What's going on?" I jerk away from Milo's touch. "Who were they? Why were they here?"

"Child…" *Toko* says in Comanche. "Come into my arms. I must hold you now."

I slowly walk forward. Milo brings his hand once more to my lower back, leading me to my grandfather.

My legs feel like rubber as I move forward. "But I don't understand. What's going on?" I look into my grandfather's black eyes and watch as the porch light brings attention to a single tear slipping down his weathered cheek.

Toko does not cry. Well, he did, when his daughter died and when Suda Kaye got married, but I've never seen him shed a tear otherwise.

I swallow and shiver as my body turns ice cold. The reality of those men in uniforms coming to a protected Native American reservation and likely having reason to do so puts pieces of a puzzle together that I'm not prepared to see.

"No." I shake my head. "No." My father's smiling face races across my mind. I gasp, trying to get more air into my lungs.

Milo rests a hand on my shoulder, giving me support.

"It is your father, child. He has left this world." *Toko's* soothing voice can't put together what his words are doing to my heart. Breaking it straight in half.

I lose my footing and start to crumple toward the ground. Milo is there with his hands at my waist, holding me up and pressing me forward until I'm in my grandfather's arms. Wrapped in his safety and love.

"No! I—I just…t-talked to him." My voice is cracking and almost unrecognizable trying to remember the quick call I'd had with him.

Toko holds me against his chest, wrapping a hand around my head. Uncontrollable tears fall down my cheeks as I sob. "Not my dad, please. *Toko*, no."

"He left us a hero, little one," he whispers. "He is to be revered."

"No, please." I fist *Toko*'s poncho tight.

He holds me while I cry. Memories of my father's short stays with us on the reservation flit across my eyes. The excitement I'd feel when he'd come home dressed in his full uniform looking like royalty. The way he'd put Suda Kaye up onto his shoulders when she was small and hold my hand. The laughter he and my mother shared.

Gone. Just gone. Forever.

"He's never coming home?" I half sob, and pull away enough to look into the only eyes I've ever trusted. "No, *Taabe*. He is not." He lifts the shiny item he has clutched in his hand. Two metal rectangles on a beaded chain.

Dog tags.

Used to identify military personnel in the event of a casualty.

He puts them into my hands and covers them with his own. Warmth wraps around my waist and I realize that Milo stayed right behind me as I crumpled.

I look down at the tags and my entire body shakes.

Adam Ross is the only thing I can distinguish through the new wave of tears flowing down my face.

As this happens, Milo turns me into his arms. I press my face into his comforting throat, breathing in against his neck. He lifts me up and places me in his lap as he sits in the chair we cuddled in just yesterday.

A lifetime ago.

A lifetime where my father was still alive.

13

My father is dead.

Adam Ross, military man of mystery, was taken out by the enemy.

After I calmed down, *Toko* sat me down and told me that the men that came were men my father saved under his command. They didn't go into a lot of detail. I knew everything my father did was dangerous, and he was up there in rank after years of dedicated service.

What I didn't know was he was one of the highest-ranking officials in his branch of the military who planned, researched and commanded many special-operations teams. The ones that did the crazy off-the-grid, black-ops-type jobs you only think are real in the movies.

They're real. I have the proof of his last mission dangling around my neck with my father's name on them.

Honestly, I thought he simply worked in counterterrorism, in an office. Preventing attacks with intel from data and computers, likely sitting behind a cushy desk with a map of the world laid out across the wooden surface with big red X's where they'd located bad guys. I didn't know his desk was often in a MH-60 Blackhawk helicopter leading teams into the type of combat I couldn't even dream up if I tried.

Every time he came home for one of his short stints, he'd make sure I knew how much he loved me. Told me over and over how proud of me and Suda Kaye he was. Sent money home twice a month, every month like clockwork when we were children. I had to actually tell him to stop sending money after I graduated college. At least he saw me walk that stage.

He'll never see me walk down the aisle.

Meet his first grandchild.

Just like my mother. Gone from my life. *Poof.*

I'm a thirty-year-old orphan and I'm not sure how to accept that fact.

Over the years, as I got older, I'd see my father less and less. His primary base of operation was in Europe. Mine was my office in Colorado Springs. A world away. Still, we kept in touch via email and by phone. The last I heard he was in Poland, but now I don't think that was true based on the information *Toko* gave last night. It seems my father was deep in the Middle East when his helicopter was shot right out of the sky and crashed into rough terrain.

No survivors.

I'll never know the truth behind his death or what led up to it. The officers told *Toko* that the mission was classified. His body was set to arrive by plane in the next ten days. He had afterlife directives and a last will. The body would be delivered to a morgue in Colorado Springs close to me, his next of kin.

My father told me in many conversations that he had everything planned out for when the time came. He didn't want me and Suda Kaye worrying about the details. Like Mom, Dad was an only child. His parents died when he was in his twenties. He met my mother in Atlantic City, on one of his leaves. It was love at first sight, they both claimed. They were married before his next deployment. Which means my father didn't have any roots of his own. Maybe that's what he and my mother had in common. Though every time he came home, we were a happy little family, and they were like lovesick newlyweds.

I've always based my idea of love on how my mother and father looked at one another. As though they were each other's whole world. But that was only when they were in the same place at the same time. Because in truth they were rarely together. We, as a family, were rarely together. For most of my years growing up, it was *Toko*, me and Suda Kaye. Until even my sister left me and the life we'd built together to find greener pastures.

And what's left now?

Tears slowly slide down my cheek, wetting the pillowcase beneath my head.

A large warm arm curls around my chest as I feel his body spoon mine. My back to his front. Our knees are cocked and fitted together. He presses his chin to the space between my neck and shoulder, just like he did after we made love on the bluffs tonight. It feels like a million eons ago, but in reality it was less than ten hours ago.

Milo.

After *Toko* told me the news about my father, Milo called Yana and asked her to drive my car back to his cabin and then he planned to drive her back to her apartment not far from here. Without a word, he packed up my things in my room at *Toko*'s, had a few hushed words with my grandfather and agreed to have me call tomorrow once I'd had some sleep. *Toko* would notify Suda Kaye.

My phone rang incessantly on the drive home, but I let the calls go to voice mail. I just couldn't talk to my sister. Not yet. Not until I got the slightest handle on my emotions.

Eventually Camden called Milo because Suda Kaye wouldn't let up. Milo provided Camden with the information he desired, that I was indeed fine, did not want to talk to anyone and would be safe with him at his cabin. That would not hold her off for long. Nor would I want to.

"I can hear you thinking, *Nizhoni*." His warm voice wraps around my battered heart as his arms hold me close.

I don't hide the tears from him or pretend to be asleep. If he wants me, the *real* me, this is part of it.

"I can't stop thinking about him. The last time we spoke. How scared he must have been when the helicopter crashed. That he'll never walk me down the aisle or meet the grandchildren he would hopefully have in the future. All of it. His life is just wiped out and I'm the only one who cares."

"That isn't true."

"It is. *Toko* thought he was a good man, but he never really got to know him. When Dad would visit, it was all about Mom and us girls. Making family-type memories. A lot of the time he'd take us to do fun things away from the reservation. Dad didn't have a problem with the way our people lived, but he wasn't one of us, and didn't feel perfectly at home in *Toko*'s house, so we'd stay in hotels most of the time."

"And what of your sister?"

I scowl and press my face into the pillow, trying not to scream. "What about her? It's not as if she really cared about him. Barely kept in touch. They didn't have a close bond. I'm not sure she's even talked to him more than a couple times since she left me at eighteen. Maybe it's because she wasn't really his, regardless of how much he tried over the years."

"Regardless of how close they were, he was a father figure—"

I rub at my nose with the tissue I've been clinging to and

cut him off. "The way Mom tells it, a year after they had me, she and Dad fought. By phone. He had only seen me once for my entire first year and that was a couple months after I was born. Mom was superyoung and living with *Toko*. Our grandmother was sick. She didn't know what to do. She felt tied down in a big way."

"Evie." Him saying my name in that guttural tone digs deep into a wound that's already barely held closed.

"Anyway, the story goes Dad wasn't planning to come home for another long while. Maybe a year. Mom was tired of being a new mother without his help. They agreed to separate for a while. Mom left me with *Toko* and took off to Chicago. Went there with some belly dancing crew and bartended in the evenings. All while her one-year-old daughter was left behind, being raised by her grandfather. When she finally made it back, she was pregnant with Suda Kaye."

"This is news," he says with a hint of surprise.

I nod. "Part of my family's torrid secrets. Mom gallivanting around the world, having fun, sowing her wild oats and getting pregnant. Apparently my dad forgave her and took Suda Kaye on as his own. His name is on her birth certificate, even though he's not her biological father. It wasn't like he was home much, anyway, and what's not to love about a beautiful baby girl? He didn't treat my sister differently, either. He actually seemed to try harder to connect with her. Though Suda Kaye is my mother's double. Lives out loud. Adventurous. Gorgeous. Funny. Vibrant. All the things that reminded him of the woman he loved."

"Wouldn't that mean she'd care deeply about his passing?" Milo surmises inaccurately.

I huff. "You'd *think*, but once she found out that Adam wasn't her real father, she started treating him like a stranger. Barely talked to him when he'd visit. Make plans with friends instead of wanting to do family things with Mom and Dad when he'd come around. And then, of course, Mom got sick. And he couldn't fix it. And he didn't stay. I raised my seventeen-year-old sister, who was still in high school when our mother died. She hated him for not taking a leave of absence when Mom passed."

"He left you alone?" His hold tightens around my body, a protective instinct I adore.

"He didn't exactly have a choice. There was some serious thing happening in his job that he had to get back to. He came for the funeral and left a week later. I was in my sophmore year of college. Suda Kaye had just started her senior year of high school. Suda Kaye only had half a year of school to finish and we're several hours from the reservation. I wasn't about to uproot my grandfather or my sister when I was an adult and perfectly capable of taking care of my sister like I had been for years while Mom was sick. Dad left us a bucketload of money and prepaid the rent and utilities. I didn't see him for another year after that, but we talked all the time. I'm not sure Suda Kaye has seen him since—even during her time traveling all over Europe."

"*Adinidiin*, you cannot assume how your sister feels about her father's passing."

"You see, that's just the thing. The second she found out that Adam Ross wasn't her real dad she wrote him off entirely." I snap my fingers. "Just like that."

"You are dealing with a lot right now. You need to eat, and you need sleep."

I can feel the movement of his words against my neck.

"I'm not hungry but I am exhausted. So tired, and yet every time I close my eyes all I see is his face. It's tor-torture." I hiccup-sob, more tears falling down my face in wet rivulets.

"Perhaps if you ate something you might feel more at ease. You haven't eaten since breakfast with my family."

The mention of food has my stomach growling.

He kisses my cheek. "Your belly agrees. Come, let me feed you." He curls his fingers around my hand and tugs until I'm sitting up. I'm still in the dress I was wearing earlier today.

"Can I have one of your shirts?" I ask.

His lips tip up at the edges and he nods once, moving into his large closet. He comes out with a T-shirt and sets it on the bed in front of me. I stand up and move to grab the hem of my dress.

He shakes his head. "Let me take care of you." He reaches down to the hem and lifts it slowly up my body. I lift my arms and he pulls it up and over my head, then through my arms. Then he reaches around me and unclips my bra.

I don't say anything, nor do I move.

He slides my bra down each arm and sets it on top of the dress. He dips his head and places a soft kiss on the plump, weighty portion of each breast. Then he crouches lower and places his lips to my navel and kisses me there. He dips even lower and presses a kiss to the center of each thigh, first the left, then the right. Then he slowly stands, kisses my bare neck on each side and then my mouth softly before pulling the shirt over my head. I push each arm through the soft cotton and, once it's covering my chest, the rest of it falls to just past midthigh.

"Are you warm enough, or do you want me to find you some pants?"

I shake my head. "I'm fine."

"I have a fire going and plenty of blankets. Would you like tea?"

"You mean the tea I never got to have the first time I was here?"

He smirks. "New tea. An herbal one that helps still the mind."

"Okay."

"Come." He holds my hand and leads me down the stairs and to the huge U-shaped couch in front of the fire and the amazing view of the moon over the lake. I sit in the center cross-legged and he grabs one of the blankets and covers my lap, tucking it in at the sides to keep my legs warm. "Now settle, I'll be right back." He lifts my chin and kisses me lightly, and then again in a sweet peck before caressing my cheek with his thumb, wiping away a stray tear I didn't know was there, before he leaves me and heads to the kitchen.

I stare out at the view. It's incredibly calm. An illusion of serenity. Everything outside is still and quiet, perfectly tranquil, and yet everything inside me is a tumultuous chaos of spiraling emotions, resurging memories and unbearable grief. I understand why people say they feel alone in a crowded room. In my mind and heart, it's crowded, filled to the brim with so much I can't control, and yet on the outside, I'm desperately trying to hold it all together.

Milo brings me a cup of tea and a plate. He sets the tea on a coaster on the table in front of me, then hands me the plate. On it is the best thing in the entire world. A peanut butter and jelly sandwich cut sideways with a thick layer of peanut butter and jelly smooshing out the front.

I immediately pick up the sandwich and take an unladylike monster bite. A sploodge of jelly sticks to the corner of my mouth as I chew the best comfort food of all time next to *Toko*'s fry bread.

Milo sits next to me, lifts his hand and wipes the smudge away from my mouth and sucks it into his.

My eyes light up at the intensity I see there. He has to be feeling just as crazy about everything as I am. From breakfast with his family, which ended up going really well, making this thing between us grow that much stronger. Then riding horses to sharing my most favorite place with him, to us opening our bodies to one another and being intimate for the first time.

I eat an entire half and then pick up the second one.

"I'm sorry about…" I shake my head. "About everything."

He lifts his hand and cups the side of my neck. "You have nothing to be sorry for." He frowns. "What happened on the bluffs—having that experience was more than I expected. I have never connected to a woman so purely." He adds a comforting pressure to my neck. "I'll cherish that time always. Nothing that came after will ever take that away."

"But it's all ruined now," I whisper, and glance down at the mostly uneaten second half of the sandwich.

"Look at me, Evie. Part of having a relationship is being there for the hard times. This is one of the hard times. There is nowhere or no one I'd rather be with than you."

I close my eyes and feel the tears starting up again. I inhale full and deep to keep them at bay. I've cried so much tonight.

"I don't deserve you and you don't deserve a broken woman." I share my fear wishing it weren't the truth. Before we came down from that bluff, the entire world felt like it was in front of us. Glowing and so bright. Milo and me. A couple. My dream come true. The rest of our lives ahead of us. The promise of so much. And now…it's like the universe spoke and smacked me upside the head with reality. Reach too far and for too much and you will get cut down to size.

My entire life changed in a single day. I accepted Milo into my heart and soul and lost my father.

"You are not broken. You are hurt, deeply. There is a difference. It's my job to help heal those wounds. And I will.

Remember what I said, *Nizhoni*. You give me your fear. Give me your hurts. We will heal them together."

"You are an amazing man." I sniff because my nose is trying to run again as the emotions build back up.

"We both have been through a great deal to get to this point in our lives. To find one another. To be at a place where we can share our highs and lows. Stick with me, *Nizhoni*. We will ride this storm as one and come out the other side stronger."

I press my lips together not knowing how to handle someone wanting to be there for me. "I'm used to being alone. Handling my own problems."

"You are alone no longer. Now is the time you learn to open the door and allow me to come inside."

"Milo…"

He holds up his hand as if to stop my train of thought. "If we had come down from the bluffs to find my father had a heart attack, would you leave me to handle his loss on my own?"

Stake through the heart.

"No, my goodness. I'd be there for you!" I blurt.

He smiles. "Exactly. And I am here for you. For anything you need. To feed you. Put you bed. To care for you. And one day, it will be me who needs you. And I suspect you will be there for me."

"You make it sound so simple." I push my hair behind my ear.

"All you have to do is be here. With me. Let me tend to you through this. Lean on me. I am strong. I can handle it." He smiles softly and it's so pure, his expression carrying so much compassion, my heart starts to pound as hope fills the air around us.

"I don't want to need you too much or take advantage." My voice wobbles a little as I stare into his eyes.

"That's not the way love works. At least not the kind of love we're building between us." His tone is so sure and direct it stuns me for a moment.

"You really believe in us. That we can go the distance. Family. Marriage. Kids. Happily-ever-after. All of it." I wait with my heart in my throat for his answer.

Milo cups my cheek and brings his face close to mine. "I not only believe it. Soon, you will, too."

"I want to. I started to but then…"

He presses his forehead to mine. "What we felt on the bluffs, that was reality. Our reality. I will work every day, every hour, every minute if I have to, in order for you to have faith in us."

There really aren't any more words to say. Instead, I take his mouth with mine, pouring my fear, my sorrow and my heart into a single kiss.

He cups my cheeks, slants my head and kisses me back harder, deeper and with more intent. A decision was made for him this night. I can feel it in the way he shifts my body, moving the plate with one hand to the coffee table, removing the blanket and dragging me up and over his lap. He settles me there and kisses me like he owns me.

And he does.

More so, I *want* to be owned by Milo Chavis.

My dream man.

The man who is living up to every wish I ever made on all the stars in the sky.

His arms wrap about my body and he holds me closer, plunging his tongue inside, devouring my mouth as if he may never get another chance. I cling to him like my life depends on it, moaning into his movements, gasping for breath before going back at his lips.

Eventually he runs his mouth down my neck, nipping and kissing, while sliding his hands up my bare back underneath the shirt of his I'm wearing.

My nipples tighten and my sex swells. I can feel he's hard as steel through the pajama bottoms he's wearing. I reach between us and palm his impressive package.

He groans and lets his head fall back. "*Nizhoni*, you are not thinking straight."

I stand in front of his spread legs and shimmy out of my panties, then lean forward and yank the waist of his pajama bottoms until he lifts his hips. Once they are off, I toss them behind me and gorge on the sight of him hard and weeping at the tip.

With quick movements, I'm back to straddling him, centering right over the wide head. "Please, I need you right now. Make some of this pain go away. Just for a little while," I plead.

His eyes light up and turn into pitch-black pools as his nostrils flare and his jaw hardens.

"We didn't use protection before…" he warns.

"I'm clean and on the pill and I trust you." I lean forward and kiss his plump lips, sucking and nipping the bottom one before running my tongue along to dip in the top one.

"I trust you with my life, and I'm safe, too," he admits, his gaze practically holding mine hostage when he slides his tip through my arousal, notches his crown at the center and pulls me down onto his length.

Heaven.

I arch back in pure ecstasy when I'm filled with all that is Milo.

He curses in Navajo and then eases me up and slides me

down slowly. I tip my head forward and take his mouth in a luxurious kiss.

For a long time I ride him slow and easy, until the heat builds between us, ribbons of pleasure shooting out in every direction making me move faster and come down harder.

Milo grips my hips as I rest my hands on his powerful shoulders. We're both still wearing our shirts and it doesn't matter. We're beyond connected in all the ways that matter. I pick up the pace and pant as every thrust takes me higher and higher, readying to rise up over the cliff and fall to the cool water down below.

He wraps his arms fully around me, smashes our chests together, takes my mouth in a blistering kiss and grinds me down over his length, crushing that bundle of nerves that makes me sing.

He groans into my mouth and I swallow it down as he takes my cry of extreme joy at the same time. Our combined release goes on and on, both of us giving and taking from one another until we're sloppily kissing and moving our hips in uncoordinated slow movements coming back down.

My body goes liquid against his form.

He takes my weight and sighs with what I know is contentment because I feel it, too.

"I'm so tired." I press my face against his throat and close my eyes, our bodies still connected in every way.

"Sleep, my Evie. Let me take care of you."

I nod against his neck and fall asleep in the arms of the man I love, content to let everything that happened today just go away…at least for a while.

14

The sun shining through the open curtains warms my face. I'm snuggled back against my own personal heating unit.

Milo's arm is locked around my waist, his body plastered to mine from shoulders to feet.

"Good morning, *Taabe*." He uses my family's nickname.

I smile and close my eyes but turn around to face him. I press my hands against his bare chest. His hair is loose, falling in black silky sheets all over him.

Not for the first time, and God willing not the last, I take in all that is the man who owns my heart. He's on his side, his broad shoulders wide and welcoming. He keeps an arm around my waist, a heavy weight that I appreciate, serving to ground me to his bed. Not that I'd ever leave when I can stare in awe at such magnificence.

"How did you sleep?"

"The best I've slept in a long time. Thank you."

He smiles softly, leans forward and kisses me too briefly. "I have canceled my meetings for the next few days and have taken a leave. I also contacted your office. Spoke to Regina and explained what happened. Left a message with Camden letting him know that you will call your sister when you are ready."

I frown. "Uh, when did you have time to do that?"

"Evie, my love, it's two in the afternoon. You've been sleeping for twelve hours."

I push my head back, turn and look over my shoulder to the clock on the wall. Holy moly, it *is* two in the afternoon. "Wh-what? I—I've never done that."

He cups my cheek and pushes stray locks of my hair away from my face and over my shoulder.

"You needed it. I got up at eight, made all the calls and came back to bed. I read for a while until I fell back to sleep."

I purse my lips and push onto my back. Reality slams into my mind.

My father's dead.

I close my eyes and hold off the tears. My eyes are already scratchy and sensitive.

"You hungry?"

I turn just my head and look at the most handsome man I've ever known.

"Do you know I wished for you?" I admit randomly.

Milo's arm locks around my waist and tugs me until I'm facing him again.

"Explain."

The memory flashes through my mind. I bite down on my bottom lip, take a fortifying breath and tell him what he deserves to know.

"Huutsuu, Taabe, come here, my beautiful loves." Mom reached for both me and Suda Kaye. I knew what was coming. Usually before one of her adventures, she'd bring me and my sister somewhere to have a chat. Even though I hated knowing what was about to happen, meaning her leaving us again, I still gravitated to her, thinking that maybe if I was a good girl and did everything she asked, she would choose to stay.

She led us up a hill and sat down near the edge. The sun had just set, and the sky was getting darker by the second.

"Come, girls," Mom called, and we both rushed up the hill. I beat Suda Kaye to the top.

Suda Kaye sat on one side of our mother, her lap filled with all the wildflowers she'd picked for Toko's dinner table. He wasn't ever happy when we picked them because it killed them, and he believed everything had a right to live. I stopped doing it, but let Suda Kaye have her fun. I sat on her other side and Mom wrapped her arms around our backs.

"Look up at the sky. You see all the stars?" she asked with awe in her tone.

Suda Kaye and I both looked up and nodded. From this spot it was like we could see the entire sky spread out before us. Bursts of twinkling lights were everywhere blanketing the view.

"Those are all the wishes of the world, waiting to come true." She pointed to the stars.

Suda Kaye's mouth fell open as she stared above. "Really?"

"Yes, Huutsuu. I'm going to teach you to wish on a star, but you must remember to not be greedy. Be thoughtful about your wish, for you only get one until it comes true. Then you can wish for another. But it could take what seems like forever for your wish to come true," Mom said.

"Wow," Suda Kaye gasped.

I just stared at each one thinking there were so many people out there making wishes that weren't yet coming true. And what if I picked a star that held someone else's wish? Would mine burn out theirs or could the star handle more than one?

I frowned, wondering how to consider my options for the best result. I didn't want to pick someone else's star. That felt mean and rude. "How do you pick one?" I asked, studying the sky intently.

Mom pressed her face close to mine, the earthy, patchouli-and-

citrus smell filling my lungs with her happy scent. "One will call to you, Taabe. Just like the sun calls to you, my golden girl." She kissed my blond hair at the crown of my head before turning to my sister. "And you, my Huutsuu. *Let the wind help you choose."*

Suda Kaye *and I sat there for a long time staring at the stars with our mom. I scanned each one with intent. Waiting for one to call to me. Wanting to feel something—anything—but nothing was happening. I didn't understand what I was supposed to be seeing. They were all bright, all pretty and shiny, but I didn't want to mess up. It had to be perfect or I could risk never making my wish come true.*

There was only one thing that I wanted above anything else.

"Did you pick one, my loves?"

I hadn't, but saw Suda Kaye *beaming and nodding so I copied her and stared straight up at the sky. My eyes landed on one and I just focused my attention on it, hoping it was meant to hold my wish.*

"Okay now, repeat after me while looking at your star." Mom's voice was soft and low. Sounding sweet like when you hear a flute.

"I wish I may..." she said.

We repeated it, our small voices filled with wonder.

"I wish I might..."

We followed along.

"Have this wish..."

And again repeat.

"I wish tonight," Mom finished, and we repeated the last phrase.

"Now make a wish on your star but don't ever tell anyone what your wish is, or it will never come true." She held us close and we stared up into the brilliant sky.

I focused on the star I chose.

That night, I wished to be the opposite of my mother. I wished to find a man one day who loved only me. A man who would never leave me for an adventure. A dream man who would want to build a family and never leave the children we brought into the world. A man who would hold my hand and love me until I died.

Staring into Milo's face after I tell him my memory, I know that after twenty years of wishing on stars I've finally been granted my wish.

"It's you I've been wishing for. I finally caught my dream but I'm so afraid I'm going to lose it. Lose you. Everything I want, all the people I love…they leave. If you choose me, you can't ever leave. Not ever. I won't survive it." I press my hand to his rapidly beating heart.

Milo dips his face closer to mine, his onyx-colored eyes focused and intent.

"I am honored to be your wish. Your dream man. For you, my Evie, are my dream woman. You are my light, my sky, the ground beneath my feet. I love you, Evie Ross. I want forever with you. All of the things you wished for I will give you. And you have my word, *Nizhoni*, I will never leave. Not willingly. Not ever."

I let the tears fall as I cup his face. "I love you, too. I'm still scared out of my mind, but I can't deny I want to be with you. I want to build a life. Let go of my fears. I'm not sure I know how, but I'll try. I promise, for you I'll try. Don't give up on me."

He presses his forehead to mine. "Never. I'll never give up. You gave me your love. It's mine now. I'm never letting it go."

Milo curls his arms around mine, eases our naked bodies front to front and kisses me full and deep.

He doesn't stop kissing me until we've made slow, sweet love, cementing everything we just committed to.

It's official.

Milo and Evie.

Together.
A dream come true.

Milo's kissing my neck and playfully splashing me with droplets of water as I attempt to do the dishes after our huge lunch.

He thawed out some of his mother's homemade fry bread, and made his own beef stew to dip it in. To top off the comforting stew and bread, he made strawberry shortcake. I think he ate more of the whipped cream off me than he did from his bowl.

Every time I took a bite, he'd squirt a dollop from the can on my shoulder, elbow, the palm of my hand. Then he'd take his time licking it away with hungry eyes and spirited nibbles against my skin. Eventually I got into the game and squirted some on his bare chest, teasing his nipples until he lost it and took my mouth in a fiery kiss.

It was fun and free. We left behind the heaviness of yesterday and instead spent time together as a couple. Eating, talking, teasing, kissing—all the things I fantasized of doing with him from the moment I saw him again.

And amazingly, it was easy. Being with him, having declared our love for one another, opened the doors to something so unique and special. For the first time, I feel like I have someone on my side, in my corner, there only for me. To keep me safe, loved, protected. And more, he wants that job. He's proud to have it. Proud to call me his.

"Can we talk about our homes again?" Milo asks.

I frown and rinse one of the bowls we used and place it in the dish drainer. Since there weren't many dishes, I chose to do them by hand. Besides, there was something gratifying about cleansing something by hand and seeing the end result, all freshly cleaned and ready for use the next time.

"In what manner?"

"My preference is you living here. I have spent a lot of time, money and effort preparing this as the home I want for my family."

"Milo, we just committed to one another fully…" I try.

"Yes, exactly. I do not wish to live apart. Ever. I would like for you to move in here, as soon as possible."

I look around his home. It's beyond amazing. Definitely way better than my small apartment and it's only five to ten minutes farther from his house to my Colorado Springs office. And his home is a bit closer to my Pueblo office, so it evens out in that regard.

"Isn't that moving a little fast?"

"Fast is getting you pregnant with my child now. Which I'm also not opposed to."

My eyes practically bulge out of their sockets. "Whoa, whoa, whoa. Now you want me pregnant with your baby!" I step back until I'm leaning against the counter and capable of keeping myself upright.

He nods. "I know that is too soon for you. It is not for me. I'm thirty-four, *Nizhoni*. I want a family. With you. Many children."

"Many? What are we talking here?"

"As many as you will give me." He crosses his arms and his biceps bulge. I watch those muscles, fascinated, wishing I'd run my tongue across that sexy surface during our food game earlier.

"I—I…" I let air out of my lungs as though a balloon were deflating. "Milo, you're making me speechless again."

"Do you not want children?" He tips his head and his brow furrows as though concerned.

"No, I do. Definitely. I've always wanted kids. I just…

I mean. We just committed to this." I point upstairs to his bedroom. "Like, a couple hours ago."

He smiles softly. "No. I committed to you a lot longer than that and you just admitted to having dreamed and wished for me for years. I am here. Right here. Ready to give you all that you desire."

I lick my lips and tap my foot. "There's an order to things, honey. Date, fall in love, eventually move in together, get married and then plan your family. We're only at step two and we just barely got there today. Perhaps we can take some time for the next steps? Besides, I'm an emotional wreck. My father just died." I attempt to go the logical route.

He shakes his head. "I don't wish to wait any longer than necessary I've waited thirty-four years of my life to have you. You gave me your love. Now I want you to give me your hand."

I jolt to attention. "Are you asking me to marry you? Now?"

He frowns. "Do I even need to ask? The stars and the universe have spoken, Evie. You are my mate."

Heat flows through my veins, making my blood get hot. I narrow my gaze. "You are not getting out of asking me to marry you!" I point at his chest. "When we've had some time together and I'm not grieving. And I want romance. Flowers. Candlelight. The whole thing. My dream man is not going to just demand I marry him! No way, no how. Think again, buster!"

His lips twitch and he moves to take a step closer to me.

I put my hand up, but he moves until his chest is right up against my hand. I can feel his warm skin and heart pounding through my palm. It almost makes me give up the fight and just jump his bones, because the man is insanely sexy and the things he can do in the bedroom are mind-melting.

"Romance. I can do this," he agrees.

I nod curtly. "Okay. Then first step after admitting we love one another is moving in together. Normal people take a few months, maybe a year or two, before they make that move."

"We are not normal people." His voice is a low and deep warning, basically stating without using words that he is not okay with a long grace period.

My resolve falters. "Why do you want me here?"

He closes his eyes and takes a calming breath. At least that's what I think he's doing when he opens them and blows me away.

"Not only do I want to take care of you, especially now with your recent loss, I need you here. To wake up to your scent every day. To feel your body close to mine as I sleep. I know now I built this home for you. For us. For our future family. If you are not here, it is not home. You are my home now."

I'm reminded of when he told me that his ex was always gone. Never stayed with him. Always off gallivanting toward her own desires and leaving him behind. My stomach lurches at the thought. Without Milo saying it outright, I fear this is one of Milo's demons. One I could so easily slay by simply agreeing to living with the man I want to be with. Overall, it's not really a huge concession. I want to be with him. He wants and needs me here to feel safe in this relationship.

"Okay," I say breathlessly, my heart bleeding, butterflies filling my belly and flapping their wings wildly. I want nothing more than a man who thinks I am his home. "I'll move in."

He smiles bright and it's a vise-lock around my heart. I put my arms around his shoulders.

"Can we go get some of your things today? Clothes, necessities. Whatever it is you need to live here now. Then we can go again throughout the week and pack up the rest. Decide what we want to keep and what we want to store or donate."

From zero to a hundred. Not surprised when it comes to this man.

"This is happening fast," I warn, reminding him that I'm as skittish as a feral cat.

He grins and it softens me again. "Yes, it is. My woman in my home. Telling me she loves me in our bed. The bed we will make children in. Once we put your father to rest, all will be good."

A wave of happiness and sorrow mingling together bubbles up in my chest and I press my head to his neck. "It doesn't change that last night I lost my father. I'm sorry I can't be as happy or as strong as you."

He wraps his arms tight around my form. "I'll be your strength. And as you deal with your hurts over your loss, you will have something positive to focus on, too. Us. Building our life here together."

I nod. It does sound lovely.

"Tell me what you're feeling." He rubs my back in soothing strokes.

"I'm sad about my dad. Crushed at his loss. I'm still not sure what to do with those feelings. They keep coming up and swallowing me whole and then you're there, and I'm reminded that I have someone who still needs me. Someone of my own. Someone real."

"And I will be here through whatever you need to feel. You can trust me with it," he murmurs, and I cling to him.

"Thank you."

"No thank-you needed. I know one day this favor will be returned. I'm not looking forward to it, but it's inevitable. In life there is loss, my Evie. Deep, heartbreaking loss. We will wade through this sadness together. Come to the other side where you can remember the good memories with your father. He will always be a part of you. And he died a hero."

I suck in a sharp breath and just barely hold back the deluge of tears and emotion wanting to pour out. Instead, I press my head further against Milo's and breathe in his strength and fortitude.

"I want to go to my apartment. Get my things. Then tonight, will you take me out on the lake? I have a new wish to make on a star."

He cups my cheeks, kisses each one, then my lips.

"Anything you want is yours, *Nizhoni*."

I hold on to his thick, strong neck. "I love you, Milo Chavis. I've loved you since I was eight years old. I love you now at thirty and I plan to love you every day from this moment forward."

He cups my cheek and runs his thumb along my bottom lip. He doesn't need to say anything. His touch, his look, the shelter of his arms, they say it all.

Milo Chavis loves me and as he stares deeply into my eyes, I know for a fact this man is never going to leave.

The safety and security that belief provides me is life-changing. The knowledge fills and feeds my soul with the sweetest serenity I've ever known.

Home.

I have a new home now. I lock my arms around him and soak in the feeling of being exactly where I'm supposed to. In the arms of the man I love, building the life I always dreamed I wasn't worthy of. He makes me believe I'm worthy. Seeing myself through his eyes is empowering. No more feeling undeserving or unwanted. This man wants me. No one else. Me. He knows all of my fears and insecurities and is willing to fight away any demons standing in his way.

I've never had anyone fight for me. But as I stand here

in the arms of the man I love, I realize that I, too, need to fight for him. Fight for *myself*. Fight for what we want to build together.

Fuck fear.

I will no longer be afraid of being happy. I'm going to grab happiness by the reins and ride off into the damn sunset with my dream man at my back helping to steer the horse and lead the way.

"Are you ready?" he asks, not having a clue about the mental war I was waging standing in his arms.

"I'm ready for anything. Today is the first day of our lives together. I'm not going to let anything come between me and you. Especially not me and my ridiculous fears." My voice rises and I stand taller. "No more worrying. No more fear. My mother always wanted me to leap first and plan later. Well, you know what, Mom?" I look up at the ceiling. "I'm finally taking your advice."

Milo's arms lock around my waist.

"I love you, honey. I'm all in. Let's pack everything we can. I'm tired of waiting for my life to start, too. All my life I felt like I was searching for happiness and it was always just outside of my reach. Well, you know what?"

Milo's lips flatten and he smirks. "What, *adinidiin*?"

God, I love it when he calls me "his light."

"You make me happy. *You*. Us. I knew the day we met that you were special. Saving me from those bullies. Taking care of me. Protecting me. You've done nothing but prove that to me over and over." I lift up onto my toes and press my lips to his, close enough to still speak against his beautiful mouth. "Let's build a life together. No more waiting. We'll move at our pace and if that's at the speed of light, then so be it."

This has Milo smiling huge, his entire body exuding joy, filling my entire being with his happiness.

"You surprise me." He kisses my lips hard and fast.

"You surprised me," I counter. "You changed me, Milo. With your relentless pursuit, your follow-through and your commitment to us. You've given me the one thing I've always wanted and needed above anything else."

"Which is?" His words are said against my lips, soft and warm, our breath comingling, becoming one.

I stare into the endless shiny black abyss of his stunning gaze and hand him my truth. Trusting that he'll take care of it.

"Someone who loves me enough to stay."

15

Being in my apartment feels strange. Cold. I glance around my living room and note the lack of joy sliding over me. It's as if my entire life changed in a single week. Heck, more like a single day. Making up with Milo's family. Being intimate with him for the first time. Finding out about my father's death. Admitting our love to one another. And last, agreeing to move in with him. To starting a new path and building our life together.

I grab all the framed pictures of me and Suda Kaye from different times in our lives off a bookcase and set them in a box. I've already turned off my phone and left it in my purse. Milo took care of contacting who needed to be called. I have no desire to speak to anyone right now. I need time in my own head and with the man I love. Everything else is unnecessary and can wait.

"Even Suda Kaye," I whisper as I run my finger over her face in the picture.

It's not that I don't want to talk to my sister; it's just that I'm not sure I can. There is so much swirling in my head related to her, my father, our mother and our past. I need more time to work through it all, so I don't hurt her or myself.

I pick up a picture of me and Dad at my graduation. *Toko*

took the photo. Suda Kaye was somewhere abroad and it didn't even dawn on her that I'd want her to see me graduate college. I didn't push it. Maybe I should have. It was one of the proudest days of my life. I'd set out to do something, be the very first of my family to graduate college, and I did it. My father's wide smile and his lock around my body, my cap tilting off my head with his exuberance, was a beautiful moment. The pride on his face is obvious.

Tears well in my eyes and I let them fall. He may not have been around a lot, but he was there when it mattered most. My graduation from high school. Suda Kaye's. Mom's death. My college graduation. I knew he did his best to be as present as he could and still be a good provider and the patriot he couldn't deny in his soul. Unlike our mother, who left for her own selfish desires.

I toss the photo into the box with the others as Milo leaves my bedroom with two enormous armfuls of my clothing on hangers.

"I'll put these in the Cayenne. We'll put the boxes in the truck."

"Okay. Thanks, honey."

His dark gaze lights up at me calling him honey. He likes it and shows me by leaning forward and stealing a quick kiss before heading to the front door. I dash over to open it for him and am greeted by my sister's sorrow-filled face. Her caramel-colored eyes are red-rimmed, her brown hair up in a messy knot on the top of her head. She's wearing a man's hoodie that goes to her midthigh, a pair of pajama pants and fuzzy slippers.

She looks like crap.

"Evie." Her voice shakes, and she throws herself into my arms.

I wrap my arms loosely around her but can't bring myself to put a lot of effort into it.

"I'll just put these in the car and then go to the box store and get more." He stands still, waiting for me to let him know I'm okay.

I wave him off. "It's fine."

After my sister finishes sobbing against my chest, she pulls herself away, tears streaking down her pretty face. She frowns, looking at my stoic, unemotional expression.

"Evie…" she croaks out.

"What are you doing here?"

Her chin trembles and her brows push together. "Evie, we need to be together. Our dad died."

I sniff. "Our dad. Now he's *our* dad. Right." I turn around, go over to the bookcase and start yanking books off and stacking them in a box I had waiting.

Suda Kaye curls her arm around my bicep. "What's that supposed to mean? And why aren't you looking at me?"

I shrug her hold off. "If you can't tell, I'm packing."

"Yeah, I can see that. Why?"

"I'm moving in with Milo. I love him, he loves me and we're not going to waste a moment of building our life together."

Suda Kaye gasps and I turn my head to look at her.

"Evie, oh my God, that's awesome," she says as though I just told her I'd won a million dollars.

"Yes, it is. So, if you don't mind, I'd like to get to it." I grab another handful of books and shove them into the box.

"What's going on? Why are you acting all cold and weird?" She rubs at her arms, then tucks her hands into the sleeves like a small child trying to hide herself.

"Am I?"

"Uh, yeah." She sniffs and wipes her running nose on the oversize hoodie she's wearing. "We need to talk about Dad's arrangements. Get things set up."

I yank another book so hard off the shelf that two others fall off and hit the floor. "Crap!" I clench my fists and turn toward her. "Dad's arrangements were already made. By him. You'd know that if you talked to him more than once a year."

Her face twists into one of pain, as if I'd just slapped her.

"You…you're mad? At me?" Suda Kaye interlaces her fingers together and dips her head.

"No. I'm busy and you're bothering me." I move to the next shelf and start grabbing handfuls, making a stack on the floor.

"*Bothering* you? Evie? What the hell is going on? You're acting weird."

I huff. "That's rich coming from you. I'm acting weird. No, I think I'm acting perfectly normal. My father just died. My father's body will arrive in just over a week and I have to put him to rest."

"He was my father, too," she whispers, tears clogging her words.

"Convenient. You sure didn't act like he was your dad growing up. Always trying to get out of spending time with him when he'd visit. Did you ever even visit him when you were traveling in Europe for, oh, I don't know, *years*? Did you even love him? At all?" I wave my arms around like a maniac. Fire and brimstone fueling my boiling anger.

My sister takes a couple steps back. Her voice is scratchy and raw when she says, "Of *course* I loved him. He's the only father I've ever known! How dare you suggest I didn't care. I'll admit, we weren't close like you and he were, but I always thought you were closer to him and I was closer to Mom. It all balanced out."

"Balance. Is that what you're calling it? More like being apathetic. You didn't care about him. Admit it. When you found out that Adam Ross wasn't your biological father, you wrote him off!" I sneer, the truth spilling out for the first time.

Suda Kaye's mouth tightens, and she crosses her arms over her chest in a defensive pose. "I'll admit when I found out he wasn't my real father it hit me hard. It still does to this day. I don't know who my biological father is, Evie! Mom wouldn't tell me. Dad wouldn't, either, though I suspect he knew. And yet neither one of them thought it prudent to share with *me*!" She points at her chest angrily.

"Oh, poor Suda Kaye. Had a mother, father, sister and grandfather who doted on her, treating her like gold, and it wasn't enough. Not for you. Always wanting more. More fun. More adventure. More of everything. And you didn't care what your selfish desires did to anyone around you." I seethe, spitting out the words through my teeth. "Just. Like. Our. Mother. Selfish to the core."

"If being selfish means I chased after my dreams while you sat stuck to your quiet little nothing life, then yeah, I'm selfish. Wake up, Evie! The world is standing before you but you're too afraid to take a step. To do anything that might be seen as risky or irresponsible."

"Because everything *you've* done in your entire life was irresponsible. Until Cam. The second time you deemed to give him your attention! Apparently you had to break a few hearts before you learned your lesson. Including mine!" I fire off the secret I've been holding forever.

Suda Kaye's face goes pale. "When have I broken your heart?" she whispers.

"Every single day you were gone broke my heart!" I blurt, tears now falling down my cheeks, too. "Every day I didn't know if you were safe. Every day I didn't hear your voice. Every day you chose a life that didn't have me in it. Just like our mother. Birds of a feather, huh, *Huutsuu*! Mom sure was apt giving you that nickname because all you ever do is fly away. Leave everyone behind wishing they were enough for you to want to stay."

She puts a fist to her chest over her heart. "Is that what you thought? That I left because I didn't want to be with you?"

"It's pretty obvious. The second you got your wheels and the money from Mom's inheritance, you were gone. I didn't see you for two years and that's because I came to *you*. Then it was three years. Again, I came to you. You were gone a decade, Suda Kaye. A freakin' decade!"

Tears track down both of our faces so fast my sister becomes blurry.

"We talked on the phone all the time, and besides, I came back," she croaks. "For you, Evie. I came back for you."

I close my eyes and let her words pierce my heart.

"You said we got past this. Moved on. And yet you're flinging it all in my face again almost a year later." She sniffs.

Pain, loss, fear and grief rip through me as though a demon is scratching at my chest with angry, acid-tipped claws. An intense rage ripples up my spine, over my chest and comes roaring out.

"A person doesn't get past her sister leaving her for a decade, Suda Kaye! Especially after twenty years of being abandoned by her mother and father!" I cry out, and fall to my knees, the hurt so overwhelming I can no longer hold up my own body.

My sister rushes to where I've fallen, my arms crossed over my chest while bone-crushing convulsions rack my body as years of pent-up frustration, fury and devastation rip through me like a tsunami of pain. Suda Kaye wraps her arms around me from behind and presses her chin to my shoulder.

"Let it out, Sissy. I'm here. Let it all out."

"Why does everyone leave!" I screech. "Why am I not good enough!" I choke on the words.

Tears fall to my shoulder where my sister cries, her arms locked around me. "I'm sorry, Sissy," she whispers. "I didn't know you were hurting." She holds me tighter.

"You didn't care!" I hiccup-sob over and over.

"I didn't know. I was stupid. I was selfish. I didn't see it. Evie…" Her voice is barely a whisper against my cheek. "I didn't see. I'm sorry. I'm so sorry."

"You're not so-sor-sorry," I accuse.

She presses her face closer to mine. "Evie, I am. I love you more than any person in this world. You are the constant in my life. My guiding star, Sissy. I always knew that no matter where I was, I had you to love me. I thought you knew the same. And now I know you felt unworthy and left behind." The sadness coating her tone is tugging at my heartstrings. Turning the tide. I don't want Suda Kaye to hurt. I never want her hurt and yet here I am, laying it all on her shoulders.

"I would die for you, Evie. In a heartbeat. In a second if it meant you could live and be happy."

"No!" I sob. Grabbing her arms around me and holding tight. "I shouldn't have said anything, I don't know why… I—I don't know what I'm doing anymore." I admit the God's honest truth. I'm wading into territory I have no map for. It's filled with dangerous emotions and broken hearts and I'm not sure what the right direction is to make it out of this place in one piece.

"I'm sorry you felt left behind. I'm sorry that my tumultuous relationship with Dad hurt you. I'm sorry that I followed in Mom's footsteps and that hurt you, too. But, Evie, I never stopped loving you. I thought of you every day even if I didn't see you. You're my big sister. The person I share my most private moments with. I think you always knew I was going to leave, but that didn't mean I was leaving *you*."

The tears have slowed but are still tracking down my face. "I wanted to be enough for you to stay."

She sighs and I can feel her warm breath against my neck. She lets go and crawls around the floor to face me, grabs both of my hands and holds them tight against her chest, then leans forward, bringing her face close to mine.

"You were enough to come home to when the time was right." The seriousness in her tone floors me.

I pinch my lips together to stop them from trembling.

"Evie, I traveled the world, saw what I needed to see, experienced what I needed to experience, but the only thing I wanted when it was time to settle down was *you*. The one person in my entire life I couldn't live without. Not longterm. I'm sorry that my need to fly free hurt you. I can't take it back, and honestly, I wouldn't. I needed that time for me. To grow, to change, to be who I was going to be outside of who I was to you."

"Sissy," I whisper.

"You give yourself too little credit. You think I left because you weren't good enough for me to stay. Don't you see I left because I didn't have anything to offer? You made me the center of your universe. There was nothing for you. Everything you did was for everyone else in your life, especially me. Not only did I leave to find myself, I left so that *you* could find yourself, too. I always knew I'd come back, or end up wherever you were, because you're my sun. You're everyone's sun. Me, Mom, Dad, *Toko* and now Milo."

"Suda Kaye." I bring her hands to my lips and kiss the tops of our clasped hands.

"Your light is so bright, Evie, sometimes it outshines everything else and everyone else around you. I had to go so I could find my own light and not be blinded by yours. Don't you see? You're the measure by which I decide if I'm good enough. Smart enough. Successful enough. Pretty enough. Woman enough. It's you. My sister is the most capable, beautiful, intelligent, successful woman I know. You have it all figured out. Your entire life mapped perfectly."

"No. Please," I murmur, hating that she felt I outshined her when I thought it was the exact opposite.

"Let me speak." She swallows and takes a breath. "When I found out Adam wasn't my father, it broke me. Deep in a place I wouldn't admit to anyone. Not even you."

I cup her cheek and watch while her eyes swirl with sadness.

"Then Mom died, and I was finishing high school and I still had no idea what to do, how to be, who I was. I compared myself to you every day of my life and found myself lacking. My grades were crap. I couldn't hold even the simplest job after school, and I wasn't good at anything. So, when Mom's letter urged me to see the world, I jumped at the chance to find myself. To figure out who I was without standing in your shadow."

"No, Sissy. You are all that is joyous, vibrant and filled with life. You live life like it could end tomorrow..."

"Because it can." She grips my hand as though to express the severity of what she's trying to say. "Our grandmother died young. Our mother, too. Now Adam, in his fifties? There isn't a moment to waste, which is why when I came up with a plan for my life, the only thing I wanted to do was come here and share it with you. It's why I work so hard at the store. I want, no, I *need* you to see that I can be responsible. I can be successful. I can be someone worthy of the devotion you've always given me."

I pull her into my arms and hold her like she might disappear at any second. "You are worthy. My goodness, and I'm so incredibly proud of you. You've built an amazing business. Married the man of your dreams and are talking about raising a family of your own."

"I'm sorry I left you, but I hope you understand why I did it."

I press my forehead to hers and clap my hands around both of her cheeks so I can hold her face only a few inches from mine. "Thank you. For telling me. For being honest. For sharing all of it, even though it hurts."

She bites her bottom lip. "Seems like we both had things really twisted in our minds."

I nod and pull her into my arms. This time hugging her with everything I have and all the love I feel for her.

"Is it over now?" she whispers against my hair.

I nod. "Mostly. I still think we both have some serious wounds, but this is the first step toward healing them. One at a time."

"Yeah," she agrees, and presses her face to my neck.

"I'm sorry I accused you of not caring about Dad's passing. That was mean and hateful, and I think I was just using you to blame so that it wouldn't hurt so much."

She nods. "I know. It's okay."

I shake my head. "It's not okay. It was wrong and I'm sorry."

"Accepted," she says instantly.

For a long time, we hold one another until my sister whispers, "I love you more than anything, Evie. I'm not going anywhere. I'm building my life here. Right here where my sister is building hers. Speaking of...you're packing up your apartment to move in with Milo. Hot, Native American macho Milo, who you've been in love with since you were a child. Can we talk about that for a little bit? I need all the details on how that went down." Her face brightens with instant joy. And it's just like her. The dark is pushed away, and the light comes out and she's beaming. Her mood changing as quickly as the ocean tides.

I grin and start laughing, which is what Milo finds as he enters with an arm filled with boxes.

He lifts his chin, ignores our huddle and goes right back into my bedroom, nothing but business.

"He's packing up your clothes?" She gestures to my bedroom.

I nod. "He's superbossy and opinionated. He wants the items I need right now in his home. Get this...so I can't leave!" I burst out laughing. After all the talk of being left behind, my man is making sure there is no need for me to leave him for any reason.

Suda Kaye snickers behind her hand. "That is awesome! What about...you know." She waggles her brows, leans forward and whispers, "Sex. He's a big guy. He's got to be packing some serious heat behind that zipper."

My entire face warms and I know my cheeks are red as a rose. For the first time in a long time I'm excited to talk about my relationship. The fact that I have a healthy one to talk about has me dipping my voice conspiratorially. "He's massive...*everywhere*." I squeal.

Suda Kaye fans her face and looks toward the bedroom. "Damn."

I smile wistfully. "Our first time was so romantic. Out in the open air, on the bluffs back at the reservation." Absolutely magical.

"Aw, that's your favorite place in the whole world," she gushes. Suda Kaye puts a fist to her mouth and cheeses out, her entire body positively vibrating with excitement on my behalf. "And his cabin? Camden says he's seen it once before with his brother and it's supposedly breathtaking."

"Oh, it is. Surrounded by mountains, pine trees, a lake with a dock and a boat. He's going to take me out on it tonight under the moonlight."

"That's amazing. I'm so happy for you, Sissy."

My sister bites her bottom lip and stares at me with her soulful eyes, no longer filled with sorrow and emotional turmoil. Hopefully we've passed that portion of our visit for the time being, because I am cried out emotionally, mentally and physically.

"Are you happy? Is he moving too fast? I mean, you're moving into his house so quickly. Also, the day after you suffered a major loss."

"Am I moving too fast? Says the woman that was moved in and married in a matter of months to her high school sweetheart after being gone a decade?"

She waves her hand in front of us. "I'm crazy and unpredictable. We know that about me. It's my grounded, careful, 'take baby steps toward major life changes' sister I'm curious about."

"You know, at first I worried it was. And then I realized I was basing my own happiness on a set of arbitrary rules, a mound of statistics, and Milo and I aren't a statistic to graph and estimate. We're two people in our thirties that have known each other for twenty-plus years and cared about one another from the start. We both have lived the ups and downs of bad relationships, him more so than me. We know what we want and it's one another. There's really no reason to wait to be happy. We're just going to move forward and let it happen naturally."

Suda Kaye smiles so wide and for so long I'm surprised her face doesn't get permanently stuck that way. Without warning she jumps up and does a full-on cheerleader splits up into the air screaming, "Woo-hoo," at the top of her lungs.

Milo rushes into the room, sees me sitting on the ground and assesses my silly, giddy sister dancing around in a circle that looks an awful lot like a made-up rain dance.

Milo's gaze comes to mine and he cocks an eyebrow.

So cool.

"I'm fine, honey. Told Suda Kaye about us. She's, uh—" I point to her still dancing "—happy about it."

He smirks and shakes his head. He's got a full French braid keeping his hair back courtesy of *moi*. After the shower, I patted the floor in front of the bed and instructed him to sit. He did so without question or comment. It looks mighty fine on my man and he was not kidding. He practically purred as I brushed and braided his glorious hair this afternoon. Something I plan to do daily if time permits.

"Your closet is done and in the Cayenne. I'm doing your drawers next. Anything you don't want me to see?"

I twist my lips into a saucy smirk. "How about you find something interesting and set it aside. I'll model it this evening."

His eyes flare with interest and desire. "Deal." His one-word reply is coated in promise. He disappears back into my room and I can hear the sound of him putting boxes together.

"Now that was hot," Suda Kaye says.

"Everything about Milo is hot."

"This is no lie," she agrees. "You two are going to make gorgeous babies one day."

"Sooner than later if Milo has his say," I grumble.

Suda Kaye's eyes light up. "Really? Maybe if you start your family first, I won't be so scared out of my mind to try with Cam. He wants me to get the IUD removed but I keep telling him I'm not ready. And I'm not. I feel like I need a year or two to really get my footing with the being a wife and business owner thing, ya know?"

I nod. "Yes, and as long as you're honest with him, I'm sure he'll understand. You both need to be ready."

"What about you? Are you ready for kids?"

I shrug, stand up and grab a new box. "I wasn't ready in the sense that it had to be when I turned thirty, but now that I am here, I'm definitely ready to talk about it. I'd like to be married to Milo before we try. Though I think that's about as far as he'll be willing to wait. That man's biological clock is ticking like a bomb ready to go off. He'd have me barefoot and pregnant as soon as possible."

"What about justice of the peace?"

I shake my head. "It's how he married his first wife."

"Vegas? I could tear up that town with my man!"

"You could lose a ton of his money gambling is what you're saying." I cock a brow and smirk.

She grins. "Probably. Never was a good poker player." Which is the truth. She has no ability to lie or bluff. Never has.

"What about something small and quaint at your new house?" She goes to my bookshelf and starts pulling more books off and setting them in the box I started.

"Maybe…we'll see. I don't want to put the cart before the horse. First, I'm moving in. Then we have to deal with Dad's funeral."

Suda Kaye scrunches up her nose. "Does he even know anyone around here?"

"I think the military sends people…maybe? I don't know. I'm going to call his attorney in the morning. I'll let you know what he says. All Dad told me was that he had it all planned and not to worry."

She nods. "Sounds like Dad. Will you call me tomorrow and tell me what the attorney says?"

I smile softly. "Yeah, Sissy. I won't keep you in the dark any longer. About anything." It's a promise I intend to keep and holds a whole heck of a lot more weight than when she first arrived.

"I miss him," she admits, her voice going a tad shaky again.

This has me moving over to her and pulling her into my arms again. "Me, too. We'll get this through this, together. Me, you, Milo, Cam and *Toko*. Okay?"

"Our family," she whispers, and squeezes me tight.

"Yeah, our little family."

16

A few days later, I'm seated in my therapist's office. Dr. Williamson crosses her supremely toned legs over one another, feet clad in a killer, drool-worthy pair of black Valentino slingbacks. I should search online for those. They'd be great with one of my suits.

"Great shoes," I murmur, taking a good gander at hers and then to my pale pink leather ballet flats. Definitely not my normal weekday footwear. Usually I'd be in something as hip and sexy as the good doctor's, but I'm still off work and packing and unpacking my belongings. So instead of my tailored work attire, I'm wearing a pair of bootleg jeans and a loose, off-the-shoulder cream-colored cable-knit sweater, with a matching camisole underneath. My hair is back in a simple low ponytail that looks stylish with my favorite pair of fourteen-carat-gold midsize hoops in my ears.

I feel put together enough to have a session with my therapist but comfortable enough to tote between my new home and my old apartment as I uproot my entire life by moving in with Milo.

"Thank you. And how are you dealing with your father's passing?" she asks directly. I had to cancel an appointment a couple days ago because of the news.

"As well as anyone, I guess. I'm sad. Cry a lot. Had a huge fight with Suda Kaye."

"Tell me about the fight." She tips her head, her dark assessing eyes focused solely on me.

I glance out the window. "It actually was good. I accused her of not caring about our father's passing."

"And how was that good?" Her voice rises a shred.

I purse my lips and pick at a frayed edge on the seam of my jeans by my knee. "It brought up a lot of unresolved issues. Her leaving and why. Me feeling like she checked out when she found out Adam wasn't her real father. I kind of lost it on her."

"Oh?"

"Yeah. I hurt her, on purpose. I wanted to hurt her."

"Why?"

"Because I wanted her to hurt as badly as I did. As badly as her leaving all those years ago hurt and wounded me."

"Aw, so you were paying her back."

"Kinda, I guess."

"And how did that make you feel?" She taps her pen on the legal pad she's holding.

"At first it felt good. Like I won something, but in reality, I lost. So much. Accusing her didn't make me feel any better about losing Dad. Though it was a catalyst for me admitting my real feelings about her leaving, and you know what I found out?"

Her lips twitch. "That her leaving had nothing to do with you?"

Shock fills my veins. "Yeah, exactly. All this time I felt left behind and the real reason she left was because she didn't know who she was. Couldn't shine on her own standing in my shadow. That's what she said. That I outshined her, and she needed to find herself."

The doctor nods as if this makes total sense.

"I've been upset with her for eleven years. The ten she was gone and this past year she's been home. And now…"

"Now?" she encourages.

I shrug, lean forward and place my elbows on my knees, my chin in my hand. "I'm confused. Relieved that it wasn't me she was running away from, but heartbroken that she felt she needed to leave me in order to find herself."

Dr. Williamson nods and writes something on her notepad. "Sometimes when we find out a person's genuine motivation it can ease the pain. Do you feel as though her rationale for leaving resolved your issues to the point where you can move forward with your sister and leave this behind you?"

I nod. "Yeah, I do, actually. Knowing that she was searching for something, trying to find herself during her time away and coming home when she did." I shake my head. "I don't know, it just feels better. In my heart, in my soul."

"And does that correlation bring up any of those same feelings about your mother leaving?"

I frown, ease back and sigh. "How so?"

She smiles softly and crosses her fingers over her lap. "Your mother left regularly when you were a child. Perhaps she was trying to find herself, too?"

"I don't see how they are related." I flatten my lips together, irritation coating my tone.

I'm granted another one of her patented Dr. Williamson "think harder" expressions.

"Catori Ross chose to become the wife of a military man. Chose to have a child with him. She chose her life. She didn't have to do any of it. Then when she had it, she chose to leave it behind while she pursued other interests."

"And that's different from your sister because…" she leads, and lets her words fall away.

"Suda Kaye was eighteen, a child, and left to find herself. Her leaving hurt me and Cam in the process and that's a cross she'll always have to bear. My mother left her child and then later betrayed the man she was married to and had another child. And left again, and again. Only stopping when her body couldn't handle the travel anymore. And then she ultimately left us by dying."

"Let's talk a little bit about that. How did her dying mean she ultimately left you?"

"She never got help. By the time she finally came home and went to see a doctor she was stage four. Maybe if she'd been home with her family, we could have encouraged her to seek treatment earlier. *Toko* has an innate ability to sense sickness of any kind. He would have seen she was acting differently."

"So, you blame her for getting cancer?" The doctor's chin lowers, and I can almost feel her judging me.

"No. What I'm saying is, if she'd been home like a normal mother who actually gave a crap about her children and had a hand in raising them, maybe she would have been around for another thirty or forty years."

"Look, Evie, I'm not suggesting you are wrong for having the feelings you have. Every single person is entitled to how they feel. And a lot of the time those feelings are weighted in grief, sadness, love, happiness and everything in between. What I'm trying to help you see is that you were not the reason your mother left. Do you understand that?"

I clench my teeth and inhale through my nose sharply. "Maybe if I was better, or if she loved me more, then she would have wanted to be a real mother."

"Wasn't she a real mother? Didn't she leave you with someone who was happy to care for you and give you a good up-bringing? She didn't leave you at the hospital after giving birth or give you to your grandfather and never return. She came home often, as you put it. And when she was home, I'm of the understanding that her entire attention was on you and Suda Kaye. Was it not?"

"Well, yeah, when she was home she would take us on miniadventures on the rez or outside of it. It's how we found and fell in love with Pueblo. She taught us how to belly dance and took us to classes where she'd dance along. Pretty much all that we did was her version of a family adventure. Living out loud, she called it. We'd go to a park in the middle of the night and slide down the slides, swing as high as we could in order to try and touch the stars with our feet, climb all over the bars."

"Sounds like you had some fun times."

I nod. "Yeah, they were. But it's not like we were in the kitchen baking cakes, and she was helping us with our homework or preparing us for school."

"Didn't you say *Toko* was there for that?"

I frown and think about it. Growing up, *Toko* served as the true parent. Made sure we got up, had clean clothes, ate breakfast, went to school, came home, did schoolwork, helped with reservation duties, had a snack, then a big family dinner with just the three of us, or four or five if Mom and Dad were home. He'd tuck us in, and tell us stories about our ancestors, teach us Comanche and Navajo, but more Comanche because he was full-blooded. Still, he shouldn't have had to do all that.

"It wasn't his job. It was hers. And my father's. He left for work. Sent money home regularly. We never wanted for the things we needed because his work paid for them."

"And your mother?"

"She would come home and share her experiences. Tell us about the world. Teach us things she learned in the countries she visited. Talked all the time about how, when we were adults, she was going to show us the world and then she would get to experience it all brand-new through our eyes."

"I have to say, learning about other cultures and lifestyles is a pretty neat way to connect to one's mother."

"It wasn't normal." I sigh heavily. "When I got my period for the first time, it was *Toko* I had to talk to about it. When I had a crush on Milo, I had my little sister. I didn't have someone to talk to about my hormones, or how they would go out of control when I hit puberty. I didn't have someone to teach me how to put on makeup or gush about the school dance and pick out a pretty dress with me. When I needed her most, she wasn't there."

"I can see how that would be painful."

"It was. And embarrassing. All the kids knowing that Suda Kaye and I were the ones whose mom left all the time. Then she'd come dancing back into our world with wild stories to tell and a suitcase full of souvenirs she picked up."

"That was nice of her," Dr. Williamson adds.

"It didn't replace her not being there." My voice turns ice cold.

"No, I can imagine having an unconventional mother would be difficult growing up."

"It was."

Dr. Williamson's phone pings on the table, signaling our time is about up.

"Here's what I'd like for you to do over the next two weeks. I would like you to spend a little time focusing on the good your mother brought to your life. The woman is no longer here for you to punish. All you're doing, Evie, is punishing yourself, over and over, by being angry with her.

236 • AUDREY CARLAN

It's time to work on letting go of that anger. It's not helping you. In fact, I believe it's hindering your progress at trusting the other people in your life."

I stand up and pull my purse strap over my shoulder. "How do you think I should do it?"

She smiles. "How about you write the good memories down, or spend some time with something that makes you think of only her."

Mom's letters.

I nod. "I can do that. Thank you, Dr. Williamson."

"Always, Evie. We'll see you in two weeks."

"Okay. Two weeks."

Back at home I ruffle through the pink envelopes that I have already opened over the years. I wouldn't dare open any of the ones that are sealed until the date that's written on them has arrived. It would feel blasphemous and cruel. Besides, I devour a new letter on my birthday each year. It's the best birthday present I have had since we received them.

I hold the letters between my hands and glance at the fire Milo built for me. I can hear him moving around in the kitchen making dinner. In the few days I've been here, the man has proven he's an excellent cook, and better yet, he loves doing it. Though I'm in charge of breakfast because it's one of the things I'm good at. I'm a master omelet and pancake maker. This weekend I think I'm going to blow my man's mind with my special overnight French toast. A definite crowd pleaser, something I learned to make from the mom of one of my high school friends way back in the day. Suda Kaye and Mom loved it when I'd make it on the weekends. I'd prep it on a Friday evening and then present it Saturday morning. I've since perfected the recipe and even I have to admit it's an impressive dish and I've come to find my man likes a bit of sweet in the morning. He also likes a soft round of lovemaking. All sleepy and sluggish, he makes me feel alive and ready to start my day after he's made love to me first thing after I wake.

The past week has been bliss, aside from the grief over losing my dad. Milo's been careful to let me lead the way regarding talk of my parents. He's not overly intrusive but listens intently when I do feel the need to share. All I know is that, with him, my life is already better. Someone who looks after me who I can look after in return. A person who holds my hand while we watch television. A man who tells me every single day how beautiful I am. And from his mouth, in his own words, I believe him.

Tomorrow we meet with Dad's attorney for the reading of his last will and testament. Suda Kaye and I are the only ones required to attend. Apparently *Toko* was mentioned in the will, but the attorney has already been in contact with our grandfather, who, knowing we'll have Milo and Cam at our sides, prefers not to attend. *Toko* doesn't attend things like funerals or wakes or anything conventionally modern involving the dead. He would attend a powwow on the rez, a celebration-of-life ceremony complete with giant drums, dancers in full dress and that sort of thing, but not a church service.

Our reservation is more likely to light a fire at the home burial on the land where the body is placed to rest and become part of the earth once more. A tribesman or family member of the deceased would keep it burning straight through for a few days in order to help guide the spirit to its final resting place.

Graveyards and cemeteries are most certainly not *Toko*'s thing. As it stands, my grandmother and mother are currently buried out on the protected land. A private ceremony was arranged and presided by *Toko* and one of the spiritual leaders on the Comanche side for both women.

I finger the envelopes and pick one up at random. It's from when I turned twenty-two.

Evie, my beloved Taabe,

By now you have likely become the first member of our lineage to graduate with a college degree. You are also likely going to continue that achievement going for your master's. I know you well, my darling girl. So smart. Capable. Driven to succeed.

I hope in all these achievements you are taking the time to enjoy what you've accomplished. Remember, my bright girl, to give yourself the time to appreciate all you've worked for. Nothing in life is handed to us. We have to go chase after it. And even if you did not chase after adventure like me, I'm proud that you chased after your own goals. Committed to them and made them real.

Sometimes I wish I was more like you, Taabe. Able to stay in one place, to plant roots. To receive fulfillment and joy from the work I completed on my own. Sometimes I think I was a little broken. That there was a piece of me that was missing.

I know you have always had a hard time accepting my need to experience the world because you were content with the world around you. I have always known there is much more to life than what's in my backyard. Not that my backyard or the reservation, or you, your sister or my father, weren't good enough to keep me happy; it's just that the urge to go, to move, to experience new things never left me. Like a liv-

ing, breathing thing in my gut, twitching and turning, yearning to find out life's mysteries.

Through it all, everything I lived, it was you, your sister, my father, that brought me back. Time and time again. My love for you is stronger than anything and when I left, and felt the connection to my family disappearing, I would race back home, running over hot coals to do so if I needed to.

I'm sorry that you found my time away hurtful. I could see it in your eyes every single time I left—the disappointment, the heartache and the anger. Still, I knew my fierce girl could take care of herself. Be the independent, strong and resourceful woman I'm certain you are today.

I miss coming home to you, Evie. Every time I'd see the light in your eyes, and your love bursting from every pore. I lived for that moment. The most beautiful part of coming home was seeing your joy.

That was the moment as a mother we all dream about. When your child loves you so completely you can not only feel it but see it shining as bright as the sun slipping through the dark clouds on a cold day.

I lived a thousand days off that moment.

Remember that, Taabe, when you have your own children. That minute in time when your child looks you in the eye and you are all that exists for them. The love so pure and real you won't ever truly be able to explain it.

Thank you for that gift, my darling girl.
With all the love in the world,
Mom

"Dinner's ready," Milo calls out.
I set the letters on the coffee table and amble over to where

Milo has placed dinner at the dining room table. Eight empty seats stretch out beyond us but in the center a single round candle sits on a pedestal, its golden light flickering.

Two plates filled with blackened chicken, beans and long-grain wild rice are placed kitty-corner to one another, his at the head, me to his right, a bowl of salad beside each plate. He holds my chair out for me like the gentleman he is and I can't help but smile at his chivalry even in our home.

"Thanks, honey. This looks amazing and smells divine."

He nods and takes his seat. After placing his napkin in his lap, he lifts his chin toward the couch. "What were you reading in those envelopes?"

Right then it dawns on me that I haven't explained the letters. Actually, I've never shared them with anyone. The only people who know they exist are Mom, Suda Kaye and *Toko*. My father didn't even know about them since she wrote them during the years she was sick and gave them to *Toko* to give to us when the time came.

"They're letters from my mother."

He cuts his chicken breast and digs his fork into the meat, and then lifts it toward his mouth. "While she was away during your youth?"

I shake my head, putting some rice on my fork. "No, she wrote them while she was sick and living in Pueblo. I always thought she was journaling, but turns out that after her death she had these huge stacks of sealed envelopes for me and Suda Kaye. One letter for each future birthday that we wouldn't have with her."

Milo tips his head, chewing thoughtfully before he taps his plate with his fork. "A profound gift she left behind, her words to you."

I nod. "It is. Extremely special. Every year I look forward to getting to open another one."

"And you reread them?" he surmises intuitively.

"Yeah, it often helps me deal with some difficult feelings. Most having to do with her loss. Her loss when I was a kid, her loss when she died, her loss now that I'm an adult."

"Does this sadden you when you revisit them?"

I purse my lips and think about his question for a minute. He doesn't rush me to answer or prod for more details. He is content to allow me my thought process, perfectly comfortable in the quiet.

"Sometimes, yeah, it does."

"Why?"

I swallow down a bite of his perfectly cooked chicken. "This is good." I point to the plate with my fork.

He nods but, once again, simply waits for me to answer his question.

"My mother's loss has been this big open wound inside of me for far longer than after she died. I think it started when I was younger, and it opened bigger and bigger every time she left. Until I started to become enraged by it. I never got over her need to leave, and even now that I understand better why she did what she did, I'm not sure I'll ever get over it."

"Some things we're not meant to get over."

"How so?" I scoop up some beans and allow the tangy goodness to enchant my taste buds and warm my belly.

"Do you think Tahsuda has gotten over the loss of your grandmother?"

I frown, taking in his words.

"She died very young, yes? Like your mother?"

I nod. "Yeah, she did."

"And did she spend her life on the reservation?"

"Yes, definitely. Back then things were very different. They met young. I think *Toko* was only sixteen when he claimed her, but they mated officially when he was of age."

"And when did they have Catori?"

"Right away. I think my grandmother was nineteen or twenty."

"And only the one?" He continues his questioning and I'm not sure where it's going but sharing our family histories is an important part of truly getting to know one another.

"*Kaku* had a very hard birth and almost died. They had to perform an emergency hysterectomy."

"And then only twenty-five years or so later she also died of cancer?"

I nod. His family definitely knew our history since we all lived on the same reservation. And especially now that I know his mother, Lina, was great friends with my mom during their early years.

"Do you wonder if perhaps your grandmother's passing before she got to see the world had an effect on Catori?"

I frown and set down my fork.

"If your mother saw your grandmother living her entire days on the reservation, although happily, but dying young, never having seen the world, perhaps that made Catori see it as a missed opportunity. In her mind, her mother didn't have the chance to truly live. She wouldn't want to make that same mistake."

"Why does it have to be a mistake?"

He smiles softly, reaches out and takes my hand. He brings it to his lips and kisses each one of my fingers. I shiver and hold his gaze with my own.

"I love that you do not see it as settling because it means you find contentment in stability, and joy in the world around you as it is. You do not need to see what else is out there to be happy."

"Right, I don't," I admit freely.

"And that is perfect for you." He kisses my palm. "And

TO CATCH A DREAM · 243

for me. We only need each other and those we love around us to make us happy. Your mother, she needed experience. She needed to have all of you to come home to. She needed the adventure in order to feel fulfilled."

"I wanted her to need *me*. And Suda Kaye. And *Toko*. She needed the world more."

"Perhaps, but that didn't mean she didn't love you with her entire heart, *adinidiin*. It just means she had a lot of space in her heart for many things as well as people."

"I guess." I sigh. My mother's intentions are such a conundrum for me. She needed to leave to feel fulfilled, but she also needed to come home to us for the same reason.

So, which was it?

And why couldn't she just choose one?

Maybe the real truth is that she didn't know, either.

17

"Mr. Fink will see you now." The short, gray-haired woman gestures to the door behind her with an outstretched arm.

The four of us stand. I follow Suda Kaye and Camden into the office. Milo keeps his hand light at my lower back. A comforting and chivalrous gesture I adore but would never admit to needing from the man I love.

Alistair Fink is tall and painfully thin. He has thinning light brown hair and a mustache around his small mouth. He's wearing a pair of silver-framed glasses that are so thick I can see the wide lens from his profile.

"Please have a seat at the conference table." He walks over to one end and the four of us sit two by two across from one another, our men holding our chairs out.

Briefly I smile at Suda Kaye, secretly expressing our good fortune in the men we've chosen. She returns with a little smile and a wink of her own.

Milo rests his hand on my thigh the moment he sits down. I cover the top of his and interlace our fingers that way, keeping his palm to my thigh, imagining it's an anchor to keep me in place from fleeing this meeting and pretending none of this is real. My father is still alive and off somewhere saving the world. If only.

The attorney sets down a file at the head of the table and takes a seat. "We are here today to read the Last Will and Testament of Adam Hunter Ross."

I inhale sharply at my father's full name. Milo squeezes my thigh. I glance at his face and find he's focused solely on me, that dark stare saying everything I need without uttering a single word.

I am here. You are not alone. You will never be alone again.

I mouth, *I love you*, as butterflies take flight in my stomach, watching him gift me a small smile.

"First and foremost, Mr. Ross did not want an official burial or service announcement. He requested his remains be cremated and his ashes given to one Tahsuda Tahsuda and placed at the gravesite of Mrs. Catori Tahsuda-Ross. Mr. Tahsuda has agreed to this request provided there are no objections by Mr. Ross's living children."

I gasp and cover my mouth with my hand. "He wants to be with Mom." The tears prick the backs of my eyelids, but I swallow through the emotion, digging deep to hold myself together.

"No objection," I whisper.

"Me, either." Suda Kaye leans to the side and presses her head to her husband's shoulder. He brings his chair closer to hers and wraps an arm around her back.

"There are four people mentioned in this document, two of whom are here. One I haven't been able to reach and a Tahsuda Tahsuda, who has declined the invitation today."

It's always entertaining to see someone say my grandfather's name as though there must be an error. When Tahsuda was younger, in order to get a birth certificate, Native Americans had to give first and last names. My grandfather has only ever had the name Tahsuda. This was common among many other tribesmen across the nation. They were

246 • AUDREY CARLAN

given a choice to choose one of the English settlers' surnames like Jones or Smith, but my grandfather wouldn't hear of it. Instead of choosing something he didn't identify with, he claimed his own name twice.

"Who is the other person?" I ask.

Mr. Fink scans the document. "An Isabeau Collins."

"Who's that?" Suda Kaye asks, her nose crinkling.

I shrug. "Never heard the name before. Does it have any additional information?" I ask at the same time Suda Kaye asks, "What's he left to her?"

"Kaye..." I warn. "It's none of our business," I say, even though I desperately want to know myself.

"None of this is confidential as this is the reading of his last directives. However, it doesn't say anything other than he's leaving her thirty-three percent of his estate."

"Thirty-three percent?" I question, surprise coating my tone. If he's leaving her that much, she had to be extremely important to him, but if that was the case, why haven't we heard of her?

The attorney nods. "Yes, and you and Suda Kaye evenly receive thirty-three point five percent equally." Now *that* I get. I would expect our father to leave us both half of whatever he thought important for us to have, but why would he leave the same to this Isabeau person? Who is she?

"Was there a contact number or address for this Ms. Collins?"

The attorney nods. "I'll make sure the both of you have it. If you get in contact with her, I'll need to set up a meeting to discuss her inheritance."

Her inheritance.

From my father.

A woman we don't know, who I've never met and have no earthly clue how she could be connected to my father.

"Where does she live?"

He reads the document. "Chicago, Illinois, it says here, but the phone number I received was disconnected. I've since paid for a people-tracking service to find additional information on this woman so that I may contact her directly. I will notify you both when I have anything."

"Thank you," I murmur, my head filling with all kinds of ideas on who this woman could be. An old friend. The wife of one of his brethren in arms. A distant relative, perhaps.

"Do you think he was cheating on Mom?" Suda Kaye voices my worst fears.

I grip Milo's hand and hold it tight. "I don't know. And we won't know until we find this woman. We should let Mr. Fink continue and discuss this later."

"Or maybe he hooked up with a woman after Mom passed. I mean, it's been eleven years and they separated long before that," she continues.

I clench my teeth and look down. The last thing in the entire world I want to do right now is think about this.

"Let's continue." Milo's voice is a demand, not a request.

"Yes, well, how about I skip ahead to the important facts and then give you both a copy so you can discuss the more personal nature privately."

"That would be excellent." I sigh. "Thank you."

He goes through every line item. And as he reads off my father's estate, I find I didn't know him as well as I thought I did. He has a home in Chicago, Illinois, and one in Washington, DC. Apparently they are both empty, but he pays services in each location to keep up the landscaping biweekly and to clean each house once monthly. Both are completely paid off.

"Did you have any idea he had these houses?" Suda Kaye asks, flabbergasted.

I shake my head.

"The home in Chicago is listed as being worth approximately three hundred and twenty thousand dollars. The condo in Washington, DC, is actually located in Georgetown and is valued at quite a bit more, with assessors listing it at eight hundred and twenty-nine thousand dollars."

"You're kidding!" Suda Kaye frowns. "I had no idea Dad had that kind of money." She shakes her head and runs her fingers through her long brown hair.

"I knew he did well in the military, but this is surprising," I agree.

"Ladies, that is not all," Mr. Fink states. "Your father had his own family inheritance that, once liquified, will add up to one point five million dollars. This money he has specifically divided four ways. To Evie, Suda Kaye, the previously mentioned Isabeau Collins and Tahsuda Tahsuda. Each of you will receive approximately $375,000 from the Ross family trust. Also, the three women will receive the disbursement of his checking account, which is currently eighty thousand dollars, and his savings account of four hundred thousand dollars, as well as any stocks, bonds and investments, of which your father had many. Not including his pension benefits."

"Okay. So let me get this straight," my sister cuts in. "You're saying that each of us is set to receive a few hundred thousand dollars from the Ross estate, which we had no idea existed, a third of his checking and savings, which is around half a million, and whatever else he invested, not to mention two houses worth another cool million."

Mr. Fink nods.

Suda Kaye stands up. "This is nuts!" she blurts out, waving her hands in the air. "Did we even know our dad at all?"

Camden stands and puts his hands on his wife's shoulders. "Sweets, sit down, we'll discuss it all later."

"Screw that. My father was loaded and none of us knew it? He had houses in two different states, which means he visited those states, and I had no clue! And on top of all that, there's a secret woman, probably some woman he was romantically involved with, who doesn't even know that he's dead! And he left her a third of his loot. A woman his two children know nothing about. Does anyone else not find this all crazy? Was the man living a double life or what?"

"Kaye, sit down. Relax. I agree. This is all news to us."

"I'm trying to understand how the heck we didn't know any of this." She points to me and then herself. Then her chin wobbles and the tears well in her eyes. "How did we not know?" she chokes out as the tears fall down her pretty cheeks. Cam curls his arm around her and brings her against his chest. She covers her face with her hands and bursts into sobbing tears in her husband's arms. He rubs her back and coos into her hair.

Such a good man.

It's hard for me to not get up and dote on her like my own baby chick, but it's not my role when her husband is around. A powerful reminder that I'm not the only person who puts Suda Kaye first. She has that in Camden now. The man devoted to giving her a good life and making her as happy as she makes him.

"Mr. Fink, is that pretty much everything? I think it's time we take our leave and digest all that we heard today."

"One more thing." He hands me a white envelope. I open it up and find a single gold key with the number 444 etched into it.

"A key?" I query.

Mr. Fink scribbles out a name and address. "It's a safety-deposit box at First National Bank in downtown Chicago, Illinois."

"Chicago?" I finger the small gold key.

"Yes."

"He left us a key to a safety-deposit box at a bank in Chicago, Illinois, three full states away from here?" I shake my head.

The attorney shrugs. "Seems so."

"What's in it?" Suda Kaye murmurs, sniffing and wiping her nose with the pocket square Camden gave her from his suit.

Mr. Fink shakes his head. "I don't know. That wasn't part of the information Mr. Ross left behind. Just that key and the name and address of the bank along with the direction to give it to his children, Evie and Suda Kaye Ross."

I tuck the key and the bank's information back into the envelope while Mr. Fink hands us both a file with all the details he just went over.

"I'm very sorry for your loss." He smiles softly at me and then at Suda Kaye.

Milo stands up and offers me his hand.

"Thank you, Mr. Fink. We'll be in touch regarding the woman mentioned in our father's will."

"If I find out a phone number and any additional contact information, I will notify you both."

The bonfire Milo made by the lake at our cabin home pops and flings little bits of burning wood and ash into the night sky.

Suda Kaye is bundled up in pajamas, complete with one of my fluffy robes and slippers. Her husband is cuddled up on the blanket behind her wearing jeans and a thermal shirt, leaning back against a log.

Along the back of our home is a path that leads to the water's edge. There's also an amazing sandy beach where Milo had a firepit built, logs to sit on and a grill. When we got back, Suda Kaye decided they were staying the night.

Milo didn't say a word and I didn't object. I want my sister close, especially after today. And besides, this weekend we'll be heading to the reservation. Dad's body is set to be cremated this week, the ashes delivered to *Toko*. Dad had it all planned out. Nothing left to decide or worry over. Just like the man himself. Always taking care of everything without our knowledge.

What I can't wrap my mind around is why all the secrecy—or lies of omission, depending on how you look at it. He never let on that he came from money or had quite a bit of his own. I mean, it's not as though we needed anything growing up. *Toko* confirmed that he sent regular payments twice a month our entire childhood. Then I knew he did the same when we moved to Pueblo, but that's as far as I would allow him to take it. Mom had left us both her life insurance policy and that paid for my schooling and the startup of my business, with money to spare.

"What did *Toko* say about the remains?" Suda Kaye asks, sucking back a large swallow of wine.

"*Toko* told me he had it all under control and that he would see us this weekend. We'll stay with Milo's parents in their spare room and the two of you can stay with *Toko*. Is that fine, honey?" I ask my man, who's walking up with two uncorked bottles of red wine and a bag of goodies hanging from his forearm. He hands me the bottles of wine. God bless him.

"*Má* will be pleased." He leans forward and gives me a slow but loving kiss. He sits down next to me on our blanket in front of the fire and tranquil water and opens up the rather big tote he brought along with the wine. He pulls out four hangers and a pair of wire cutters. He cuts the hangers and proceeds to create looped fire pokers. After he's done, he pulls out a bag of giant marshmallows, four huge chocolate bars, graham crackers and a stack of plates and napkins.

"You have such a sweet tooth," I tease, pressing my chin to his shoulder. He turns his head and I'm in awe of the way the firelight makes his harsh yet handsome features seem smooth and serene under this light. He brings his face closer to mine, steals a quick kiss and smacks his lips. "Mmm, sweet," he murmurs.

I grin and leave my chin at his shoulder, watching him while he presses big fat marshmallows onto the wire pokers.

"Camden, Suda Kaye." He offers two pokers loaded with the white fluffy treats. He then hands them a package of the graham crackers and two chocolate bars. He repeats the process for us and gives me one of the wires.

"You know, the last time I roasted marshmallows was with Dad that time he took us camping in Castlewood Canyon. What were you? Twelve, maybe? I'm pretty sure I was ten. Dad had just come back and stayed three weeks during the summer. We spent a full week camping as a family. Remember we were hiking and found this cool waterfall and Mom talked us into swimming in our shirts and undies?"

"I remember our legs getting supersunburned because we swam for hours but had only protected our faces and arms." I chuckle. "Mom had to coat us with aloe at night and listen to us gripe about how hot our skin was. Dad got our minds off of the burns by suggesting we roast marshmallows and make s'mores."

"It was a good trip together, all four of us." Suda Kaye sighs and twirls her treat over the fire.

"Yeah, one of the best," I agree.

"If you think about it, Sissy, we had a lot of those. Most of the time when Dad came back we had a blast."

And we did. Thinking back from an adult's frame of mind,

I realize that we did have a lot of family vacations. At least two a year because that was the only time when both our parents were together. And they did everything they could to make them memorable and feel everlasting.

"What are your thoughts on this Isabeau Collins?" Suda Kaye asks.

Milo maneuvers his big body behind me, his legs on either side of mine. He tucks his arm around my waist and pulls me against him more fully. I lean back and sigh into the comfort of having him at my back. He kisses my temple and a dreamy ease slides over me.

"I don't know. She could be anyone. Maybe we weren't supposed to know about her. Maybe he would have told us the next time we saw him. Honestly, without him being here to explain, we might never truly understand her importance in his life."

Suda Kaye scowls. "No way. We have her address. We have to go visit. Find out if she still lives there."

"To Chicago?"

"Well, we also need to see what secrets he left behind for us in that safety-deposit box, right?"

I frown and let out a long breath. "You've got a point there."

Suda Kaye's mouth slowly tips up until it becomes a huge smile. Then she lifts her arms into the air and hollers, "Road trip!"

I scoff. "No way in hell am I sitting in a car for that long. We'll book flights."

"I'll have to figure out my shifts at Gypsy Soul." She pouts. "Last week I actually put up a Help Wanted sign and already have a handful of applications."

"Anyone strike your fancy?"

"Actually, yeah, a waitress from Porter's pub. She can't

254 • AUDREY CARLAN

work nights because she's a single mom. During the week the store closes at six, which works perfectly because her mother watches her son after school until she gets off work at the pub. Right now she's only working the lunch crowd, which isn't giving her enough hours. My job comes with full-time pay and health coverage for her and her son. Porter highly recommends her. Says she'll be a loss but also understands he doesn't have the hours she needs to provide for her and her son."

"Sounds like you could be helping out a woman in need."

She smiles. "Exactly. Gypsy Soul has changed my life, and I like the idea of it changing someone else's, too. Plus, of course, she'd have Addy's help in the afternoons."

"What are you waiting for, Sweets? Hire the woman already. You need the help. You were just saying you were running out of time to even review new products and artists."

"Speaking of artists, Milo's mom, Lina, makes incredible Navajo-inspired jewelry."

Suda Kaye lifts her chin toward Milo's choker. "She make that piece?"

He nods.

"And the bolo ties he wears, and some amazing cuffs, rings and everything in between. All real silver, intricate and from the earth. I've got her website and they said they'd work you a huge deal on the price. She's already lowballing the pricing of her work unnecessarily, so you'll be able to turn it around and make an excellent profit."

"Awesome. Maybe I can see some of her stuff this weekend? And I'll pay what's fair based on what I see."

"I'm sure she'd like that." I smile. Lina will probably want to make my sister a big feast if she's interested in her jewelry. I'll let Milo give her the good news.

"So, when should we plan to fly out to Chicago?"

"Maybe next weekend, meaning the week after we lay our father to rest. At some point I'm going to have to get back to work. Regina and the rest of my financial planners are holding down the fort, but I don't like knowing my burdens are theirs. It's just hard…with Dad and all." I take a full breath and Milo rubs his hand along my hair.

Suda Kaye presses her lips closed tight and stares into the fire. A melancholy blanket of emotion slips over the four of us.

"I'd like to make a toast." I hold up my wineglass. Milo, Cam and Suda Kaye do the same. "To us. All of us. Milo and me, our home and the life we're building together, and to you and Camden in your marriage and your future. We all have so much to be grateful for. The four of us are a family. We're going to have children one day that will be raised to appreciate not only the beauty in our backyards but the world at large."

Suda Kaye smiles wide and Cam grins, kissing her cheek.

"And to Adam Ross," I continue. "Though he obviously had his secrets, he was also a patriot, a caring husband and a loving father."

"Hear, hear." Suda Kaye lifts her glass.

"Cheers," Cam says.

I sip my wine and turn to Milo as he does the same. His dark gaze meets mine and his lips twitch in that way that makes me think of sexy times, big breakfasts, thoughtful dinners, deep kisses and messy sheets.

He wraps an arm around me and takes my mouth in one of his mind-melting, panty-dropping, soul-fulfilling kisses. His tongue dances with mine and I can taste the sweet berry and jam notes from the wine mixed with the sticky marshmallow goodness in his kiss.

I cup his scruffy cheek and give it my all. Allowing my

emotions to soar and spill into this kiss. The grief I feel over my dad's passing along with the happiness that I have Milo here to hold me. The gratitude I feel in his presence. The hope I have for our future. The love that's growing bigger and bigger between us each and every day.

I give it all over to him.

And he takes it, kissing me hard, then soft. Deep, then simple featherlight pecks until I forget we're sitting outside, with my sister and brother-in-law.

He cups the back of my head and eases back so he's all I see.

"I will always be here for you, *Nizhoni*."

I rub my cheek against his palm and say the two words I know he wants to hear, but more that he wants me to believe straight down in my soul. "I know."

And I do. I know his support and love are in my life for good. I no longer feel the need to question it.

"Good." He stands up and puts his hand out to me. I take it and he pulls me to my feet. He then walks over to the grill in the corner, about twenty feet from where we're camped out. He lifts the lid and pulls out a huge bouquet of yellow roses. There has to be at least two dozen. He walks back over to me and hands me the roses.

I smile huge. "Honey, these are beautiful and such a nice surprise…" I start to say, but then he kneels down in the sand, backlit by the lake's beauty and the flickering bonfire. He pulls something out of his pocket and holds it up between us.

A ring.

A simple, sparkling, diamond ring.

I gasp and hold the flowers to my chest, my other hand to my lips.

"Oh my God," Suda Kaye breathes in awe from just behind us.

"Give me your hand, Evie," Milo says softly, and my hand

jets out so fast he chuckles. He holds on to it and sets the ring just at the edge of my ring finger. "Evie Ross, I want you to be my wife. To one day bear my children. To spend the rest of your days with me. I will devote all that I am, and all that I have, to you and our life together. Will you be mine for eternity?"

Tears fill my eyes and I nod. "Yes, yes, I will marry you." The tears slide down my cheeks. He eases the ring up and onto my finger. He presses his lips to the ring where it sits on my finger, then rises, pulls me into his arms and presses his face to my throat. He kisses my pulse there, then he dips his head and kisses me over my shirt where my heart would be. Then he lifts his head, cups my cheeks and takes my mouth.

Suda Kaye and Camden cheer and carry on, their applause whisked off into the night like an echo over the mountains as my man kisses me, sealing the next phase of our life together.

It's the best kiss I've ever had, and it was given to me by my fiancé.

18

The drive to the reservation is long and mostly quiet. We take the Cayenne as it's a bit more comfortable than his truck for a long car ride. For the first two hours we hash out the details of merging our businesses together. Weighing the pros and cons have made it clear that, professionally, it's a really great idea. I've been meaning to look at expanding and Milo's got an entirely new market of clientele with the tribes. He's also got several meetings set up to discuss the corporate financial planning side with the surrounding casinos. Securing even one casino would be a huge boon to both of our businesses. And since we're committing our lives to one another, it makes sense to merge. I no longer need to count on myself for everything. Each day with Milo I'm learning the benefit of having someone else looking out for you, on your side in all things and prepared to work hard toward the same goals.

Once finished with the business conversation, hand in hand over the center console, Milo randomly asks, "Why do you not like to drive?"

"You'll think it's weird." I press my back against the soft leather seat and turn to watch his profile.

He let me tie his hair half up, leaving the bulk of his silky thick hair falling down his back and shoulders. Put him up on his horse Dezba and he'd be a Native American warrior come to life. My own personal hero. Which is how I've been seeing him lately.

Everything Milo does seems to fit so smoothly into my life. Even with my father's passing, the fight with his parents, the strife between me and my sister and my cluttered feelings about my mother, he's been a solid presence. My rock. Something for me to lean on, whisper my fears to in the night without fear of judgment or backlash. The one person who is solely focused on me and my health and happiness.

His lips twitch and I sigh.

"I do not think anything about you is weird. Sweet, yes. Silly, sometimes. Strong, always. Weird, no."

I grin. "I don't like to drive because when Mom was teaching me, I crashed the car. She hit her head on the passenger side window and needed stitches. She was already sick by then so getting into a car and teaching her sixteen-year-old daughter how to drive already took a lot out of her, but I was determined to learn. I needed to be able to drive us to school, to the grocery store, and take her to her doctors' appointments or to the hospital when she was really sick."

"You are worried you will crash again?"

I shake my head. "No. I was just learning then and made an error, thinking I was turning onto a four-way-stop road when it was only a two-way stop. The other car had the right of way and crashed into Mom's side."

"I see."

"Ultimately I only get nervous when I'm driving and someone else is in the car. It's too much responsibility. Having someone else's safety in your hands. I don't like it."

"And what of our children?"

I twist the sparkly engagement ring around and around

my finger in the sunlight, loving how the sun's rays glint and shine off it.

"You'll teach them," I state flatly.

He grins. "No. What about when you have them in your car?"

I frown. "We're going to have to have some serious car safety restraints. Baby in the center for sure. Maybe we should look into SUV safety ratings and airbags."

That has him chuckling and squeezing my hand. "We will ensure we have the best and safest vehicle."

I nod. "So, your parents are okay with us staying at their house?"

He lifts his chin.

"Do we have to sleep in separate bedrooms?" I tease. "I could sleep on *Toko*'s couch, you know."

He brings my hand up to his lips, eyes focused on the road. He kisses my fingers. "No one will separate us. You sleep in my arms."

I turn in my chair and bring our hands to my lips, kissing his fingers this time. I bring his thumb into my mouth and run my tongue along the pad, feeling the grooves in his fingerprint.

"Evie," he warns, and his dark brows seem like accusing slashes on his handsome face.

"What?" I flick his finger with my tongue and bite down on the tip. "Just showing my man a teaser of what's to come in his childhood bed." I suck the digit and let it go with a plop.

He shakes his head. "I will see to this show tonight, *Nizhoni*. You will be rewarding me for my patience."

I grin and nod. "I so will!"

He chuckles and holds my hand back in the center as we pull up toward the gate of the reservation. Milo rolls down the window and greets the man in Navajo. The gatekeeper drags open the gate. We drive through, and instead of going straight to his parents' home to unload our things, he leads the Cayenne toward my grandfather's.

Camden's shiny car is already parked out front. Milo pulls up alongside it. My grandfather opens his front door and walks to the edge of his porch.

Seeing his stoic form has the emotions swirling around me like a whirlpool. Milo exits the vehicle and comes around to open my door, giving me his hand as I get out.

I slowly walk up to my grandfather. He holds out his arms and I face-plant right against his barrel chest. He smells of sandalwood and smoke, similar to Milo but with a unique difference that's all *Toko*. He cups my head and holds me for a long time.

I hear the door behind us slap closed and footsteps pounding along the wooden planks.

"Hey, hot stuff," Suda Kaye says, and I smile into *Toko*'s chest.

He lifts my face and stares into my eyes for long moments. "You are okay, *Taabe*?"

I nod. "Yeah, I'm okay, *Toko*."

He kisses my forehead and then his gaze rises to a height somewhere behind me. "You have taken care of mine own?"

"Yes, Elder Tahsuda, and I always will," Milo says in perfect Comanche.

I turn my head and my mouth falls open in shock. "You speak Comanche!" I blurt.

He grins. "Enough to get by."

I point a jaunty finger at him. "I can't believe you!"

Suda Kaye giggles and rests her butt on the wooden railing. "You're full of surprises, Milo."

"He sure is!" I chuckle.

"Show *Toko* the other surprise he dropped on you a few days ago," Suda Kaye urges.

I spin around and hold out my hand, happy as a clam. "I'm getting married, *Toko*!"

Toko stares at my hand, then at my smiling face, and then up at Milo. Then his weathered cheeks rise up along with his lips into a beatific smile.

"This I know as young Chavis called to request your hand. Today is a good day. We will celebrate."

I shoot the biggest smile at Milo. "You called *Toko*?"

He nods and winks. I fall even more in love with him for giving *Toko* that honor.

Suda Kaye pops off the railing and does a little jig. "Oooh, I hope our celebration comes with some peace pipe action! And dancing. And all the wine."

Toko shakes his head. "You are not old enough to smoke," he says, matter-of-fact.

She frowns. "I'm almost twenty-nine! That means I've been an adult for eleven years, *Toko*." And she's right. We share the same birthday, which means in a couple months I'll be thirty-one.

"Like I said. Too young." And that is that. *Toko*'s word is law.

I snort while Suda Kaye starts listing off all the reasons she is old enough to smoke with the elders. It's been something she's wanted since she was about five years old. *Toko* always says she's too young.

Camden comes out of the house with two glasses of iced tea.

"Babe, tell *Toko* I'm old enough to smoke the peace pipe."

"You guys do that?" he asks *Toko*.

He shakes his head. "It is not a peace pipe. That is a stereotype." *Toko* narrows his gaze at Suda Kaye.

"It brings you peace in the mind, doesn't it?" She narrows her eyes, cocks a hip and puts her hand to it. Oh, man, she's getting riled up.

"Sweets, smoking isn't good for you," Camden adds.

Her head jerks back. "You're on his side? No way! You are legally bound to be on my side any time I have an argument with anyone!"

He shakes his head and smiles. "Not when it's with your grandfather. I'm not stupid. And if he says you're too young to smoke something you shouldn't be smoking, anyway, then I'm on his side."

"No sex for you!" she screeches instantly.

This has my man, who's standing behind me, laughing heartily. I playfully elbow him in the gut. "Don't get involved. She's hell on wheels when riled. And she often gets riled about the peace pipe."

"If it makes you feel any better, Suda Kaye, I have not partaken of the pipe, either," he states for her benefit.

She harrumphs, pouts and stares at Milo, I'm assuming trying to assess his honesty. "That blows! Does anyone else feel like this is a rite of passage for a Native American? I need to channel my people, the spirits and the gods!"

"You need to channel reality, Sissy, and realize that you are not ever smoking from that pipe!" I tease.

She scrunches up her face and flounces over to the chair, plopping down the same way a petulant child would.

Crisis averted. She'll stew in her irritation until something else sparkly or exciting happens and then she'll be over it.

Milo turns suddenly, hooking his arm around my shoulders at the same time. I see his parents walking up and around our vehicles.

Both of them come up to us and Milo hugs his mother and father. I do the same.

"Hey, did you see us drive up?" I ask.

"Yes, and I was too excited to wait." Lina walks away from me and bows her head to my grandfather. "I hope you don't mind the intrusion. I was looking forward to seeing my son."

"No mind. Welcome, Lina and Sani." He turns to Suda Kaye. "*Huutsuu*, can you get our guests a cold drink?"

She hops up, her ire gone as quickly as a breeze. "Sure thing."

I introduce Milo's parents to Camden as Suda Kaye brings out two glasses of iced tea and hands them to Lina and then Sani. "Hi, I'm Suda Kaye, *Toko*'s other granddaughter."

Lina smiles softly. "Yes, Catori's youngest child. You carry many of her beautiful features."

"Aw, thanks. Good to meet you. I love your son, and I can't wait until they get married."

Lina's face pinches into an expression of confusion. "Married?" She turns her head to her son and speaks in rapid-fire Navajo so fast I can't keep up. Whatever she says, though, has *Toko* happy based on the small way his lips tilt up and his eyes sparkle with happiness.

She reaches for my hand, admires the ring and throws her arms around me. "Finally! The woman meant for my boy!" Tears fall down her cheeks and onto my shoulder as Sani pats her back.

"*Shimá*, Mother, you can let her go. Evie isn't going anywhere." Milo curls his hand around my arm and tugs me toward his side. Once there he wraps his heavy arm around my shoulder.

"We have to celebrate!" she cries, wiping her tears.

"Party on the rez!" Suda Kaye whoops from her seat next to Cam on the porch.

"We will make a feast! Invite everyone!"

Milo puts his hand out in a stop gesture. "*Shimá*, remember we are here because Evie and Suda Kaye lost their father. They are putting his spirit to rest with their grandfather. They are not here for a party."

Lina covers her mouth. "Yes, my sweet girls, I am sorry," she whispers in Navajo.

"A dinner for our two families would be good. A small feast?" Sani suggests his gaze, flicking to *Toko*'s. He nods his head in return.

"*Aoo', Aoo'.* A feast to bring our families together during a happy and sad time," she agrees, her head falling forward.

I grab her hand and she lifts her watery gaze. "Thank you. A meal together would be lovely." I pat the top of hers.

Lina nods and steps back. Sani hooks his arm around her waist. "There is much to do to prepare."

"Suda Kaye and I can help! And *Toko* makes amazing food."

"I will bring my fried corn, bread and wine," he offers. The wine was a given.

"Perfect, Elder Tahsuda. Thank you. I would love your help, Evie and Suda Kaye. Perhaps the men can show Camden some of the reservation?"

"Would love that." He rubs his hand up and down my sister's arm. "I've been hearing about a pair of horses from Evie. Dezba and *Adinidiin*."

My eyes light up. "Oooh, how is our little one?" I ask Sani.

"Right as rain. I have her in a pasture with Dezba and Chenoa. Milo can bring you when you are ready."

I hug Milo's side. "I can't wait until we can bring them home. It will be fun to see them every day."

"It will," Milo murmurs against the top of my head before planting a kiss there.

"See you guys soon." Lina hands Milo her tea glass and

Sani does the same before taking his wife's hand as they make the trek back to their home.

"Dinner was so fun." I hum as I pull off my sweater and toss it on the floor.

Milo shuts and locks his door.

I unbutton my jeans and shimmy them down my legs. The wine my grandfather loves so much swimming warmly through my veins. I list to the side and fall to my bum on the bed realizing I didn't take off my suede booties.

Laughter bubbles out from my mouth as I fumble with the zips in my shoes. Eventually I yank them off and push off my jeans.

"Yay!" I gleefully cheer.

"*Nizhoni*, you have a promise to uphold." Milo's deep voice rumbles through my chest even from across the room.

I look up and find him leaning back against the door, muscular arms crossed over his wide chest.

"Excuse me?" I stand up, put my hands to my hips and tilt my head to the side.

He unfurls his arms, unbuttons and unzips his jeans and opens them enough to pull out his very hard cock.

My throat goes dry even as my mouth salivates. I swallow and lick my lips, watching him run his large hand down one seriously monstrous erection.

"On your knees, my love," he commands, gifting me the sight of another stroke. The tone, timbre and serious nature of his need is a powerful aphrodisiac.

I curl my arms behind me and unfasten my bra, letting it fall to the floor. Wanting to give him everything his heart could possibly desire. I ease down my lace panties until they land next to my bra. Milo's eyes blaze like fire as he takes in my naked body.

"Nizhoni," he utters as though caught in between pleasure and pain as he strokes himself.

I take the few steps and place my hands to his chest. I unbutton his shirt and shove it down his massive frame. He lets go of his cock so I can push the shirt off. His hands come to my head and he pulls me to him, crushing his lips against mine in a searing kiss.

Heat fills every ounce of my body as I plaster my naked body against his. I reach down between us and circle his length with my much smaller hand. He grunts into my mouth and plunges his tongue deep, owning my mouth while I run my hand up and down his virile length.

He devours my mouth to the point where I can't breathe. I rip my mouth away as I circle his tip with my thumb, spreading the moisture there until all I can think about is putting my mouth on him and driving him insane.

I fall to my knees and yank at his jeans until he helps me get them down his legs and to his ankles. He's already taken off his boots and I help him step out of his jeans. Once done, I cup my hands around his mighty calves and slide them up the backs of his large legs. Once I get to his ass, I squeeze hard. His hips thrust forward, his penis only an inch from my face.

I grin and look up, pressing my cheek to the velvety appendage before I place a small kiss just at the base. He's completely shaved, no hair to speak of, and my man keeps this up daily, so the skin is silky smooth when I press my nose there and breathe in his earthy scent. His chest is also free of hair, but that's a genetic gift.

"Do not tease me." He threads his fingers into the hair at the side of my head and grips a handful at the roots, tugging until I gasp, and arousal races down my body to settle hotly between my thighs.

I grin and run my lips along his cock until I reach the wide crown. I flick my tongue against the tip, and he tightens his hold in my hair but doesn't force me on him. He's content to let me lead and, right now, I'm all about leading my man to the most intense orgasm of his life.

With my gaze zeroed in on his, I wrap my lips around the head and suck hard. He hisses through his teeth and tips his head back against the door.

I remove my mouth. "Eyes on me, baby," I dictate, and his black eyes dance with pleasure as I swirl my tongue around the tip before taking him down my throat once more.

With my hands I run up and down his straining thigh muscles, over his chiseled ass and around and up his toned abs.

He groans when I wrap one of my hands at the base and jack him while I give attention to the first few inches. With my hand and mouth working in perfect synchronicity, I run the flat of my tongue along the sensitive gland just under the head, while simultaneously rolling his heavy balls in the palm of my other hand.

Milo's breath catches as I work him over and over, sipping the drops of his essence that seep at the tip. I rub the wide crown all over my lips before taking him inside again. I get so into it, I ease one of my hands down my body and between my thighs, finding myself slick and ready. I circle the tight knot and moan around his length until I'm humping my hand and humming around his length.

"Evie," he warns, his hips moving with my efforts, seeking his release. His body is slick with sweat, his veins protruding. Milo breathes sharply through clenched teeth and grips my hair.

"Make me," I whisper, and watch fascinated and completely turned on as his nostrils flare, and he tunnels his other hand into my hair and thrusts into my mouth as far as he can go.

I'm so relaxed from the wine and the arousal oozing through my veins I'm able to breathe through my nose as he pushes his beast past my tongue and down my throat. It's a tight fit, constricting and brutal, and I love every freakin' second of it.

Milo's entire body is vibrating with pleasure as he takes my mouth in a series of deep thrusts. His body goes stiff, every muscle throbbing and straining with his efforts.

I hold on to his ass with one hand and roll his balls with the other until I can feel the heat of him in my hand, his seed rushing through his sac, up his length and powering into my mouth in jet after jet of his release.

"My Evie," he moans.

I suck him down and swallow until his body shivers beneath my hands, the intensity of his movements lessening until I feel him relax against the door. He eases his length out of my mouth, leans over and pulls me up and into his arms. He walks us over to the bed and sets me down, taking my mouth in a long, blissful kiss.

My head is swimming, my body aching for his, but I don't have to wait long. When he's done taking my mouth, he works his lips and tongue over my neck, then down to my breasts. He sucks, nibbles and tortures each one with his talented mouth until I'm about to come from that alone.

"Milo, baby," I whisper, arching up.

He sucks one tip so hard I cry out and grip the wooden slats of the headboard.

"Shh, you don't want my family to hear your pleasure," he reminds me even though they are on the opposite side of the house and at dinner he told me they sleep like the dead.

Still, what we're doing feels illicit and taboo in his childhood home and yet all the more exciting because of it. I clamp my mouth shut and he smiles, his hair sliding along my rib cage and down my belly, following the path his mouth is taking.

"Open for me," he demands, and I cock my knees up and butterfly them wide. No hesitation. I know exactly where he's headed and I'm here for it. Completely. Milo has proven these past couple weeks that he's a very creative and giving lover.

He growls low in his throat like an animal about to feast, only I'm what's ready and waiting.

With both of his hands he holds my thighs down and looks his fill of my sex.

"My Evie." He runs his thumb down my center, then presses it inside me. "Hot for me," he murmurs, and it sends chills down my back.

"Yes," I answer.

"Wet for me."

I shiver. "Please." I ease my hips up, making it clear what I want.

"All mine." He pets my sex reverently before placing his mouth over me.

I cover my mouth as a cry rips through my chest. He holds me down fast, so that I'm forced to enjoy every lick, suck and kiss of his incredible mouth.

"Honey." I reach for his head with both hands and weave my fingers through his glorious hair.

He snarls low in his throat and presses two fingers deep, then latches his lips over my clit and sucks hard.

I was so primed from sucking his cock and him worshiping my body that I instantly orgasm. He continues to work me with his fingers and mouth, until I'm greedy for more and gasping for air.

One orgasm turns into two and he still doesn't stop. With incredible speed and agility, he flips me over onto my stomach, yanks my body toward the end of the bed and runs his tongue from my sex and over that secret pucker no one has ever touched before. He spreads my cheeks and circles the tiny rosette with the tip of his tongue until I'm keening and pressing back to get more. To get everything he's giving.

Before I can even assess how I feel about that new sensation, he stands behind me, notches his now hard length at my sex and eases inside, all the way to the hilt. I swear I can feel him in my stomach. He reaches forward, curving over me, and curls his hand around the back of my neck. His thumb on one side, his four fingers on the other, holding me captive. I tilt my bum up and arch into him as he thrusts once.

"Oh God, so deep," I gasp, and he does it again, slowly, easing in and out, letting my body get used to this position.

When the glide is a bit easier, he slides his hands down my rib cage and to my hips.

"You ready for hard, *Nizhoni*?"

"God, yes!" I whisper, but before I can catch my breath, his body is slamming into me with such powerful thrusts my knees actually leave the bed. He lifts me and hammers inside, filling me completely, endlessly, until I don't even know where I am. I lose all train of thought that doesn't involve his massive length plunging inside of my body, making me feel loved, connected, whole.

I start to rock my hips back, forcing him to take me harder. He does. Gripping the fleshy part of my hip tight as the other hand goes into my hair. He tugs my head back, arching my body until I push up to where I'm just on my knees, hung up on him.

I reach behind me, my arm locking around his neck. One

of his arms wraps tightly around my waist and the other goes straight between my legs where he manipulates me perfectly.

"Give me what's mine. I want all your pleasure," he growls into my ear before sinking his teeth into the meaty muscle of where my shoulder and neck meet.

I gasp as my body burns, overheating, electricity sizzling through my limbs sparking each nerve ending until I explode. He shoves his fingers coated in my essence into my mouth so I can't scream. I suck them hard as the orgasm destroys me one molecule at a time.

Milo keeps up the ravenous pace, relentlessly tweaking my clit until I'm one endless orgasm, never starting or stopping, just stuck on blastoff, jerking wildly against his hold.

Lights flicker behind my eyes and my heart races. Eventually his own body goes off, his arms locking me in place, and I lie there, a spent and sated rag doll, my form plastered to his front while his body convulses in aftershocks behind me.

As he comes down, he removes his fingers from my mouth, turning my head so he can kiss me. He tastes of him and me, everything good and right in the world.

"You move me, *Nizhoni*. Every time is wonder and magic."

I smile, using all the strength I have left to lift my head forward and suck on his bottom lip.

"It was good for me, too."

He chuckles against my lips and eases out of me. I moan and wince.

"I took you too hard." He frowns and pets my lips with his thumb.

I lick it and wink. "You took me perfectly."

Still, he lifts me up and carries me to the en suite bathroom. Now this would be an amazing feature in *Toko's* house.

Milo sets me bare-bottomed on the vanity. "Shower?"

I shake my head. "Too sleepy," I murmur, closing my

eyes and leaning back against the mirror. The water turns on and soon my legs are spread and Milo washes away our lovemaking with a warm cloth. I'm too tired to care or be embarrassed that I'm not doing this myself.

When he's done, he lifts me back into his arms, takes me into the bedroom and pulls back the covers. He sets me in the center of the bed, then slides his naked body in. I turn to my side and he wraps an arm around my waist and cuddles me close.

I yawn. "Good night," I mumble.

He presses his face to the side of mine. "With you in my life, safely tucked in my arms, I will always have a good night."

I hum and smile. "Love you."

"Love you. Good night, my Evie."

19

The walk through the dry, desertlike climate is stifling, filling my throat with bitterness and sorrow even though it's late in the day and the sun is far off to the west at our backs. The sky is already starting to change color into the brilliant orange, purple, pink hues that make the land magical on a normal day.

Today is not normal. We are laying my father to rest in the manner in which he requested.

Toko leads the way, in full headdress and chest plate, wearing an appropriately simple robe, and with his hair braided. He's not dressed for a powwow, which would include head-to-toe dress, but he's still respecting the position my father held in this family.

The headdress is stunning and incredibly intricate. It's made of golden eagle feathers that go from a stunning white to a muddy brown, then pure black. The headpiece was passed down to him from his father and grandfather, who were real-life Comanche warriors. The beaded band over his weathered and lined forehead is a stark bright red-and-white pattern of triangles representing the mountains. A circular beaded medallion in the shape of a six-sided star sits on each side of his temples where a series of unique feathers hang down from leather thongs.

The beaded chest plate is the same one he wears for special ceremonies even in these modern times. He wore it to Suda Kaye's wedding not long ago and I hope he'll wear it to mine, too.

Milo squeezes my hand as we continue to walk to the one place I haven't visited in eleven years. When we arrive, there is another elder from the Navajo side waiting for us. Since my mother was both Comanche and Navajo, it stands to reason there would be an elder representing her, although my father wasn't Native American.

We get to the tree that sits uniquely shaded by a rock wall behind it. It's the perfect location for a mourner to visit since they get the natural shade from the tree and the wall. About three feet from the base of the tree are two flat gravestones. They're not the contemporary ones you see in a normal cemetery. These are made from actual rock and were chipped and chiseled by my grandfather's own hand. I stare at my grandmother's, which bears a single name, TOPSANNAH, all in capital letters with a flower etched next to it. There are no years and no last names because it is not needed. Her name in Comanche meant "prairie flower" and I think it's beautiful, but we only ever called her *Kaku*, which is "grandmother" in our tongue.

About five feet from her stone is another with my mother's name on it, CATORI, and etched in her stone are stars at the top, waves on one side, a mountain on the other and below her name a few swirls that I think are meant to represent the air. Proving that even *Toko* knew his daughter was a free spirit. Which incidentally is what *Catori* means.

I lick my dry lips and bring Milo's hand closer to me until

I'm wedged up against his side. He says nothing but stands strong and supportive.

Camden and Suda Kaye stand beside us. None of us speak as the Navajo elder uses a shovel at the base of my mother's stone and digs a hole about eighteen inches deep. *Toko* speaks in Comanche and holds up the urn containing our father's ashes. He whispers the words I remember him saying at my mother's ceremony.

Once the hole is big enough, *Toko* uncaps the urn and pours the ashes straight into the earth. He stands back up and looks to me.

"*Taabe.*" He gestures to the mound of dirt sitting next to the hole. I let go of Milo's hand, my heart in my throat. I dig my fingers into the dry earth and grab a handful.

"Goodbye, Daddy. Rest in peace with Mom. I'll make sure your legacy lives on, and your grandchildren will know the hero you were to us all." I drop the earth over his ashes. "I'll love you forever." Tears fall down and drip right onto his final resting place. I turn around and move straight into Milo's arms, pressing my face against his chest, my ear to his heart. It thumps loud enough to settle me.

I turn in his arms and he wraps me up, plastering his front to my back, putting his chin in his favorite spot and pressing his cheek to mine. His stability and rock-solid support gives me a burst of strength to get through this.

"*Huutsuu,*" Toko states softly.

My sister swallows and shakily walks to the dirt pile, leans over and takes a handful.

"Goodbye, Dad. Thank you for accepting me as your own. Thank you for loving me. Mom will take care of you now. Be at peace." Her voice shakes as she drops the earth over mine. Her own tears fall and mingle with mine over his ashes.

"Men?" *Toko* offers them, and Milo lets me go and walks to the pile.

He picks up a large handful and holds it in the air as he speaks. "I will love and take care of Evie until my last breath. On my honor." He drops the handful.

My body bucks and I sob as his moving words pierce straight through to my soul. He comes back to me and embraces me front to front, our bodies shifted to the side so I can hold him and participate at the same time.

Camden follows Milo's lead, grabbing a handful and holding it up. "Suda Kaye will always be my priority. She will be loved and protected her whole life long." He drops the dirt on top of ours.

Toko says a few more words and goes to the pile. He holds up his hand and speaks in Comanche.

"Let the earth, the sun, the air and the fire guide your spirit." He drops the handful over, then the other elder covers the rest and packs it down with his bare hands, whispering his own words of guidance.

The six of us go quiet as *Toko* moves to a bag the other man must have brought. The first thing he removes is an American flag folded in the shape of a triangle.

My gasp is loud and tortured. *Toko* walks solemnly to me. "As the eldest living kin, this is for you." He presents me with the flag I'm sure he received from the men in uniform a couple weeks ago but neglected to mention. Now I know why. He wanted it to be part of us saying goodbye.

Toko presses the gift into my shaking hands. I grip it and hug it to my chest. Suda Kaye loses her cool and sobs into her husband's chest.

Milo cuddles me from behind. "We will display it proudly in our home and speak of his service to our children. They will know him through you."

I nod as a river of tears falls down my cheeks.

Toko moves back over to the other elder and digs into the bag. Together they remove the items they need to build a small fire and light it. I vaguely remember *Toko* doing this at my grandmother's ceremony, but I was only around six years old so the details are vague.

"We will keep this fire burning in order to help guide the spirit to its final home," he announces.

I frown. We didn't do that for Mom, but we did for *Kaku*. I distinctly remember every second of my mother's ceremony as the entire tribe was there in the distance paying their respects but not getting too close. Suda Kaye was only seventeen and I nineteen but it's not something I would forget.

Toko finishes the ceremony and we stand staring at the fire burning for a long time. *Toko* nods to the elder as another member of the tribe approaches but stands respectfully off to the side.

"Who's that?" I ask *Toko*.

"He will help keep the fire burning. And in a couple hours someone will relieve him and so on for the next few days. It is their service to their people."

Toko gives the man a chin lift and in return the man bows his head in deference to his position as an elder in the tribe.

My grandfather leads us away from the gravesite. We walk for about fifteen minutes until the burning question will not leave.

"*Toko?*" I ask, and his steps falter from leading the pack. "Why did we not have a fire burning for Mom when she passed?"

His lips flatten and he takes a slow breath.

"My Catori's instructions to me were not to let her spirit leave until the time was right."

I frown and Suda Kaye comes up behind me. "But it's been eleven years." She takes the words right out of my mouth.

Toko nods. "Her spirit is not done."

"What more is there left for her spirit to do?" I question. That my mom didn't get her full due to lay her spirit to rest is pissing me off.

Toko shakes his head. "When the time is right, we will know when my Catori is ready. She is not."

I point to the land behind us. "Her husband is dead. His ashes are buried at her feet. His spirit is being guided on its journey right now. Is that not the perfect time? Should we light two fires?"

His lips flatten and once again he shakes his head solemnly.

"That doesn't make any sense!" Suda Kaye fires off her own anger, lighting up and fueling mine.

"It is not for you to understand. Catori's wishes are being respected. That is all." He turns his moccasin-wearing feet back toward his home, leaving us to ponder this turn of events.

"I don't understand," Suda Kaye gripes.

"Me, either," I say through clenched teeth, ready to race after *Toko* and give him a piece of my mind, until Milo places his warm hand on my shoulder.

"Evie, it is not for you to question," he says softly.

I narrow my gaze. "How do you figure that? It's my mother. I can damn well question anything I want!"

His lips twitch and his features soften to one of concern.

"Some things are meant to be the way they are. The truth will be revealed in time. Patience, *Nizhoni*."

"He's keeping this from us for a reason." I pout.

Milo nods. "Your grandfather is a fair man. If he is keeping this to himself, there is a reason. One not meant for you to know now. I believe he will explain when the time is right."

"I think it's crap!" Suda Kaye fires off.

Camden smiles softly and hooks his arm around her shoulders. "It may be, but I don't think you're going to get anything out of the man any time soon. If he wants you to understand, he will share. Until then, you just have to trust that he has your and your mother's best interest at heart."

I frown because Camden is right. *Toko* doesn't lie to us. He never sugarcoats anything. Whatever reason he has for the things he does are his own. And he'd die before hurting us or our mother. Apparently whatever it is was a private agreement he made with my mother. And as her father, it's up to him what he wants to share. Even with us. Her children.

A breeze flows over my skin as though it were my mother's own touch, soothing my ire. "I trust *Toko*," I murmur, and watch his retreating form get farther and farther away from us.

Suda Kaye sighs long and loud. "Me, too. Even though I still think it's crap."

Camden chuckles. "Come on, Sweets. Let's get you ladies fed and drunk on some more of that wine."

I turn to Milo. "Can we go to the bluffs after dinner to look at the stars? We never did go out on the boat back home so I could make a new wish and teach you how to wish on stars."

He leans forward and kisses me sweetly. "We can go where you want."

Milo and I both carry a lantern as we trek up to my favorite spot. Even more so now that we had our first intimate moment there.

When we get to the top, the sun is almost completely behind the mountain. Milo wraps his arms around me from behind.

"How are you?" he asks.

I know he's concerned. I didn't say much through dinner or drinks with my small family.

"I want to go home tomorrow. Finish unpacking everything. Go back to work. Start my life again. Put our heads together about merging our businesses and how that would best benefit us."

He holds me closer and presses his head to my cheek. "If that is what you want, we will go. The work will always be there, and we can start the process of merging whenever we want. Your health and happiness is most important."

"Your mom will be disappointed."

"She will understand your need to get back to your life after your loss. It's the natural way of things. Besides, I want you all to myself."

"You know she's gonna be all over us to plan the wedding, right?"

He hums. "What do you want?"

"I just want you and me, forever. Nothing else matters in the grand scheme of things."

"What about here?"

I jolt back and turn around so we're facing one another. "Here, here? As in the reservation?"

He shakes his head and kisses me softly. "No. Here as in the bluffs. Me, you, *Toko*, your sister and brother, my parents and sister. And one of our people to officiate. No more, no less. Mom and Dad will put on a small feast and we'll celebrate, then go on a long honeymoon."

I grin wide. "Really?"

He nods.

"That sounds magical and absolutely perfect." I wrap my arms around his neck and kiss him for a long time.

A kiss to seal our fate.

He pulls away first and lays the big blanket out over the ground where we first made love. He lights his lantern as I light mine and place it on the opposite side of the blanket. From a satchel he carried he pulls out a bottle of wine and two metal goblets.

I sit down on my knees as he uncorks the wine and pours me a glass in one of the incredible goblets. "Did your mom make these?"

He nods. "Yes, she made them for us, for our home."

I smile wide. "Our first present as a couple." I lift up the weighty cup. "I didn't know her work extended to metal-work like this."

"Father helped. It's something he does as a hobby. He crafted them and she hammered and worked the designs."

I hold up the goblet to the light and take in the intricate swirls cut into the metal, the perfectly placed hammered div-ots blending hard and soft together. Just like Milo and me.

Once he's poured his own glass and is facing me, he holds it up. "To our life together, may it be long, and happy for-evermore."

I clink his glass. "Absolutely." I sip the fruity wine, lean over until he gets the hint and does the same so that we can kiss under the stars.

I'm the first to pull away. "Okay, now look up."

He does.

"You're supposed to pick a star that calls to you."

His brow furrows. "Why?"

"Just do it." I scramble across the blanket to sit right next to him. He wraps his free arm around my back and hooks his hand at my waist.

"Okay, shall I show it to you?"

I shake my head and look up until I find one that instantly calls me, unlike when I was a child and worried I'd pick the wrong one.

"Now, repeat after me. I wish I may," I say, and wait until he repeats it.

"I wish I may." Milo side-eyes me and smiles.

"I wish I might," I continue, and he repeats it.

"Have this wish." I bite into my bottom lip until he says the words.

"I wish tonight," I finish, and wait until he says it.

"Now what?"

"You make a wish on that star. But you can't tell me because it won't come true."

He frowns. "You told me your wish."

I grin. "True. But that was after it had already come true. Now focus on your star and make a wish."

For a few minutes we both stare up at the sky. I hold that little blinking light in my vision for as long as I need until my heart's desire comes to me.

I wish to have a family one day. A strong and healthy black-haired boy just like Milo and a happy, beautiful girl that always knows she's loved, wanted and needed by her family.

Together we sit and watch the stars and drink our wine. We talk more about what we'd like to see for our wedding and pick a date. Three months from now when we've had some time to settle into our home and our new life. We will do it either first thing in the morning when the sun rises over the land or perhaps at sunset. That night we'll sleep in a tent up here on the bluffs and make love for the first time as husband and wife under our stars in the place where we first became one.

20

"Stop wiggling around, you're driving me crazy." I place my hand firmly over Suda Kaye's bouncing thigh as we sit in the waiting area at First National Bank in downtown Chicago.

The last week has been filled with incredible highs and the lowest lows. Milo has been there through it all. Comforting me when I break down and cry for what seems like no reason or laugh uncontrollably at something I remember Dad saying to me as a kid. Cooking up some of the eclectic dishes Mom told us she had during her travels. Anything that would make me feel close to them.

It's been interesting to the say the least. Trying to experience my parents through the veil of good memories has been a trying task, but one I needed. Milo helped, asking me questions about different things we did, keeping them alive for me in his own way.

After we got back from the reservation, he moved everything off the mantel above the fireplace. He set my father's flag right in the center and requested we get a picture of him to place next to it. Of course, the very next day I was at the printer getting one made up. I also printed pictures of Suda Kaye and Camden from their wedding, the selfie I took of Milo and me on our bluffs, pictures of Milo with his family, one of his sister, a stoic image of my grandfather in his head-dress and chest plate and a stunning image of my mother. She was wearing a colorful flowered dress in deep blues and purples. She had a black-and-white dotted scarf around her neck and big silver hoops in her ears that had five inches of dangling beads and chains. Her pitch-black hair was pulled up just at the top and falling all the way down to her waist as she sat, legs crossed, hands held together, contemplating the world. *Toko* said she was about twenty in that image and, for me, it epitomizes exactly who she was.

A thinker. A dreamer. A free spirit.

Suda Kaye jumps up from her chair and reaches for my hand as the banker we were waiting for appears.

"I am ready to take you down to the safety-deposit boxes." He gestures with his arm for us to go in ahead of him.

"I'm so freaked out," Suda Kaye whispers, and grabs my hand, holding it like a little girl afraid to cross the street by herself.

I squeeze her hand. "I would have assumed you'd be excited. Finding out one of Dad's secrets," I tease, and wink to help offset her fear.

"Why aren't you freaked?" she accuses, and scowls.

I shrug. "We can't fret about things that haven't happened yet, right?"

She glares at me. "Since when did you become the open-minded, chill one in this family?" She nudges my shoulder. "It must be Milo. He's the chillest human I know."

"Chill? Nah. More reserved and thoughtful."

"Well, whatever it is, it's wearing off."

The banker brings us into a huge room with nothing but a wall of golden plates with keyholes and numbers etched into them. There are rows and rows of the same size and then bigger ones and even tiny ones.

He leads us over to a midsize one and inserts his key into the left side of the box. "Now you, Ms. Ross." He gestures to the key I've had a vise-lock on since we entered the building and had to sign all the forms and prove our identification.

I insert the key and we unlock the box. I open the door and he nods and walks toward the exit. "I'll leave you two alone."

"Thank you," I mutter, pulling the long heavy box out of the crevice and setting it down on the table in the center of the room.

Suda Kaye is positively vibrating with nervous energy next to me. I place my hands on her shoulders and stare into her pretty face. "Sissy, relax. Whatever is in there doesn't change anything about us. We're sisters, we're with the men of our dreams and we're happy building our lives."

She nods. "Right."

We both take a deep breath and let it go.

"Okay." I lift the lid and jump when it smacks the other side of the table.

Suda Kaye starts to giggle and then we both end up laughing as we stare into a box that holds more of Mom's pink envelopes. Except there's a ton of them.

"More letters from Mom. Stacks and stacks of them by the looks of it?" Suda Kaye reaches in but then she moves over the pink ribbon we're both familiar with and reads the name on the first one.

Her hands shake as she shows me the inscription. "Isabeau."

I lift out the stacks and set them on the table. At the bottom there is a bigger yellow envelope that has *Evie and Suda Kaye* scribbled in my father's handwriting on the front.

"This one's for us." I open it and dump the contents out onto the table. There's another smaller envelope with our names on it in our mother's handwriting. A handful of photographs and a full sheet of paper with our names at the top in Dad's scrawl.

Suda Kaye picks up the pictures and lays them out one at a time. They are in order. The first is of a baby wrapped in a pink blanket with a pale green hat on. The next, one of our mother holding that baby in her arms in a hospital bed.

"What the…" Suda Kaye tapers off as she sets the next one down.

A picture of a redheaded toddler in front of a birthday cake with two candles on it. The next a picture of the same girl at maybe five or so standing in front of a school, smiling wide. I know that smile well. It's the same as mine and Suda Kaye's, because we got it from our mother. The next image is of the girl when she was maybe ten years old baking a cake with a red-haired, good-looking man. Jesus, that must be her father. The next is of the girl as a preteen in a party dress. Maybe before going to a junior high dance. The last picture is the redhead in a cap and gown at what is likely her high school graduation.

"Oh my God, oh my God, oh my God." Suda Kaye backs up and slams into the wall of boxes. Her caramel-colored eyes are wide and scared.

I hold up my hands. "We don't know what we're seeing." I try to put the pieces together.

"Yes, we do! That girl is our sister! Mom had a baby with that red-headed dude!" she states, both of her hands going straight into her wild hair and tugging at the roots. "This. Is. Nuts!"

I lick my lips and press my hands into the table, staring at each image of the redheaded girl who I'm now assuming is Isabeau. As I'm staring at the images trying to understand how this can be, I notice the full-size letter and the envelope from Mom.

"Come here. Let's read this." I set it on the table in front of us both so we can read at the same time.

Evie and Suda Kaye,
If you are reading this letter, it means your old dad is gone. First, I want to say I'm sorry, my little ones.
Sorry for not being honest with you about the dangerous nature of my work.
Sorry for not being there for you as you create families of your own.
Sorry for not always being there as you grew up to teach you the things a man should teach his daughters.
Sorry for not knowing how to help you through your mom's loss.
Sorry for keeping this secret.
Your mother had another child. A daughter. It was intentional, and I knew about it from the beginning. It's very hard to explain and I hope the letter your mom left for you will do what I can't. Just know that this baby was a gift to a pair of men that she felt she owed. In large part because one of them is Ian Collins, Suda Kaye's biological father. They couldn't have children of their own and asked your mother for help. She agreed to be their donor and surrogate.
It happened when you girls were around five and three.
Her name is Isabeau Collins.
Your half sister.
Your mother agreed to let Isabeau be raised by her fathers solely, without her involvement. It would have been devastating and confusing for all involved.

*It was the most selfless thing she could have done.
I admire her for it.*

*Please understand why we couldn't share Isabeau's
existence. She doesn't even know her mother nor that
she has two half sisters. Regardless, your mother always loved her and Isabeau's fathers kept in touch
by sending these pictures every few years even after
your mom passed.*

*I couldn't keep her existence from the two of you
any longer. With the both of us gone, I'm leaving the
decision up to the two of you. My smart, beautiful and
loving girls. The last known address I have for Isabeau
is written on the back of this letter.*

I miss you both. I'll miss you forever.

*Just know that I'll love you and your mother until
the end of time.*

Your Dad

"My goodness this is a lot to take in." I fold the letter in half and run my finger down along the crease. Isabeau's address is written in blue ink sitting in front of my eyes like a challenge.

Suda Kaye blows out a long breath. "So, we have a sister."

"We have a sister," I repeat, not knowing how to believe all that we've read and seen.

"And I now know who my biological father is."

I squeeze her hand and nod, then grab up the rest of the items in the box, all the letters, images, and shove them back into the envelope before stuffing the lot into the empty tote bag I brought.

"Let's take this back to the hotel."

"And discuss over copious amounts of tequila," she suggests.

"Definitely," I agree.

★ ★ ★

When we get back to the hotel, Suda Kaye orders us both huge burgers and fries and a full bottle of Patron Silver tequila. We sit on the bed munching on fries and sipping tequila from cocktail glasses. We could have stayed in Dad's Chicago house, but it felt weird and intrusive. We're still not sure what we're going to do with it or why he had a home there in the first place. Washington, DC, I can understand because of his work with the military. Unless he kept an eye on Isabeau from afar? Which I wouldn't put past either him or my mother to do.

"Think we had enough to drink to open Mom's letter?" Suda Kaye breaks me from my musing while swirling a French fry in a vat of ranch dressing.

I shake my head. "Nope," I admit, and pour myself another finger's worth of tequila in my glass and slam it back, letting it burn a fiery trail down my esophagus.

"When do you think we should open it? Before or after we visit Isabeau?" she asks as though it's a foregone conclusion.

"Are you sure we should? I mean, she's gotta be at least…" I count the years on my fingers, then recount them because of tequila. "Around twenty-five-ish?"

Suda Kaye pours herself another shot while nodding. "Exactly. Old enough to be able to handle finding out she has a pair of sisters."

I shrug. "Maybe. What if her fathers already told her?"

She shakes her head. "No way. She'd have tried to find us."

"I don't know. Honestly, we don't know anything about this woman. She could be as mean as a snake."

Suda Kaye sucks back a shot and slams it down with an, "Ahhh."

"Mom's genetics would have to come through a little,

and Mom was awesome. Loved everyone and everything."
She shrugs.

"Yeah, but she has two fathers. Two men that raised her."

Suda Kaye points at me. "Two gay men or at least one
of them has to be bisexual. That one being my father. That
factors into the coolness possibility. All the gay men I know
are open-minded, and cool as hell."

I think about that for a while and run through all the
people I know that happen to be gay. And she's right, they
are pretty cool and open-minded. "Technically that's ste-
reotyping. I'm sure there are plenty of gay assholes in the
world, too."

"Well, I'm glad I haven't met any," she teases. "In reality,
though, Sissy, I can't keep this under wraps. I have to know
her. She's our sister. Has our mom's blood running through
her veins. Plus, one of her dads is my real father. If I have
the chance to meet him, I need to take it."

"I know." I reach a hand out and cup her cheek. "It would
be a shame for them to not meet you."

She smiles and I caress the apple of her cheek, the same
ones I have, the same it looked like Isabeau has in her pictures. The bone structure we got from our mother. I drop
my hand away and glance at the tote bag on the dresser.

Suda Kaye grabs my hand. "Can you really know she exists and not want to meet her?"

I shake my head, because if we don't try, I'll think about
her forever. And more than that, I think Suda Kaye needs
the closure of finally knowing who her biological father was
even though she's playing her feelings on that very close to
her chest. Almost as if she's not giving it the same attention
as she is the issue of Isabeau, but it has to be running through
her mind that her real dad is alive and raising her half sister.

"Fine." I get up and ruffle through the tote bag with all

the letters addressed to Isabeau, not knowing what we're supposed to do with all of those, either.

I grab the letter and come back to the bed. "Pour us another. I'm going to need it."

Suda Kaye wiggles in her spot and pours two more shots of tequila and hands me my glass, then holds hers up.

"To Isabeau, our sister from another mister." She grins.

"May you be ready to take on two Ross women in your life," I agree.

We slam the shots back and I open Mom's two-page letter to us.

To my darling girls, Evie and Suda Kaye,

Your father asked me to write this letter to you in the event that both of us have passed. I hate the thought that you are alone in the world but hope by now you will have found the men you're meant to be with and are living happy, wonderful lives.

It's my greatest wish for you both.

As you now know, you have a half sister.

Isabeau.

In order for you to understand, I have to go back to before Suda Kaye was born. Adam and I had just had Evie and you were a year old. I was going through severe postpartum depression. He was off fighting a war no one knew about, and I was at the reservation with Toko, my mind filled with endless thoughts that I was failing as a mother and a woman.

Toko urged me to go to find some solace. He understood that the wind is where my soul flourished. Adam was angered by my need to leave our daughter when he was out fighting for his country and providing for his family.

We agreed to separate. To find our own happiness and come back together a year later. Evie, you were too young to understand the relationship your father and I had. I'm not sure anyone could.

I loved Adam more than any man on this earth. There was a part of our souls that were only content when we were together. Though we weren't meant for a conventional marriage of the "father and mother in the home" type, raising their kids together. It didn't work for us. We understood that and accepted that when we were together we'd live and love fully. Then we'd separate and go our own ways.

It sounds odd to say our marriage was open, but it was. He had women he spent time with during the many months and years he was gone. I dabbled in other men when I was moved to do so.

Still, your father and I loved one another and respected each other very much. He's the greatest love of my lifetime and has always been my best friend.

Your father, Suda Kaye, is Ian Kamal Collins. He is married to Casey Collins, Isabeau's biological father. I met Ian at a festival. We clicked. We became lovers and great friends. I found out I was pregnant. He wasn't ready to be a father; I wasn't ready to share a child with him. My child would be raised by me and Toko and have Adam Ross as her father. After many moons and endless talks, he ultimately agreed it was best, and I left.

Close to three years later, I received a desperate request from Ian. To be a surrogate and donor to Ian and Casey's child. They'd already had a woman agree using donor sperm but her egg. Once the child was born, she refused to give them the baby, and since it wasn't biologically theirs, they had no recourse legally.

I prayed hard about the decision and ultimately agreed. Adam accepted my decision. I went through in vitro and they chose Casey to be the biological father. I got pregnant the first attempt as though it were meant to be. When I was about six months along, I left you both with Toko. I spent the end of the pregnancy and the first three months of Isabeau's life with Ian and Casey.

And then one morning, I knew it was time. My feet were itching. My wings ready to fly. And my heart calling for the two of you and our home with Toko.

I kissed my daughter's head, told her I loved her and left. I never went back, though they sent a picture every so often.

It was the hardest thing I ever did, but also the one thing I knew I was meant to do.

I hope you can find it in yourselves to understand. I'm sorry, my darlings, I never told you about Isabeau, but she was never meant to be mine.

Toko knows of her existence because he had to console me through the months without her. He claims that he will not leave this earth until he is able to hold his blooded granddaughter in his arms and look into her eyes.

I've left that up to fate.

Be well, my lovely girls.

I'll love you until all the stars fall from the sky.

Mom

"That was intense," Suda Kaye whispers as if talking too loudly will break our connection to our mother.

"Mom says here that Isabeau was never meant to be hers."

"Yeah? So?" My sister frowns.

"I guess the real question now is, was she meant to be ours?"

21

The house at the address Dad gave us is in a small and quaint neighborhood with huge trees that have been there a long time. The type that meet up over the center of the road making the landscape lush and green. The actual home itself looks tidy and small. It's split-level with front-facing bricks and windows that meet up with the line of the lawn.

Suda Kaye and I stare at the house as though it has a dangerous explosive device attached to it and could explode at any moment.

I reach for her hand and take hold. "We don't have to do this. We can find her number and call her."

"What if my biological father is in there right now?" Her chin trembles and tears well in her eyes. "What if he doesn't want to see me?"

I press my lips together wondering when *she'd* finally start worrying about seeing *him*. I feel sure it will hit her at some point, but she hasn't brought it up yet.

"Do you want me to go first?"

Her eyes widen. "And let you go by yourself? No way." She squeezes my hand so hard it hurts but I don't let it go. "It's all or nothing with us, Sissy."

I frown. "Maybe we should have brought Milo and Cam.

They would be no-nonsense and go straight up to the door without a care in the world, even if they had to drag us kicking and screaming."

Suda Kaye laughs and focuses her gaze on our clasped hands. "Promise me something." She lifts her head and her amber eyes are devastatingly beautiful. That swirling yellow brown like hot caramel melting over a flame.

"Anything." I promise.

"Whatever happens in there, whether they want us in their lives or don't, or act weird, or excited. Whatever it is, and however this goes down, in the long run it's always going to be you and me. Promise you will not let this woman or Ian get between our connection?"

I cup both of her cheeks and match my gaze with hers. "Me and you, Sissy. Always me and you."

She nods and then we both jump when there's a knock on my window on the passenger side.

We both screech and stare at the redheaded, bearded man with kind green eyes. He waves and makes the motion to roll down the window.

My heart is beating double time and my fingers are shaking as I press the down button enough that I can hear him, but not enough so that he can reach an arm or hand inside the car. Safety first and all that.

"Hello, ladies. Are you looking for someone?"

Suda Kaye doesn't speak. She literally goes mute.

"Um, yeah, actually. Is this the address for Isabeau Collins?" I swallow down the giant emotional golf ball stuck in my throat.

He smiles. "It is now! She's home from school. Just graduated." He frowns a little and looks at my face, then at Suda Kaye's. "Are you guys school friends of hers?"

Me. A college friend. That nightly skin-care regime I've

got going must be doing me a lot of favors if he thinks I'm young enough to have been in college with his daughter.

"Not exactly, but we do know someone in common," I supply vaguely.

He smiles again and waves his hand. "Well, come on in. She's in the kitchen making homemade donuts." He holds up a bag. "I just hit the store for a couple ingredients."

"Oh, you know, we don't want to intrude…"

He shakes his head. "Come on in. My firecracker always makes enough to feed a football team. The girl doesn't do small servings." He chuckles and reaches for my door handle and opens it for me. "I'm her dad, Casey."

I lick my lips and make big eyes at Suda Kaye. "Now or never, Sissy," she says shakily, but opens her door and folds out of the driver's side. My sister is in one of her flowy maxi-dresses in a riot of reds, oranges and teals and a pair of flat beaded sandals. I'm wearing a white pair of capri pants with a silk peach tank tucked in that I paired with a thin gold belt around my waist, a simple pair of gold sandals and hoops that match. Both of us have our hair down. Mine with soft beachy waves, Suda Kaye's with a bit of wild curl to it.

We follow the tall man into the house holding hands. He leads us inside his house as if he doesn't have a care in the world, definitely not keen on the two women behind him who are freaking way the hell out.

"Izzy! You have some visitors." He leads us into the kitchen.

"I want mine covered in chocolate. You know how I love me a good dose of chocolate goodness." A tall, athletically built man rubs his hands together excitedly. He's wearing a pair of lime-green jeans tucked into yellow combat boots with black laces, a silver shiny bomber jacket with a black tank underneath and has frosted golden hair that's spiky on top.

"Jasper, you just love chocolate *men*," comes the sassy and sweet sound of a redhead elbow-deep in dough, her gaze on the food she's making. Her hair is a deep auburn halo of curls and waves running past her shoulders just like ours. She has amazing high cheekbones, plump lips much like my own, a smallish nose with a smattering of freckles across it. Though it's her smile that punches me straight in the gut.

Mom's smile. My smile. Suda Kaye's. This young, vibrant and beautiful woman has the exact same smile.

Sitting at a six-seater table that's been shoved into a kitchen nook is an incredibly attractive man. Dark brown hair, skin the color of toasted almonds and a devil-may-care smile. Though that's not what has my sister gasping and putting her hand over her mouth. No, that would be his amber eyes, the exact shade of my sister's unique and now teary ones.

The man who I know is Ian drops the paper in front of him and stands suddenly.

Casey sets the shopping bag on the counter and everyone looks at us. "These ladies were sitting out in front of the house and said they were here to see Izzy?"

I open my mouth to speak and look at each person one by one. "Um, maybe we, uh, should come back another time?" I try.

Suda Kaye grabs my forearm and digs her nails straight into my skin. I grind down my teeth.

"I'm sorry. Have we met?" Isabeau asks while wiping her hands off on a towel and canting her head to the side.

"You look so much like her," Ian whispers, coming closer to the two of us. "Catori." He raises his hand as though to touch my sister's face, but she steps back, pulling me with her as the tears fall down her cheeks. "Suda Kaye?" He chokes out her name as tears fill his eyes.

"It can't be?" Casey comes up to his husband and wraps an arm around Ian's back.

Ian's gaze switches to me. "Evie?" His gaze traces my features. I nod.

"Anyone going to tell me what's going on?" Isabeau goes over to the young, wildly dressed man she called Jasper and he takes her hand.

"Izzy, baby girl, your father and I have something to tell you," Casey announces to the entire room while Suda Kaye and I stay deathly silent.

His words jolt me into action because it's obvious she doesn't know anything about our mother or the two of us. It's not fair that we sit here through her world being shaken upside down.

I dig through the satchel I brought and pull out Mom's letters and the copy of Dad's will.

"Forgive us for coming without calling. Unfortunately, I have some things I need to give you."

Isabeau frowns and presses her lips together. "Who are you?"

"I'm Evie and this is my sister, Suda Kaye. We'll let your dads explain in more detail." I pull out the stacks of Mom's letters and hand them to Casey. Then I pull out the folder I've brought with us. "This is our father's Last Will and Testament…"

Ian winces and looks at Suda Kaye as though she's an oasis and he's stuck straight in the center of hell.

"And Catori?" Casey asks.

"She passed eleven years ago… I'm sorry," I state flatly, barely holding on to my own emotional turmoil. I didn't know what to expect but I guess them never having talked about Mom or us hurts more than I thought it would.

I swallow. "This document will explain things." I press the file into Ian's hands. "He's left Isabeau quite a lot and his attorney needs to get in touch with her."

"What? Who left me what? And why did you mention my mother's name? There can't possibly be many women named Catori in the world."

I close my eyes as the tears surface. I breathe in as my sister cries into my shoulder, pressing her body behind mine.

"Why would Adam do that?" Casey looks at me with gentleness and compassion.

"Because he loved our mother and the children she bore, regardless of if they were his blood. He wants her legacy protected."

"Her children. Are you saying that you two—" Isabeau points to me, then Suda Kaye, who lifts her watery gaze "—are my half sisters?"

I lick my lips and glance at Casey and then at Ian, who cannot stop looking at Suda Kaye with so much longing I can practically hold it in my arms like a squiggly eager puppy.

"Catori Ross was your mother, too? Oh my God!" She smiles huge. "You were donor eggs, too, and you found me! This is awesome!" She claps and jumps up and down. "I'll betcha there's tons of us!"

I tilt my head as her incorrect assumption filters through my mind. "Not exactly. Like I said, we needed to bring these items and we'll be on our way." I reach into my purse and pull out my card and set it on the counter closest to us. "When, uh, you've had some time, and if you want to, feel free to call that number. It's my cell phone. We'll be in town for a couple more days."

"Where do you live?" Ian asks Suda Kaye, his attention all about his long-lost daughter.

"We live in Colorado. I'm in Pueblo and Evie is in Colorado Springs." It's the first thing she's said since we arrived and I'm proud of her for it.

"Suda Kaye, we need to talk," Ian says, then glances at me. "We all do."

I nod. "Yes, and we're open to that, but I think you have something more important to talk about." I lift my chin toward Isabeau, who frowns.

"You're not from donor eggs. Are you?"

I shake my head.

"I don't understand." Jasper wraps her into his arms and places a kiss to her temple.

"You will soon. Thank you for having us. We'll be going."

As we turn around, Ian tugs Suda Kaye's arm and pulls her straight into his arms. His face goes into her hair and tears fall down his face. She shakily lifts her arms and puts them around him.

"I've dreamed of this moment. Every day of my life for the past twenty-eight years I dreamed of holding you. My daughter." He pulls back and cups her cheeks. "You are stunning. Just like your mother. A true gem."

"Your *daughter*?" Isabeau gasps, her hand going over her heart, shock coating every one of her pretty features.

"Babe, let her go." Casey puts his hands around Ian's waist and attempts to pull him away.

"I don't want to let her go. Never again. I wish I never had…"

That has my sister ripping from his hold and racing out of the room and out of the house.

Ian crumbles into his husband's hold, sobbing against his neck, his arms wrapped around him, fingers digging into his back as though he's being ripped apart from the inside out.

"I'm sorry. We shouldn't have come." My voice cracks as I back farther out of the room.

"No, you definitely should have. Only I wish it was twenty-five years ago," Casey says solemnly. "We should have

TO CATCH A DREAM • 303

pushed harder. We knew it after Catori left, when Isabeau was three months old, but the three of us made a promise."

"Some promises are never meant to be broken," I say, my heart in my throat, my entire body turning cold.

I turn around to leave and walk out the door. When I get down the steps leading to our rental car where Suda Kaye is now sitting in the passenger seat, I hear, "Hey!" from the house.

I stop halfway down the walk and stare at my half sister. Her auburn red hair glints off the sun in striking color. She's wearing yoga pants and a simple ribbed tank that show off her very curvy hourglass figure.

"When all of this is figured out, in there—" she hooks a thumb toward her house behind her "—I'll call," she says softly.

"I'll answer."

She smiles and it pierces my heart. I want to run up and hug her, tell her that no matter what it will all be okay, but there are no guarantees when life, love and family are involved. We just have to take it day by day.

"Will she be okay?" She lifts her chin toward where Suda Kaye is sitting, her face in her hands, her shoulders shaking.

"Suda Kaye will be fine. I'll make sure of it. It's what sisters are for. We take care of one another," I whisper.

"Something to look forward to." She smiles once more and waves before going back inside and shutting the door.

I drop my head down and feel the breeze sliding along my skin in a loving caress of my senses.

"We'll make it happen, Mom. Everything will eventually come full circle," I whisper into the wind, then turn around and go back to the car.

When I get inside Suda Kaye turns to me. "I'm sorry I ran out."

I shake my head. "Don't be. They'll call and we'll work through this new stage in our life together." I grab her hand and she holds mine with both of hers.

"I can handle anything as long as I have you, Evie."

"We have each other." I focus on her watery gaze. "And soon, I think we'll have Isabeau, too."

"And Ian?" Her voice cracks.

I smile. "Sissy, he wanted to hold you and never let you go. It will take some time. The two of you have a lot of history to go over but I'll be right there by your side in any way that you need."

That very night my phone rang. Ian wanted to talk to Suda Kaye. I moseyed around the hotel room from the bathroom, to the beds, to the outdoor balcony, to give her privacy but also to ensure she didn't feel alone. They spoke for two full hours. One time she was crying so hard I came up behind her and wrapped my body around hers the way Milo does to me. She held on to me but stuck through it, getting out her frustration that she never knew him, that he didn't demand to see her and everything in between.

The conversation was messy, emotional and gut-wrenching but when she ended the call there was hope, and that's all we could wish for right now.

The next day we spoke to Isabeau on speakerphone. She sounded tired and uncertain of her role in this new connection to her biological mother's children, her half sisters, and asked for some time to wrap her mind around it.

Honestly, Suda Kaye and I need the same now that we all know of one another's existence. It will be a long road but where there's a will there's a way.

I reach for my sister's hand as the plane from Chicago lands in Denver. We didn't speak much on the flight, both of us lost in our own heads.

Hand in hand, we walk down to baggage claim and find Milo and Camden waiting side by side. Two forces of nature, waiting patiently to take care of us emotionally, mentally and physically.

I look at my sister, smiling wide, and she looks at me, smiling like a loon herself, and we both let go of one another and run to our men. Suda Kaye flies into Camden's arms, legs up and around his waist, waiting no time at all before plastering her mouth to his.

Milo catches my form and wraps his arms around me tight. His glorious hair is down, and I press my face into it and breathe in his earthy leather-and-smoke scent. He cups my cheeks and looks into my eyes for a long time.

"You are hurting," he surmises accurately from a single look.

"Love is painful sometimes," I admit.

"Not with us." He traces my features with his fingertips as though this is the first time he's seeing me in months, instead of a handful of days.

"No, but I have faith everything else will all work out as it's supposed to."

He kisses me softly, slowly and for a long time. I sigh into his kiss and let my heart fill with everything good and happy. Like recharging my emotional batteries for another life-changing event.

"Let us go home." He wraps his arm around me.

I see Camden pulling Suda Kaye's large checked bag off the belt. Me, I packed light enough to have a carry-on. I wave at my sister.

She waves back, all smiles and joy.

"Miss me!" she screams across the open area, patrons of the airport looking up to evaluate what's happening.

I burst out laughing. "Miss me more!" I holler back, and hold up my hand, palm facing out and flat toward her. She does the same as though we're touching from a distance.

"Always!" She keeps her hand up and smiles, reminding me of all those years ago when she did the same and left to find herself.

Only this time, she's not leaving for a decade. She's going home with her husband where she'll be safe and sound and loved beyond reason and only a thirty-minute drive from my home with Milo. It's all I could ever have wished for.

Milo curls his hand around my waist.

"Let's go home, *Nizhoni*. I missed you and I want to welcome you properly. Privately," he murmurs into my hair, sending chills of excitement and happiness of my own racing down my spine.

I stare up at the man of my dreams, the one who will soon be my husband, and lean my head up against his powerful frame as he leads me to his truck to take me home.

Our home.

Well, maybe Suda Kaye's happiness isn't all I wished for...

EPILOGUE

Just over a year later...

The wind picks up my long hair and flicks it around my face as the sun shines high overhead. I lift my face and let it warm me straight through to my bones. Milo unclips one belt and then the other, hefting the precious cargo into each hand, and comes around the car.

I move into action, being careful with my body after such a trying but incredible experience. Turning the knob, I push open the door of my childhood home.

"*Toko!*" I call out, surprised that he wasn't ready and waiting outside like he always is. I enter the living room and find his form sleeping soundly, his chest rising and falling. He has his fingers interlaced at his stomach as though he fell asleep waiting for us.

Milo follows me in and sets each carrier on the love seat.

"*Toko?*" I touch his hand and his black eyes open.

"*Taabe*, you took a long while."

I chuckle. "We had to make a stop for an unfortunate blowout of someone's stinky mess."

Toko rubs his hands together and puts his palms facing up. "Bring them to me," he states flatly like there is zero time to waste.

Milo unbuckles the latches and picks up our daughter. Her dark hair is completely covered by a pink cap. I do the same on the other latches and bring my bundle safely to my chest. I walk over to my grandfather and set my son into his arms.

"*Toko*, meet Adam Tahsuda Chavis." His dark gaze lifts to mine at hearing his own name. His lips twitch into a small smile and his chest puffs up with pride. He pulls off the baby's light blue cap and curls his weathered hand around the back of my son's head. My son sleeps through the entire greeting.

Toko dips his face and presses a long kiss to his forehead and whispers to him in Comanche.

"You are of mine own blood. You are Comanche, a warrior by birthright. The sun and moon will guide you your whole life long." He kisses his forehead again, then each of my baby boy's palms. "You are loved."

The pregnancy hormones are still going strong through my body since I only gave birth a week ago today and his words make me bite into my bottom lip so I don't burst into tears. Still, I couldn't wait to bring them to meet their great-grandfather.

"And my girl." He raises his other hand and empty arm like a professional childcare giver, not as though this were his first time holding a pair of twins.

Milo hands my daughter off to me and I present her to my grandfather. "And this little love is Sannah Kaye Chavis."

Toko's gaze pierces mine and I can see the emotion swirling behind those onyx eyes. He puts my son into the cradle of his legs as he reaches for my daughter.

"*Kaku* would be honored, as am I." He takes Sannah into his arms and pulls off her cap, smiling full out when he sees the wild tuffs of pitch-black hair, like her daddy, her grandma Catori, her *Toko* and her namesake Topsannah. Though she opens her eyes and they are a brilliant crystal-clear blue like mine and my father's. Her tiny hand pops out of the blanket and rests against *Toko*'s face as though she knows he is family.

He kisses her hand. "You are of my own blood. You are Comanche, a healing light. The sun and the earth will guide your healing energy your whole life long. You are loved, my prairie flower." He presses a long kiss to her forehead and once again to the center of each hand.

Milo tucks me into his arm after I pull out my phone and take a picture of *Toko* and my children. It will have pride of place on our mantel back home.

Later that day when the sun is cresting over the bluffs, I sit on a fluffy blanket with my daughter in my arms. Next to me my husband sits with our son in his. Both of us are facing the light.

"See, Sannah, this is where your daddy and I got married ten months ago. Isn't the sunlight magical?" I whisper into her ear.

Milo presses a kiss to his son, who's looking up at Daddy, not at the sun disappearing behind the bluffs. "Son, this is our place. Your mom and me, you and your sister." He lifts Adam up so his son can see everything before tucking him back to his mighty chest. "One day you will fall in love and you will bring that person here, to share in the magic."

I smile, lean over and press my lips to Milo's shoulder. He turns his head and takes my mouth.

We kiss until the sun disappears behind the mountain and we're left with a darkening starry sky.

"I wished for this," I admit to my husband. "When we were here the night we put my father to rest, I picked my star and I wished for a son and a daughter. A family of our own."

His lips twitch and he starts to laugh heartily.

I nudge his shoulder. "What?" I smile and cuddle our daughter close to my chest.

His beautiful gaze is filled with wonder as he stares at me.

"This was my wish, too. A boy and a girl. A family of our making. It's all I've ever dreamed of, Evie. Me, you, our children. It's all I'll ever need."

I kiss him hard, pouring every ounce of my happiness into it until I can't breathe, and I have to pull away.

"Should we make a new wish?" He glances up at the sky.

I shake my head. "No. I have everything I ever dreamed of. Let's save all the wishes for the people who need them."

Together, with our children in our arms, our bodies pressed side by side, I look up and whisper, "Wherever you are, I hope you're seeing this, Mom. You were right. Wishes do come true."

And as we sit there, a warm comforting breeze smelling of patchouli, citrus and the earth glides along our skin like a caress.

I smile, close my eyes and welcome her spirit to experience this with us.

★ ★ ★ ★ ★

ACKNOWLEDGMENTS

To my husband, Eric, for supporting me in everything I do. I love you more.

To the world's greatest PA, Jeananna Goodall, for being my absolute biggest cheerleader and for this series, sharing your heritage and allowing me to create a fictional universe surrounding it.

To Jeanne De Vita, my editor, for enthusiastically jumping into this project and helping to make it sparkle.

To my alpha beta team, Tracey Wilson-Vuolo, Tammy Hamilton-Green, Gabby McEachern, Elaine Hennig and Dorothy Bircher, for being willing to read this book chapter by chapter. Sharing your feedback as you read is such a gift. I can't express how much knowing what your experience is through the rough drafts helps the final story come to life. Just trust me, it does!

To Susan Swinwood, lead editor on this project with HQN, I appreciate you believing in this series and these sisters as much, if not more, than me. You're an awesome lady to work with and HQN rocks!

To my literary agent, Amy Tannenbaum, with Jane Rotrosen Agency—girl, you get me. You so get me. Thank you for finding beautiful homes for my book babies with superawesome publishers!

To foreign literary agent Sabrina Prestia, with Jane Rotrosen Agency, you are amazing, spreading the love for the Wish series abroad. I can't wait to see all the translations in the future!

To the readers, I couldn't do what I love or pay my bills if it weren't for all of you. Thank you for every review, kind word, like and share of my work on social media and everything in between. You are what make it possible for me to live my dream.

AUTHOR NOTE

Hello, new friends,

I hope you enjoyed *To Catch a Dream*, and meeting Evie Ross. If you read the first book in my Wish series, *What the Heart Wants*, you will know the story of Evie's sister, Suda Kaye. I developed the idea for this series after my dear friend and longtime personal assistant, Jeananna, told me her family history. Her mother is the real-life Suda Kaye Ross and *What the Heart Wants* is loosely based on her. Jeananna's aunt is also Evie Ross, though everything that happens in *To Catch a Dream* is pure fiction.

This series is inspired in part by the sisters being half–Native American. Through Jeananna's account of her mother's rich history, and her family line extending through the Comanche and Wichita Native American lines, I couldn't help but come up with my own story of what life could be like for a woman who grew up on and off a Native American reservation.

Much of what I've included here is the result of hours of research, including a great deal of focus on the Comanche and Navajo language in order to be as accurate as possible with the few words I've used. Jeananna also shared some of her family's personal experiences, which allowed me to spin a fictional tale that I believe will resonate with women everywhere.

Still, as a fiction writer I took a lot of liberties and would never wish to offend anyone. I know how rich and diverse the Native American culture and tribes are, and I'm thrilled to have been able to shed a little bit of light on such beautiful people.

Like Evie, I believe many of us have a fear of spreading our wings too far. Of taking chances that may end up risking more than we set out to achieve. I hope in my fictional world you learn that taking risks can often have the biggest rewards, and that you are never too old or young to chase after your dreams.

As for sisters, well, I have three biological sisters and a couple soul sisters. I come from a very large Italian family where your sisters are always a part of every facet of your life, very similar to the way that Suda Kaye and Evie are with one another.

My greatest hope is that a small piece of Evie, Suda Kaye, Milo, Camden, *Toko* or any of the characters' experiences resonate with you, and you've finished this story thinking about a dream of your own you want to chase. Maybe this book will give you the nudge you need to throw caution to the wind and go after what it is you want in life.

I promise…it is never too late.

Madlove,
Audrey

P.S. If you'd like to read more about the Ross sisters, most specifically their secret half sister, Isabeau, watch for *The Sweet Side*, the next book in the Wish series, coming soon.

ABOUT AUDREY CARLAN

Audrey Carlan is a No. 1 *New York Times*, *USA TODAY* and *Wall Street Journal* bestselling author. She writes stories that help the reader find themselves while falling in love. Some of her works include the worldwide phenomenon Calendar Girl serial, Trinity series and the International Guy series. Her books have been translated into over thirty languages across the globe.

She lives in the California Valley, where she enjoys her two children and the love of her life. When she's not writing, you can find her teaching yoga, sipping wine with her "soul sisters" or with her nose stuck in a sexy romance novel.

NEWSLETTER
For new release updates and giveaway news, sign up for Audrey's newsletter: https://audreycarlan.com/sign-up

SOCIAL MEDIA
Audrey loves communicating with her readers. You can follow or contact her on any of the following:

Website: www.audreycarlan.com

Email: audrey.carlanpa@gmail.com

Facebook: https://www.facebook.com/AudreyCarlan/

Twitter: https://twitter.com/AudreyCarlan

Pinterest: https://www.pinterest.com/audreycarlan1/

Instagram: https://www.instagram.com/audreycarlan/

Readers Group: https://www.facebook.com/groups/AudreyCarlanWickedHotReaders/

Book Bub: https://www.bookbub.com/authors/audrey-carlan

Goodreads: https://www.goodreads.com/author/show/7831156.Audrey_Carlan

Amazon: https://www.amazon.com/Audrey-Carlan/e/B00JAVVG8U/

BOOKS BY AUDREY CARLAN

Wish Series
What the Heart Wants
To Catch a Dream
On the Sweet Side

Soul Sister Series
Wild Child
Wild Beauty

Love Under Quarantine

Biker Beauties
Biker Babe
Biker Beloved
Biker Brit
Biker Boss

International Guy Series
Paris

New York

Copenhagen

Milan

San Francisco

Montreal

London

Berlin

Washington, DC

Madrid

Rio

Los Angeles

Lotus House Series

Resisting Roots

Sacred Serenity

Divine Desire

Limitless Love

Silent Sins

Intimate Intuition

Enlightened End

Trinity Trilogy

Body

Mind

Soul

Life

Fate

Calendar Girl

January

February

March

April

May

June

July

August

September

October

November

December

Falling Series

Angel Falling

London Falling

Justice Falling